Hi and Lois®

"WHISTLE FOR FORTUNE"

by MORT WALKER and DIK BROWNE

TOR®

A TOM DOHERTY ASSOCIATES BOOK
NEW YORK

HI AND LOIS: WHEELS OF FORTUNE

Copyright © 1984, 1990 by King Features Syndicate, Inc.

World rights reserved.

A Tor Book
Published by Tom Doherty Associates, Inc.
49 West 24th Street
New York, N.Y. 10010

ISBN: 0-812-50749-5

First edition: June 1990

Printed in the United States of America

0 9 8 7 6 5 4 3 2 1

Don't miss these other Hi and Lois titles published by Tor Books

HI AND LOIS: COUCH POTATOES!
HI AND LOIS: CROQUET FOR A DAY
HI AND LOIS: DAWG DAY AFTERNOON
HI AND LOIS: HAPPY CAMPERS
HI AND LOIS: HOUSE CALLS
HI AND LOIS: HOW DO YOU SPELL BAD?
HI AND LOIS: "IS DINNER READY?"
HI AND LOIS: MOM, WHERE'S MY HOMEWORK?
HI AND LOIS: MODERN CHAOS
HI AND LOIS: SAY "CHEESE"

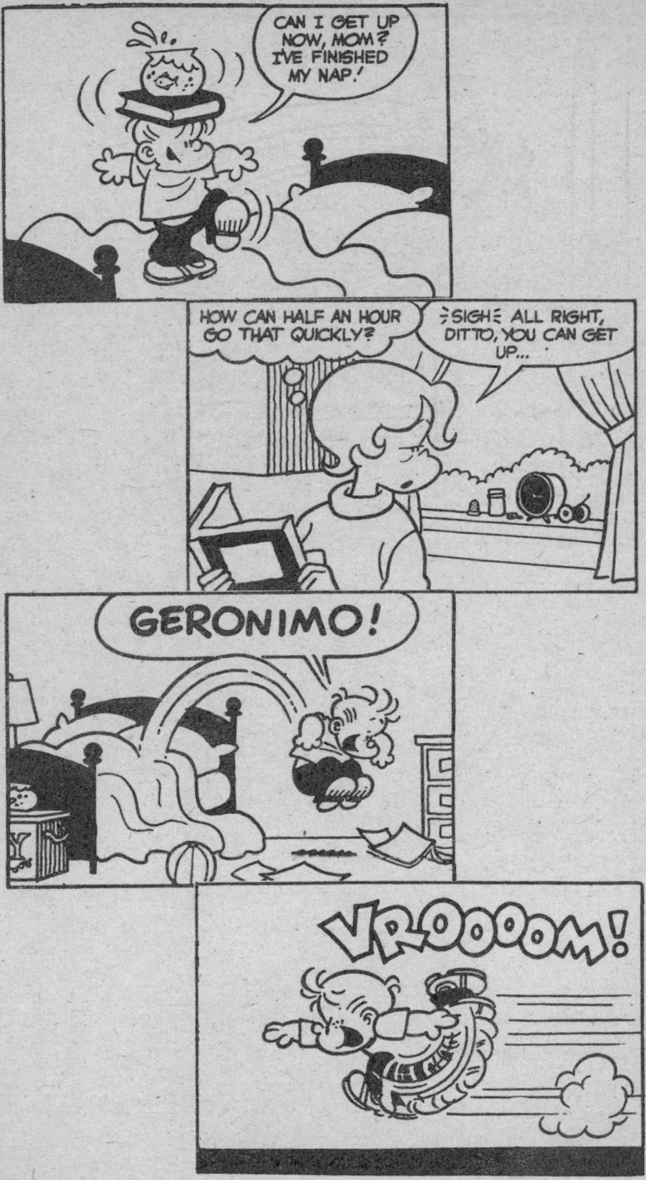
CAN I GET UP NOW, MOM? I'VE FINISHED MY NAP!
HOW CAN HALF AN HOUR GO THAT QUICKLY?
≡SIGH≡ ALL RIGHT, DITTO, YOU CAN GET UP...
GERONIMO!
VROOOOM!

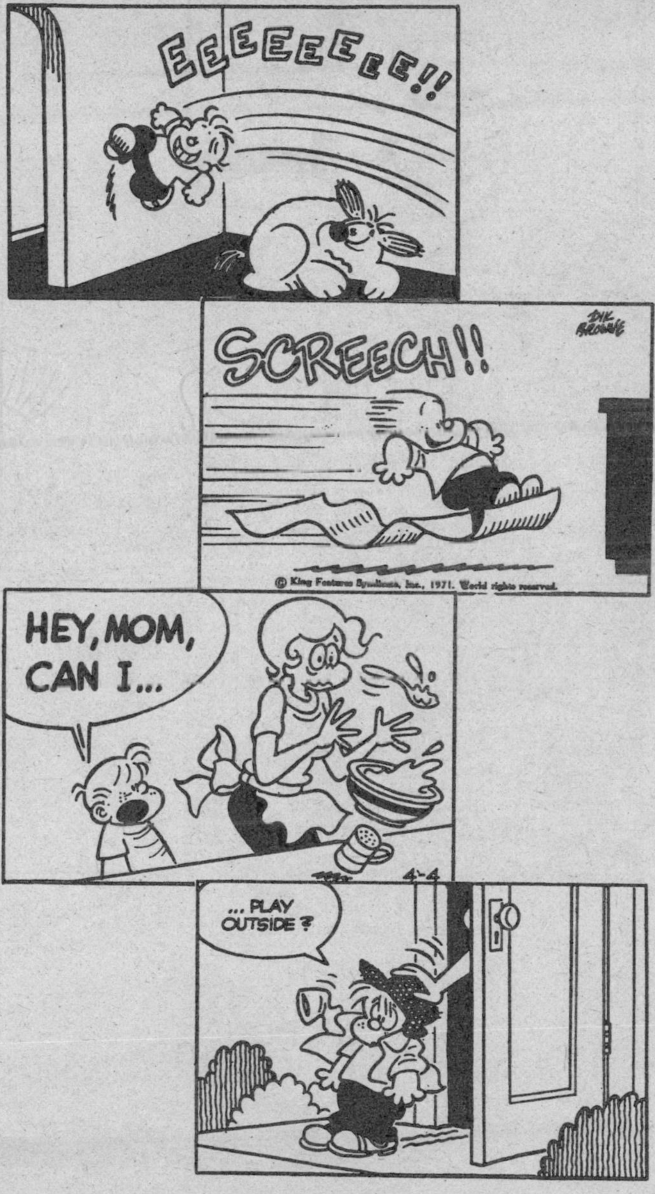
EEEEEEEE!!
DIK BROWNE
SCREECH!!
© King Features Syndicate, Inc., 1971. World rights reserved.
HEY, MOM, CAN I...
4-4
... PLAY OUTSIDE ?

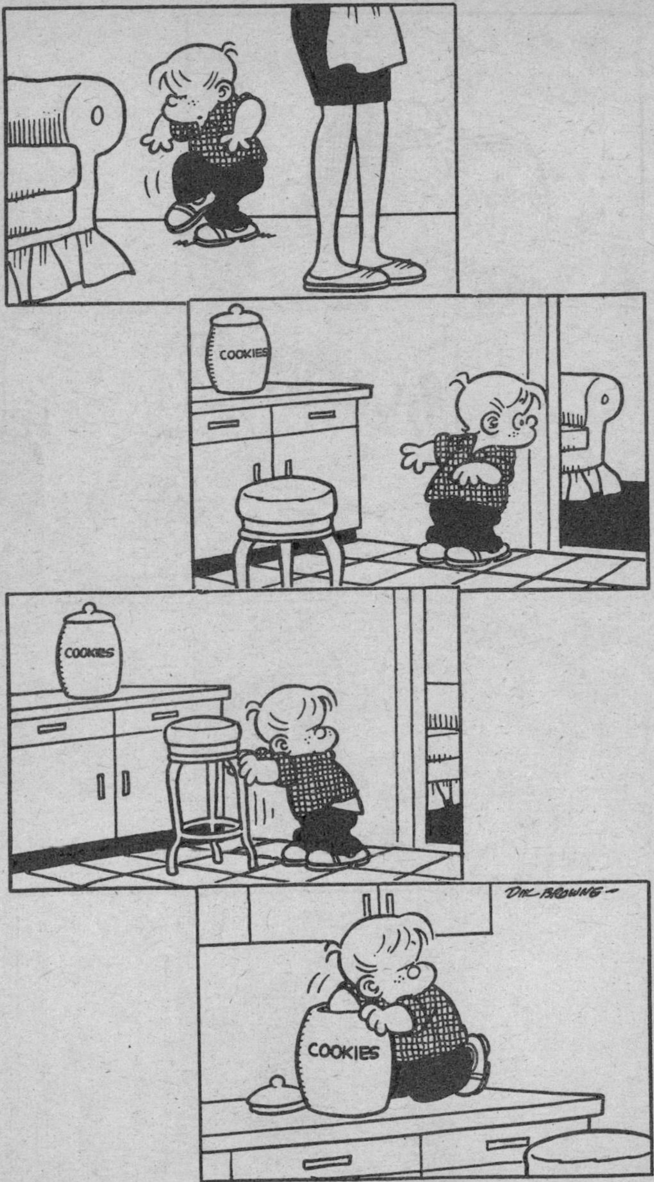
COOKIES
COOKIES
DIK BROWNE
COOKIES

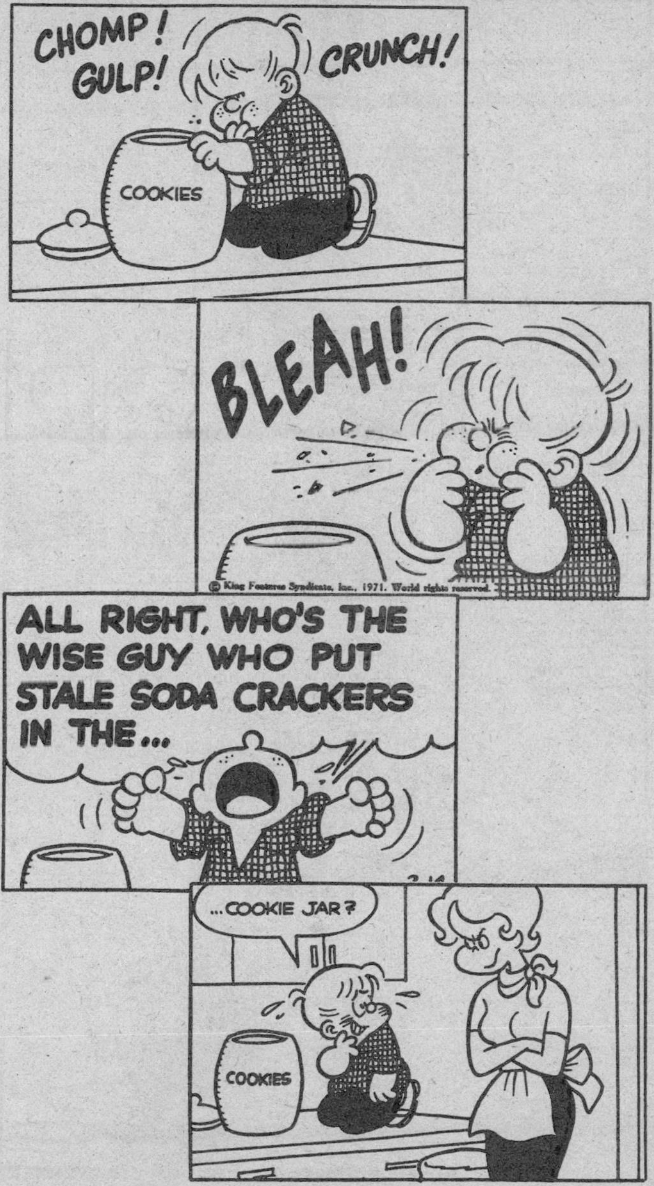
CHOMP! GULP!
CRUNCH!
COOKIES
BLEAH!
© King Features Syndicate, Inc., 1971. World rights reserved.
ALL RIGHT, WHO'S THE WISE GUY WHO PUT STALE SODA CRACKERS IN THE...
...COOKIE JAR?
COOKIES

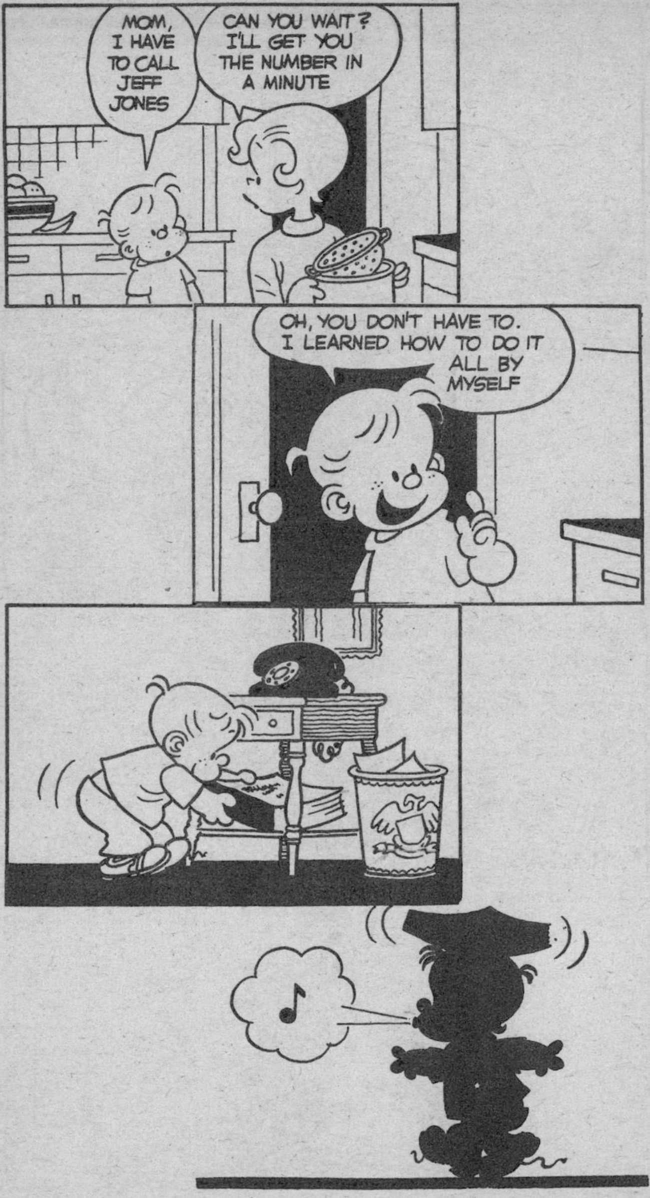
MOM, I HAVE TO CALL JEFF JONES
CAN YOU WAIT? I'LL GET YOU THE NUMBER IN A MINUTE
OH, YOU DON'T HAVE TO. I LEARNED HOW TO DO IT ALL BY MYSELF

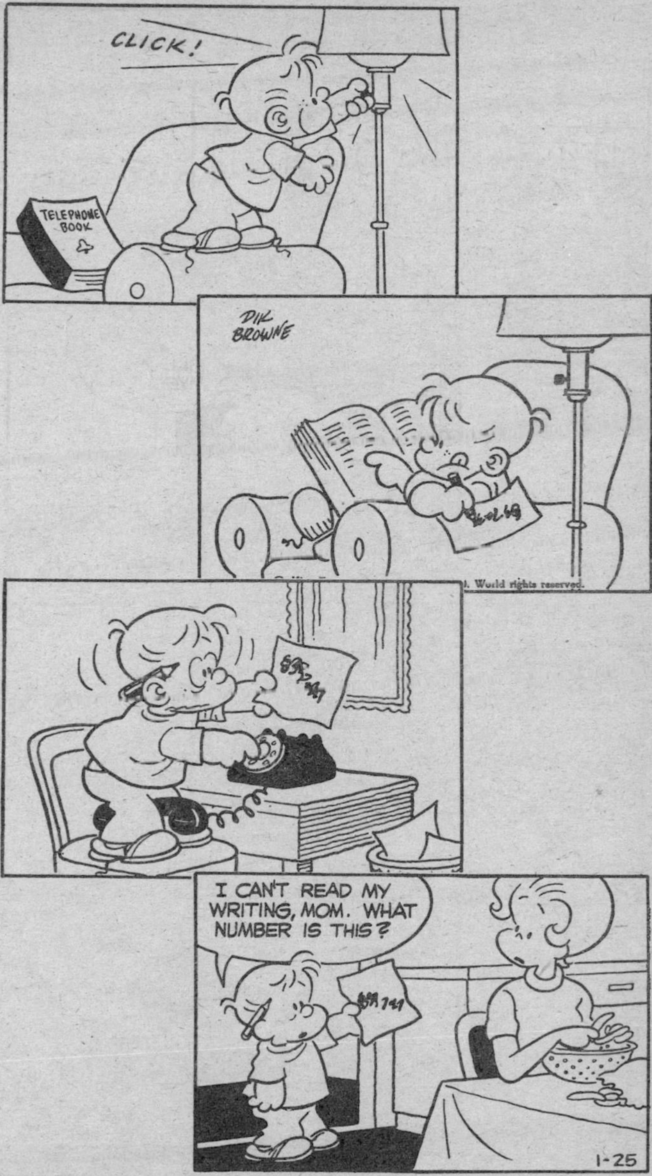
CLICK!
TELEPHONE BOOK
DIK BROWNE
World rights reserved.
I CAN'T READ MY WRITING, MOM. WHAT NUMBER IS THIS?
1-25

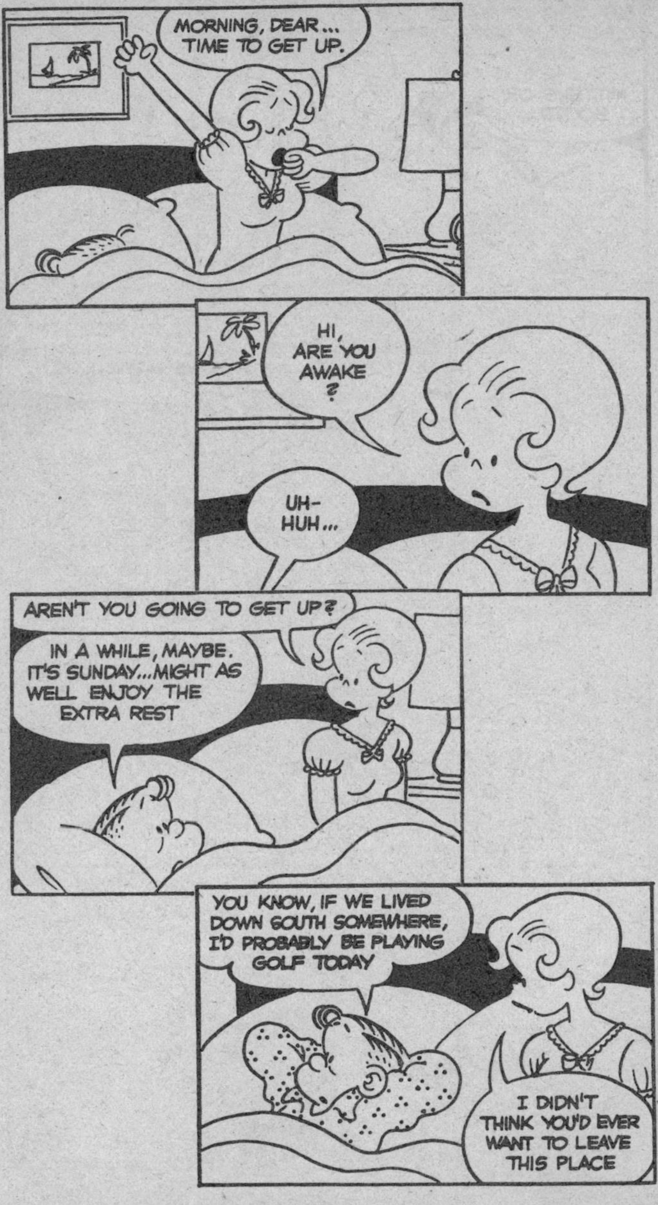
MORNING, DEAR... TIME TO GET UP.
HI, ARE YOU AWAKE ?
UH-HUH...
AREN'T YOU GOING TO GET UP?
IN A WHILE, MAYBE. IT'S SUNDAY...MIGHT AS WELL ENJOY THE EXTRA REST
YOU KNOW, IF WE LIVED DOWN SOUTH SOMEWHERE, I'D PROBABLY BE PLAYING GOLF TODAY
I DIDN'T THINK YOU'D EVER WANT TO LEAVE THIS PLACE

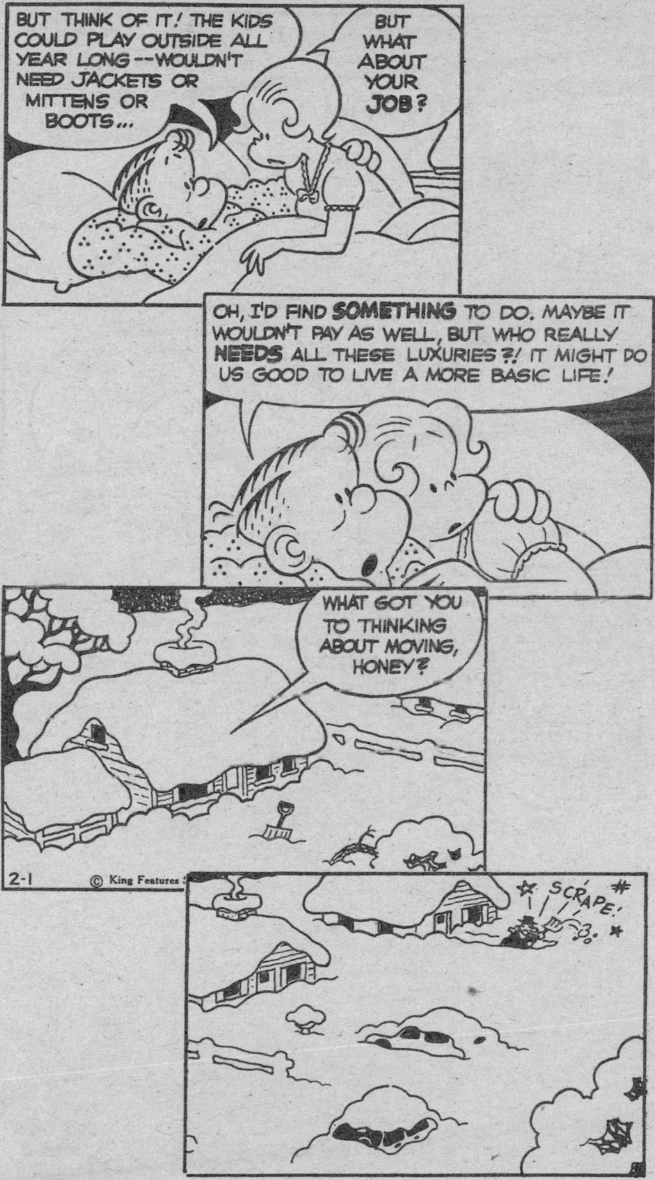
BUT THINK OF IT! THE KIDS COULD PLAY OUTSIDE ALL YEAR LONG--WOULDN'T NEED JACKETS OR MITTENS OR BOOTS...
BUT WHAT ABOUT YOUR JOB?
OH, I'D FIND SOMETHING TO DO. MAYBE IT WOULDN'T PAY AS WELL, BUT WHO REALLY NEEDS ALL THESE LUXURIES?! IT MIGHT DO US GOOD TO LIVE A MORE BASIC LIFE!
WHAT GOT YOU TO THINKING ABOUT MOVING, HONEY?
2-1 © King Features
SCRAPE!

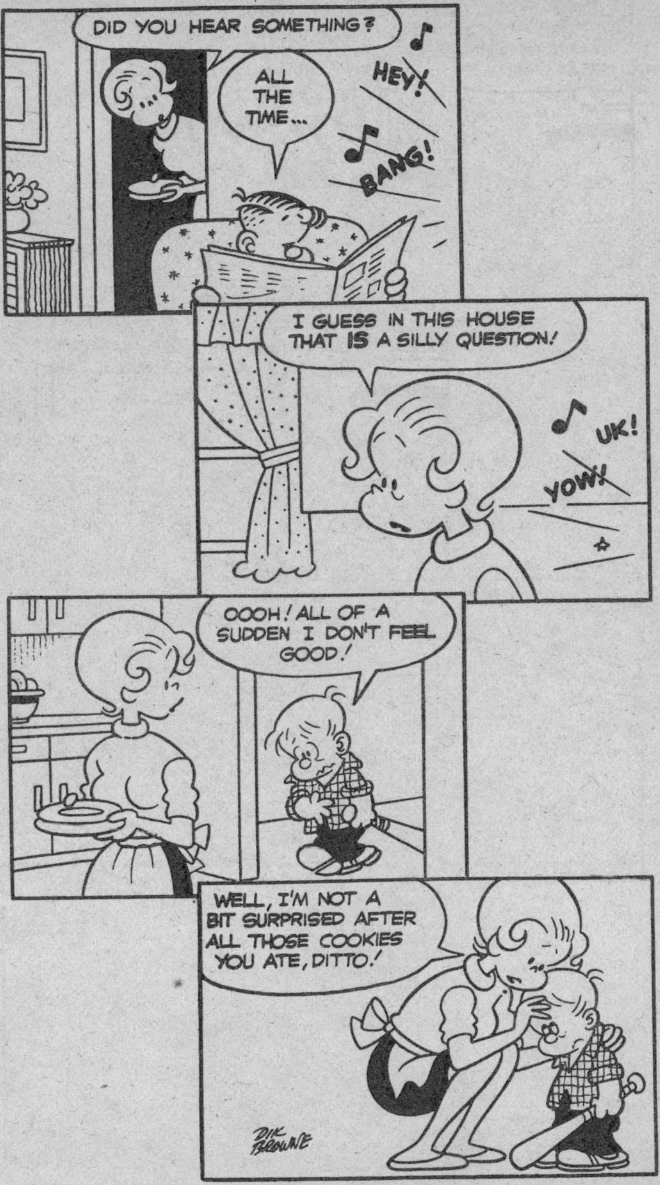
DID YOU HEAR SOMETHING?
ALL THE TIME...
HEY!
BANG!
I GUESS IN THIS HOUSE THAT IS A SILLY QUESTION!
UK!
YOW!
OOOH! ALL OF A SUDDEN I DON'T FEEL GOOD!
WELL, I'M NOT A BIT SURPRISED AFTER ALL THOSE COOKIES YOU ATE, DITTO!
DIK BROWNE

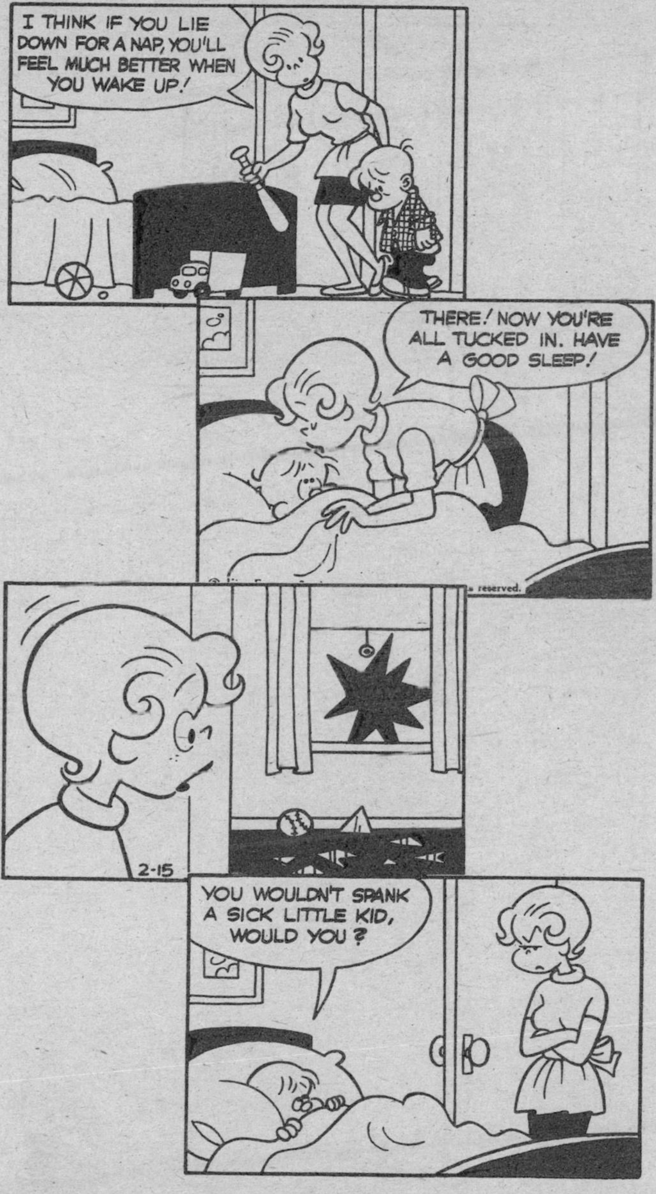
I THINK IF YOU LIE DOWN FOR A NAP, YOU'LL FEEL MUCH BETTER WHEN YOU WAKE UP!
THERE! NOW YOU'RE ALL TUCKED IN. HAVE A GOOD SLEEP!
2-15
YOU WOULDN'T SPANK A SICK LITTLE KID, WOULD YOU?

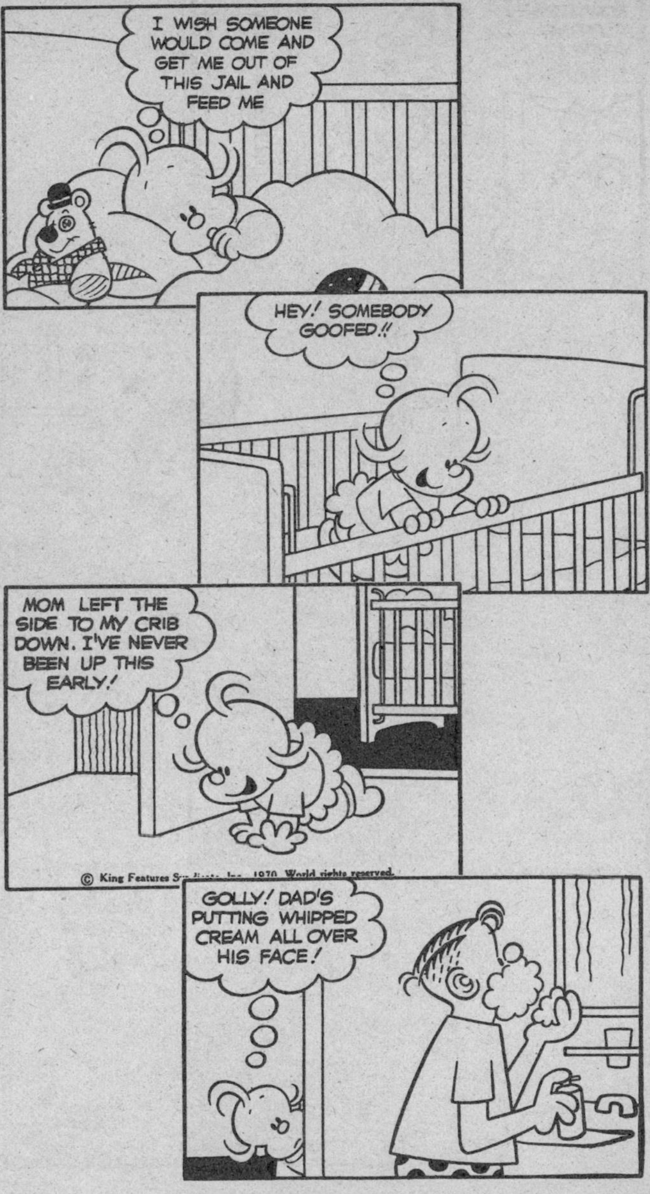
I WISH SOMEONE WOULD COME AND GET ME OUT OF THIS JAIL AND FEED ME
HEY! SOMEBODY GOOFED!!
MOM LEFT THE SIDE TO MY CRIB DOWN. I'VE NEVER BEEN UP THIS EARLY!
GOLLY! DAD'S PUTTING WHIPPED CREAM ALL OVER HIS FACE!

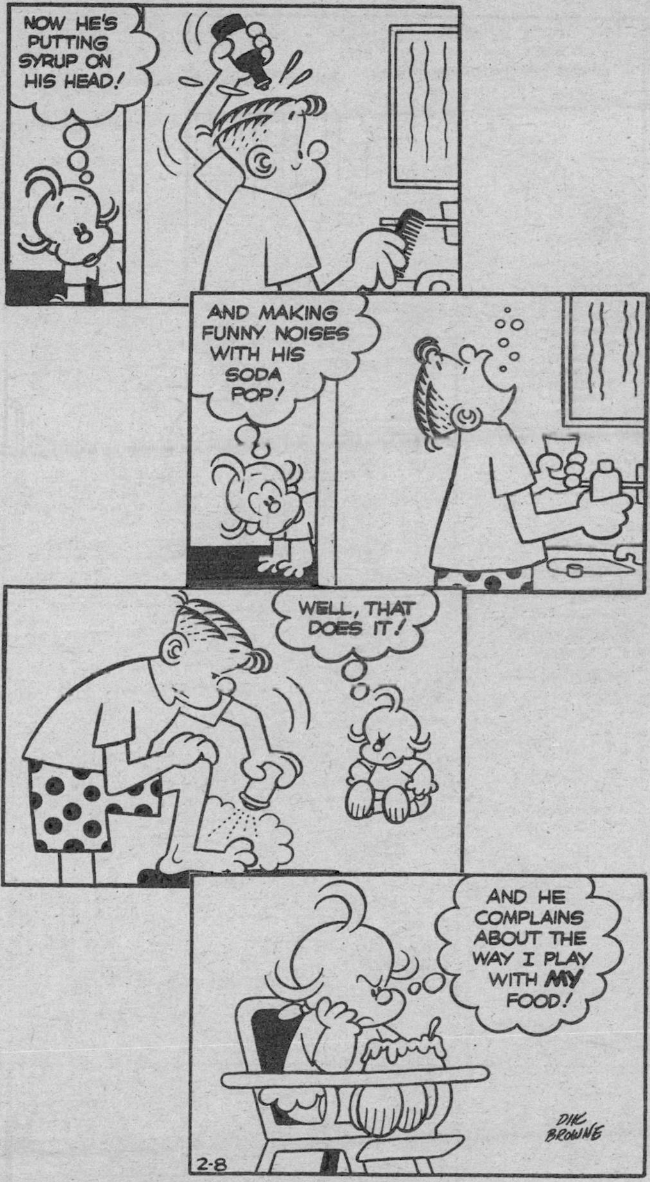
NOW HE'S PUTTING SYRUP ON HIS HEAD!
AND MAKING FUNNY NOISES WITH HIS SODA POP!
WELL, THAT DOES IT!
AND HE COMPLAINS ABOUT THE WAY I PLAY WITH MY FOOD!
DIK BROWNE
2-8

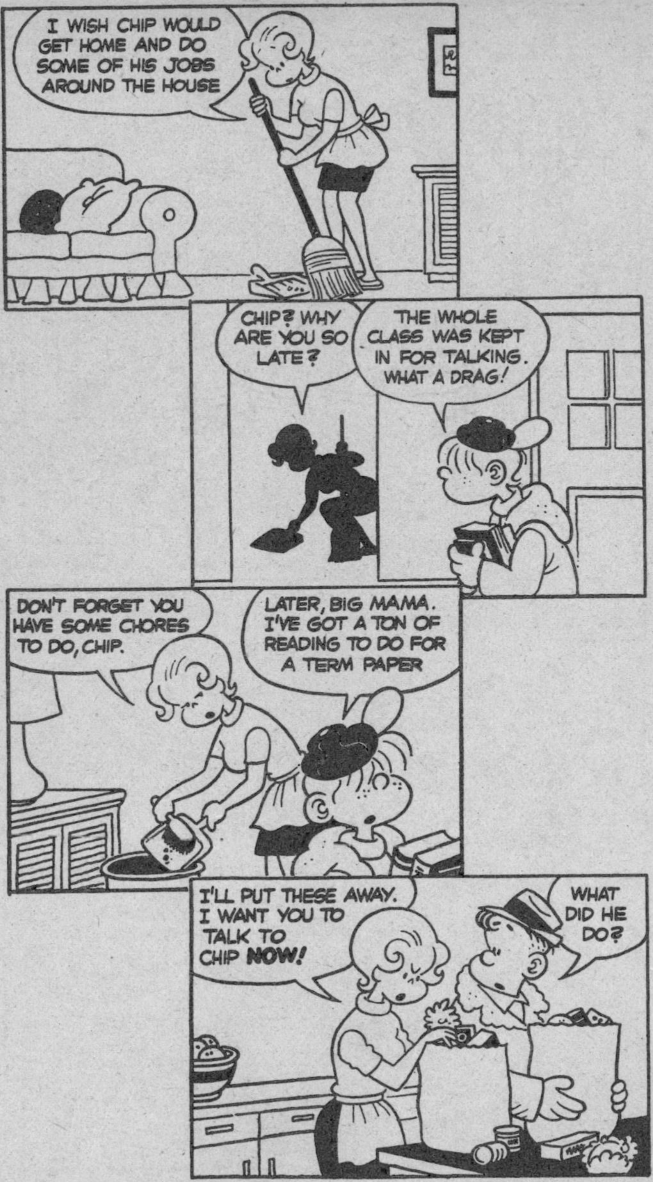
I WISH CHIP WOULD GET HOME AND DO SOME OF HIS JOBS AROUND THE HOUSE
CHIP? WHY ARE YOU SO LATE?
THE WHOLE CLASS WAS KEPT IN FOR TALKING. WHAT A DRAG!
DON'T FORGET YOU HAVE SOME CHORES TO DO, CHIP.
LATER, BIG MAMA. I'VE GOT A TON OF READING TO DO FOR A TERM PAPER
I'LL PUT THESE AWAY. I WANT YOU TO TALK TO CHIP **NOW!**
WHAT DID HE DO?

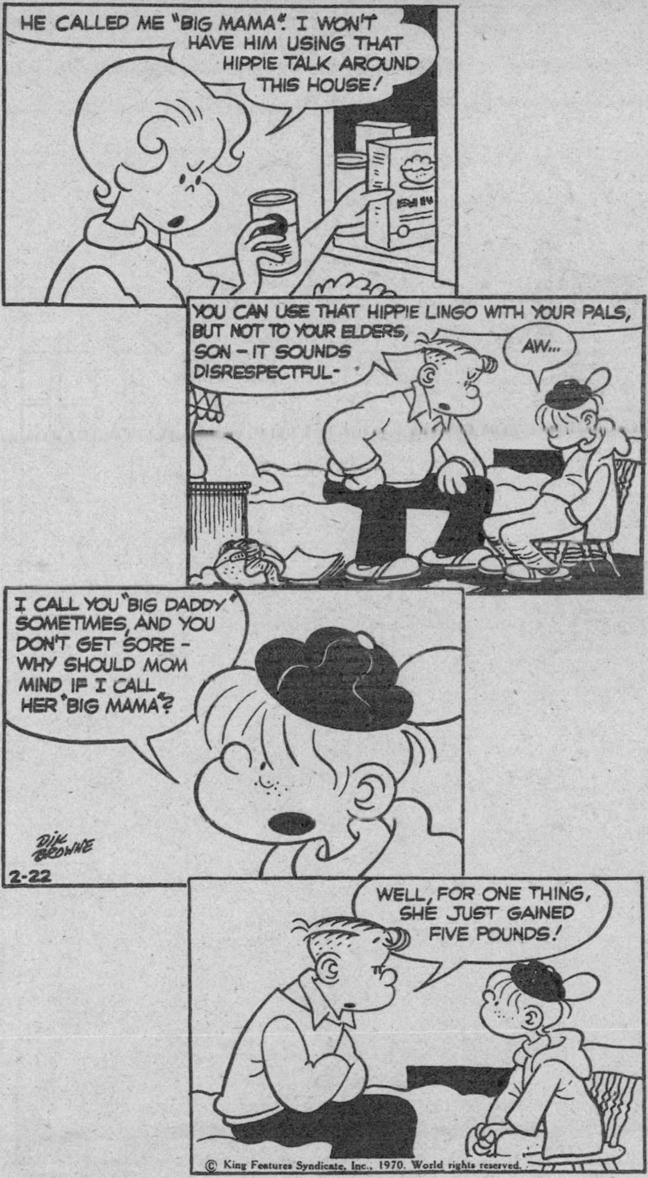

HE CALLED ME "BIG MAMA". I WON'T HAVE HIM USING THAT HIPPIE TALK AROUND THIS HOUSE!
YOU CAN USE THAT HIPPIE LINGO WITH YOUR PALS, BUT NOT TO YOUR ELDERS, SON - IT SOUNDS DISRESPECTFUL-
AW...
I CALL YOU "BIG DADDY" SOMETIMES, AND YOU DON'T GET SORE - WHY SHOULD MOM MIND IF I CALL HER "BIG MAMA"?
DIK BROWNE
2-22
WELL, FOR ONE THING, SHE JUST GAINED FIVE POUNDS!

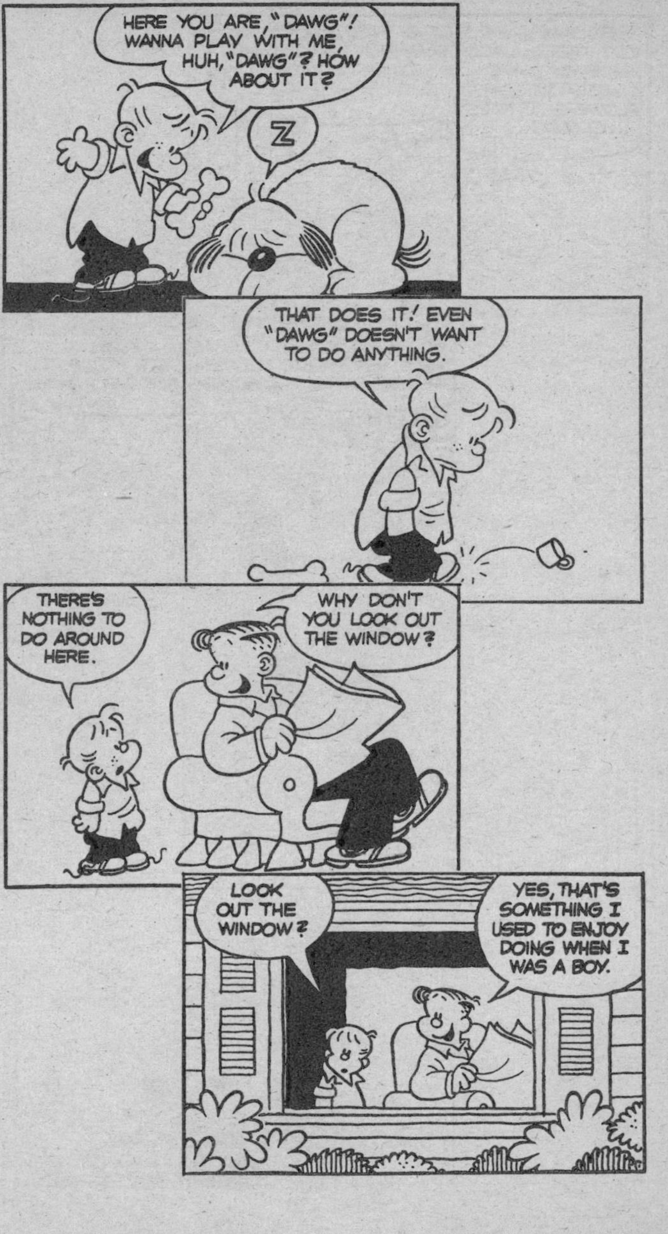
HERE YOU ARE, "DAWG"! WANNA PLAY WITH ME, HUH, "DAWG"? HOW ABOUT IT?
Z
THAT DOES IT! EVEN "DAWG" DOESN'T WANT TO DO ANYTHING.
THERE'S NOTHING TO DO AROUND HERE.
WHY DON'T YOU LOOK OUT THE WINDOW?
LOOK OUT THE WINDOW?
YES, THAT'S SOMETHING I USED TO ENJOY DOING WHEN I WAS A BOY.

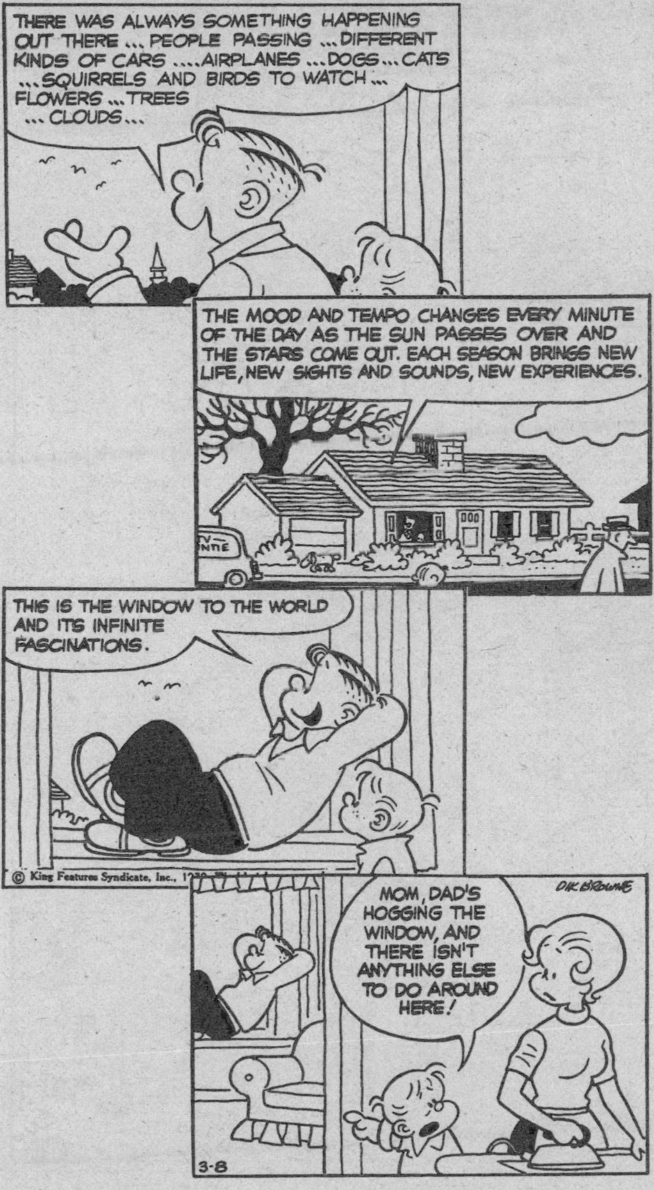
THERE WAS ALWAYS SOMETHING HAPPENING OUT THERE ... PEOPLE PASSING ... DIFFERENT KINDS OF CARS .... AIRPLANES ... DOGS ... CATS ... SQUIRRELS AND BIRDS TO WATCH ... FLOWERS ... TREES ... CLOUDS ...
THE MOOD AND TEMPO CHANGES EVERY MINUTE OF THE DAY AS THE SUN PASSES OVER AND THE STARS COME OUT. EACH SEASON BRINGS NEW LIFE, NEW SIGHTS AND SOUNDS, NEW EXPERIENCES.
THIS IS THE WINDOW TO THE WORLD AND ITS INFINITE FASCINATIONS.
© King Features Syndicate, Inc.,
DIK BROWNE
MOM, DAD'S HOGGING THE WINDOW, AND THERE ISN'T ANYTHING ELSE TO DO AROUND HERE!
3-8

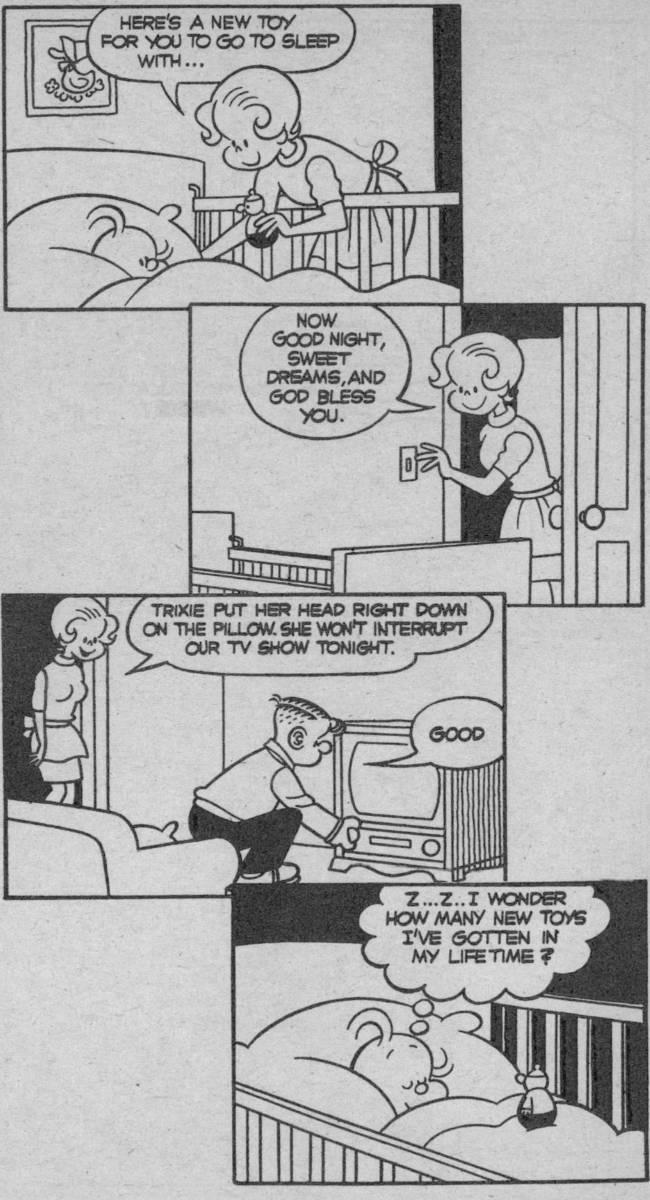
HERE'S A NEW TOY FOR YOU TO GO TO SLEEP WITH...
NOW GOOD NIGHT, SWEET DREAMS, AND GOD BLESS YOU.
TRIXIE PUT HER HEAD RIGHT DOWN ON THE PILLOW. SHE WON'T INTERRUPT OUR TV SHOW TONIGHT.
GOOD
Z...Z..I WONDER HOW MANY NEW TOYS I'VE GOTTEN IN MY LIFETIME ?

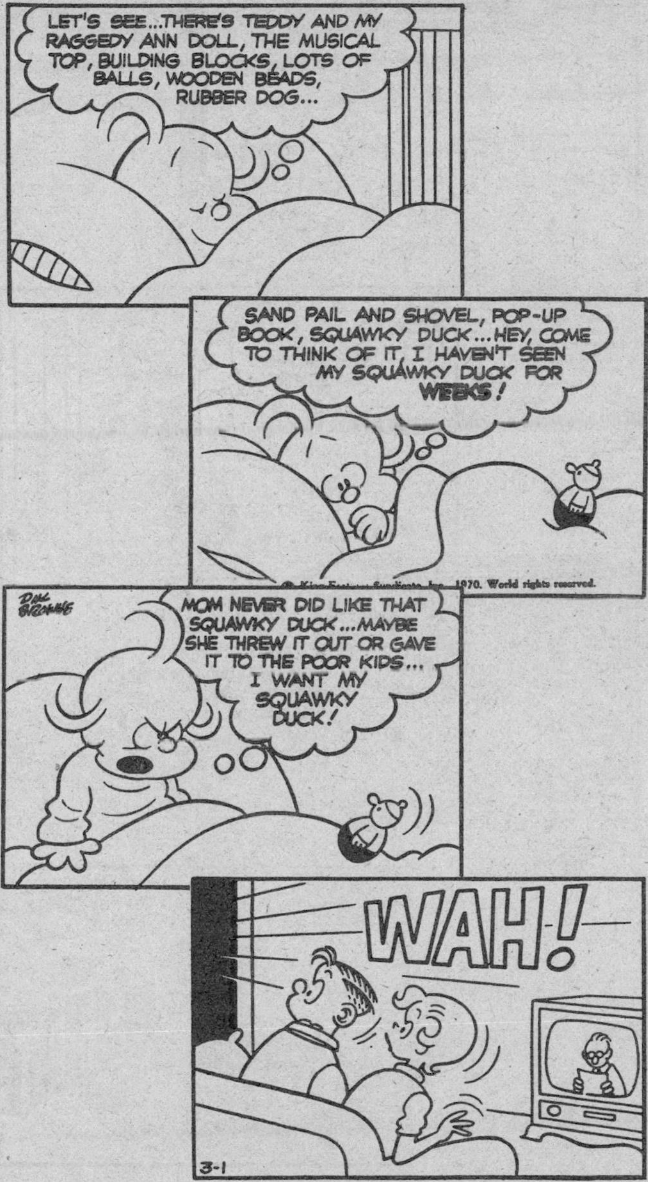
LET'S SEE...THERE'S TEDDY AND MY RAGGEDY ANN DOLL, THE MUSICAL TOP, BUILDING BLOCKS, LOTS OF BALLS, WOODEN BEADS, RUBBER DOG...
SAND PAIL AND SHOVEL, POP-UP BOOK, SQUAWKY DUCK...HEY, COME TO THINK OF IT, I HAVEN'T SEEN MY SQUAWKY DUCK FOR WEEKS!
1970. World rights reserved.
MOM NEVER DID LIKE THAT SQUAWKY DUCK...MAYBE SHE THREW IT OUT OR GAVE IT TO THE POOR KIDS... I WANT MY SQUAWKY DUCK!
WAH!
3-1

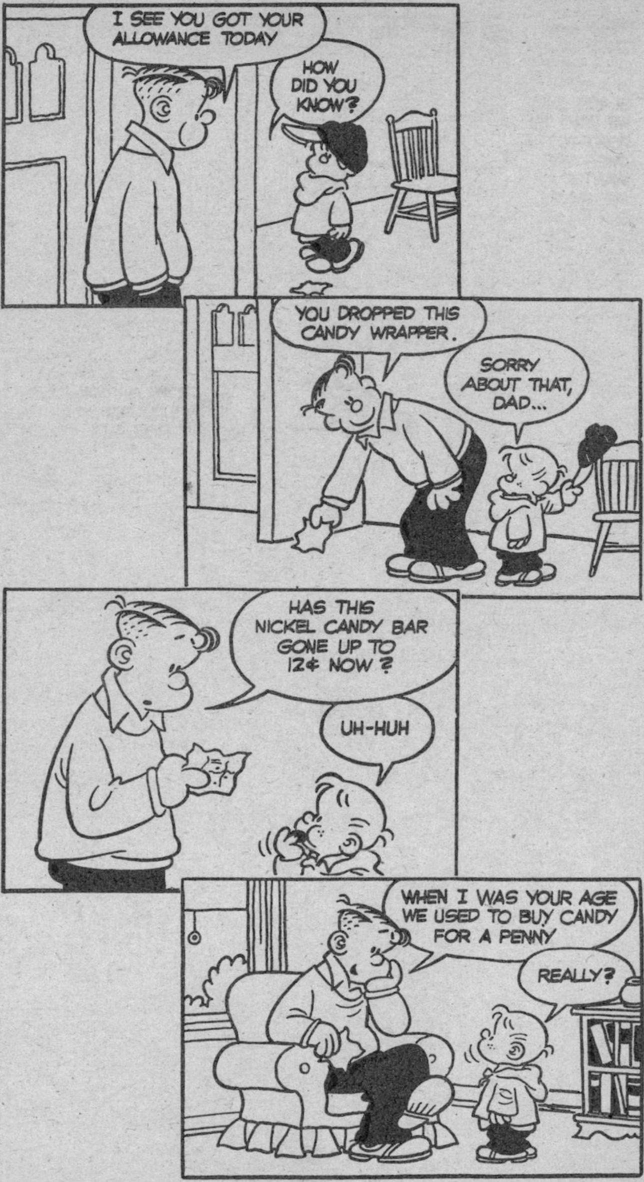
I SEE YOU GOT YOUR ALLOWANCE TODAY
HOW DID YOU KNOW?
YOU DROPPED THIS CANDY WRAPPER.
SORRY ABOUT THAT, DAD...
HAS THIS NICKEL CANDY BAR GONE UP TO 12¢ NOW?
UH-HUH
WHEN I WAS YOUR AGE WE USED TO BUY CANDY FOR A PENNY
REALLY?

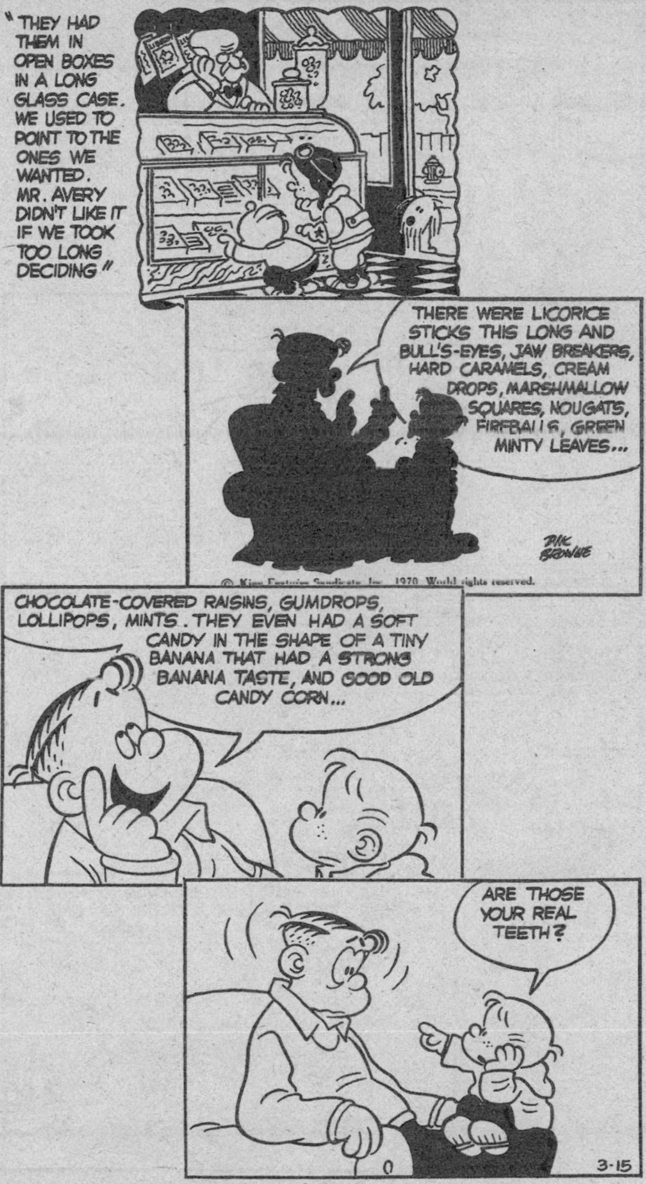
"THEY HAD THEM IN OPEN BOXES IN A LONG GLASS CASE. WE USED TO POINT TO THE ONES WE WANTED. MR. AVERY DIDN'T LIKE IT IF WE TOOK TOO LONG DECIDING"
THERE WERE LICORICE STICKS THIS LONG AND BULL'S-EYES, JAW BREAKERS, HARD CARAMELS, CREAM DROPS, MARSHMALLOW SQUARES, NOUGATS, FIREBALLS, GREEN MINTY LEAVES...
DIK BROWNE
© King Features Syndicate, Inc., 1970. World rights reserved.
CHOCOLATE-COVERED RAISINS, GUMDROPS, LOLLIPOPS, MINTS. THEY EVEN HAD A SOFT CANDY IN THE SHAPE OF A TINY BANANA THAT HAD A STRONG BANANA TASTE, AND GOOD OLD CANDY CORN...
ARE THOSE YOUR REAL TEETH?
3-15

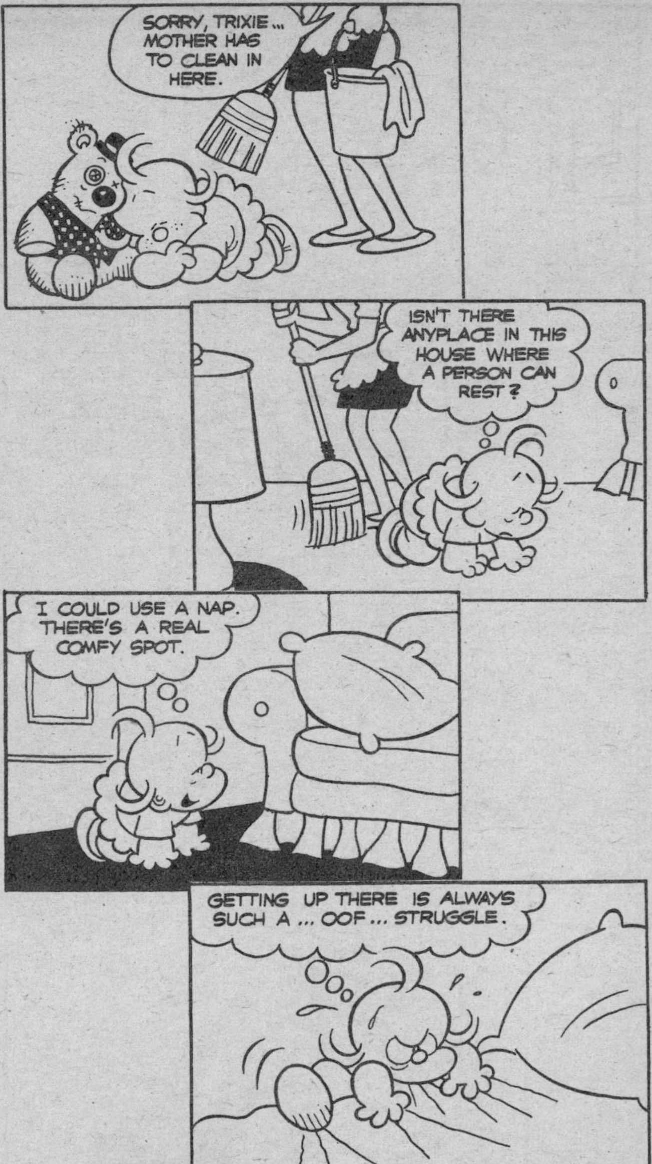
SORRY, TRIXIE... MOTHER HAS TO CLEAN IN HERE.
ISN'T THERE ANYPLACE IN THIS HOUSE WHERE A PERSON CAN REST?
I COULD USE A NAP. THERE'S A REAL COMFY SPOT.
GETTING UP THERE IS ALWAYS SUCH A ... OOF ... STRUGGLE.

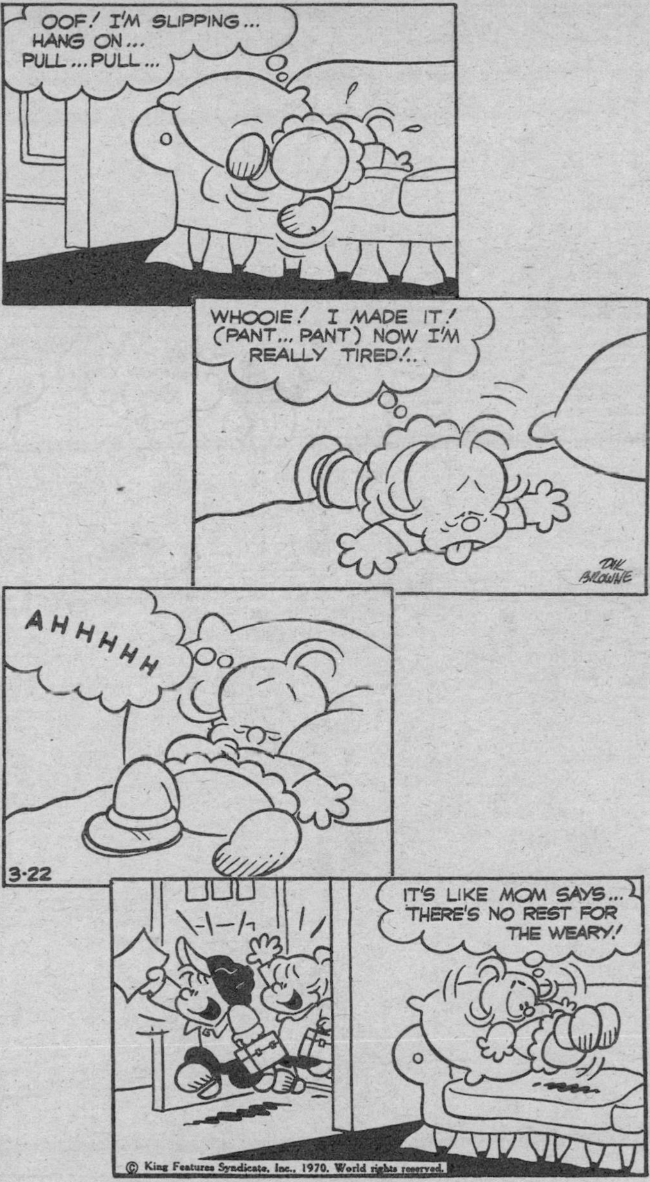
OOF! I'M SLIPPING... HANG ON... PULL... PULL...
WHOOIE! I MADE IT! (PANT... PANT) NOW I'M REALLY TIRED!..
DIK BROWNE
AHHHHHH
3-22
IT'S LIKE MOM SAYS... THERE'S NO REST FOR THE WEARY!

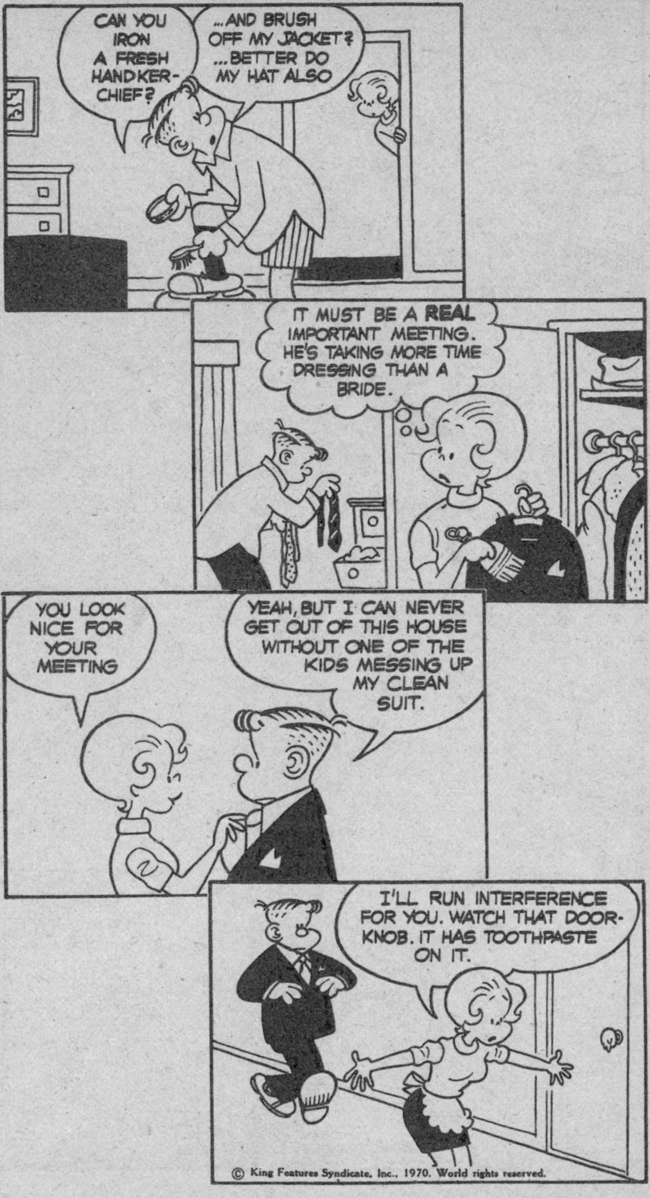
CAN YOU IRON A FRESH HANDKER-CHIEF?
...AND BRUSH OFF MY JACKET? ...BETTER DO MY HAT ALSO
IT MUST BE A REAL IMPORTANT MEETING. HE'S TAKING MORE TIME DRESSING THAN A BRIDE.
YOU LOOK NICE FOR YOUR MEETING
YEAH, BUT I CAN NEVER GET OUT OF THIS HOUSE WITHOUT ONE OF THE KIDS MESSING UP MY CLEAN SUIT.
I'LL RUN INTERFERENCE FOR YOU. WATCH THAT DOOR-KNOB. IT HAS TOOTHPASTE ON IT.
© King Features Syndicate, Inc., 1970. World rights reserved.

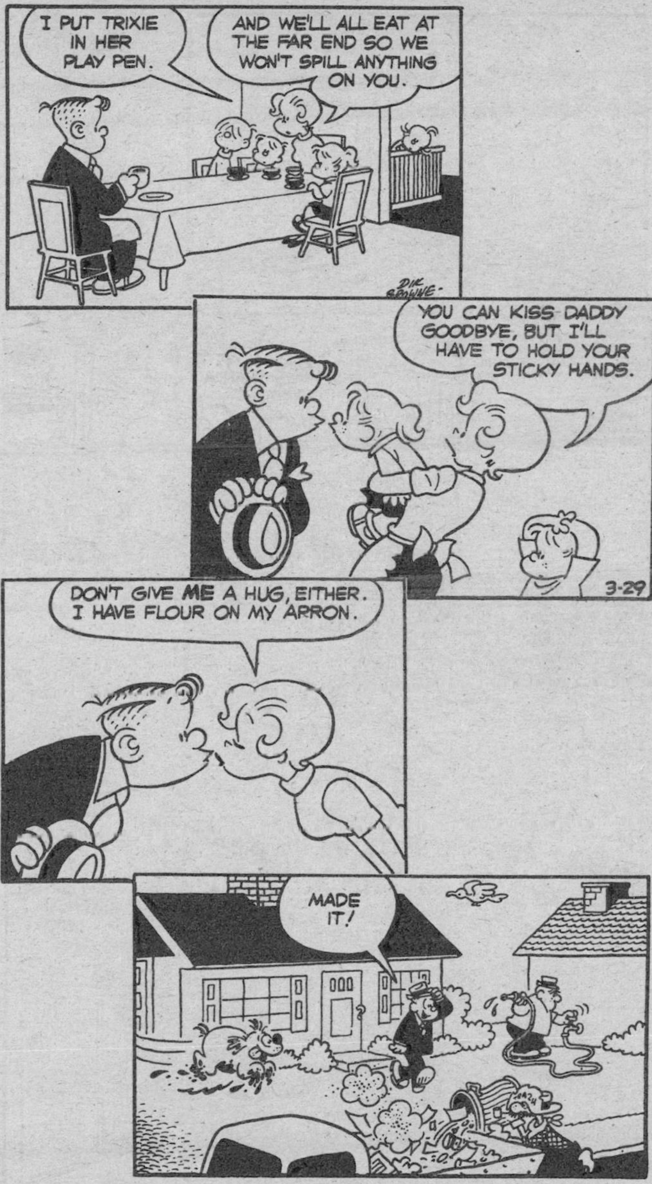
I PUT TRIXIE IN HER PLAY PEN.
AND WE'LL ALL EAT AT THE FAR END SO WE WON'T SPILL ANYTHING ON YOU.
DIK BROWNE
YOU CAN KISS DADDY GOODBYE, BUT I'LL HAVE TO HOLD YOUR STICKY HANDS.
3-29
DON'T GIVE ME A HUG, EITHER. I HAVE FLOUR ON MY ARRON.
MADE IT!

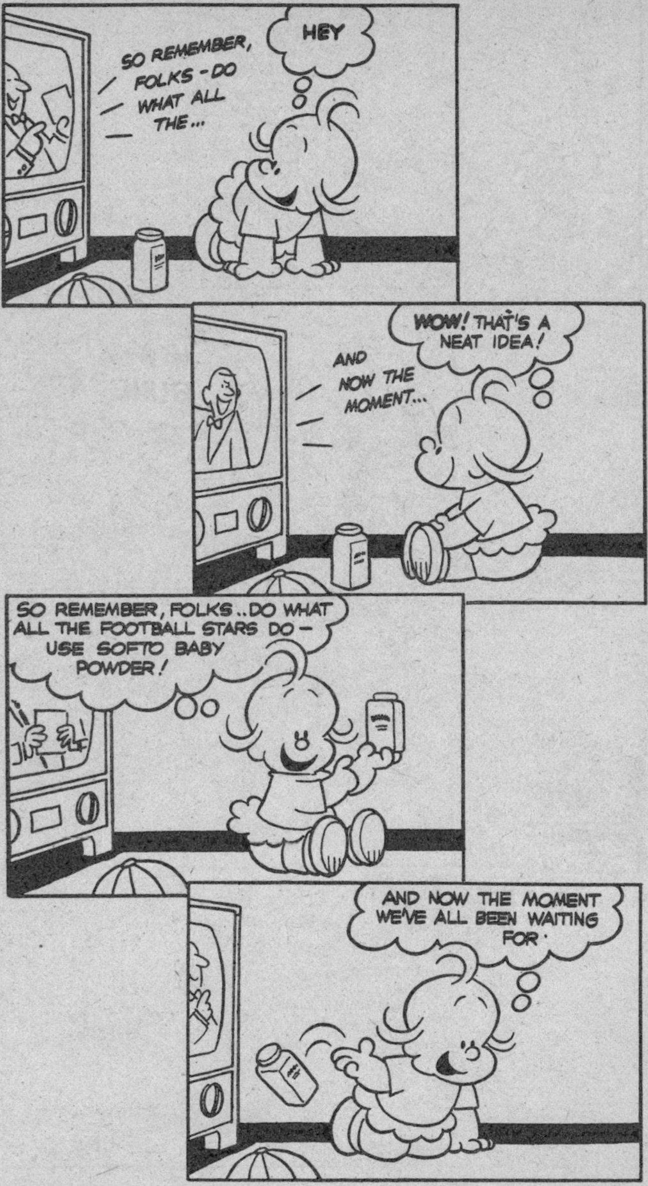
SO REMEMBER, FOLKS - DO WHAT ALL THE...
HEY
AND NOW THE MOMENT...
WOW! THAT'S A NEAT IDEA!
SO REMEMBER, FOLKS..DO WHAT ALL THE FOOTBALL STARS DO - USE SOFTO BABY POWDER!
AND NOW THE MOMENT WE'VE ALL BEEN WAITING FOR ·

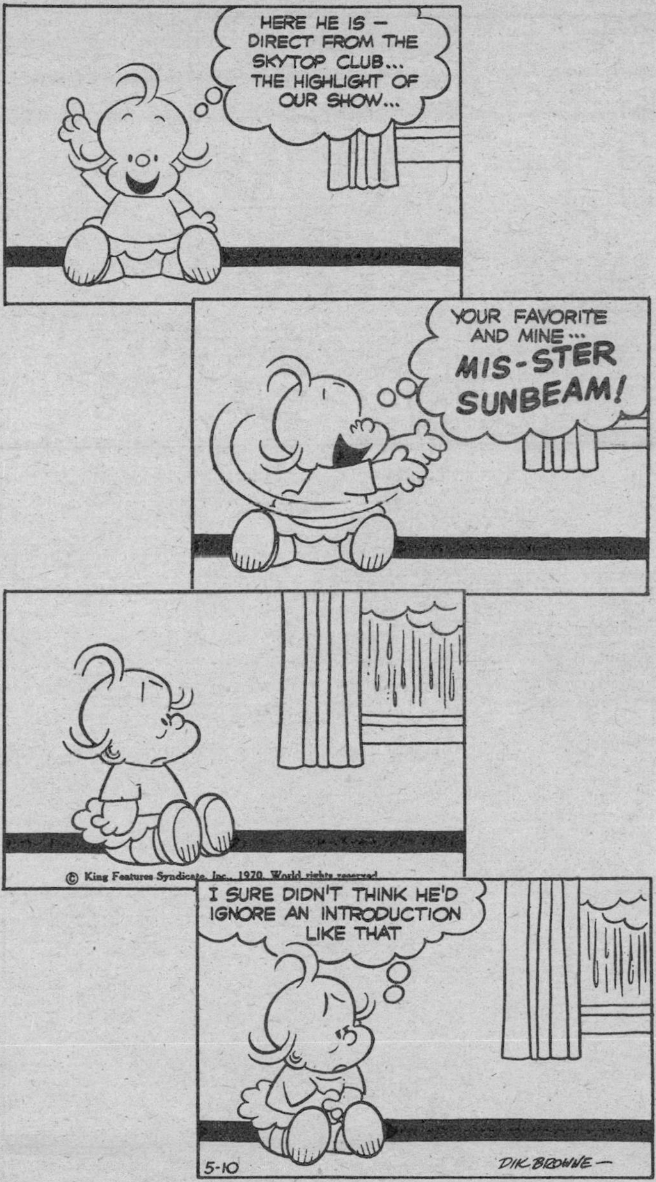
HERE HE IS — DIRECT FROM THE SKYTOP CLUB... THE HIGHLIGHT OF OUR SHOW...
YOUR FAVORITE AND MINE... MIS-STER SUNBEAM!
I SURE DIDN'T THINK HE'D IGNORE AN INTRODUCTION LIKE THAT
5-10
DIK BROWNE

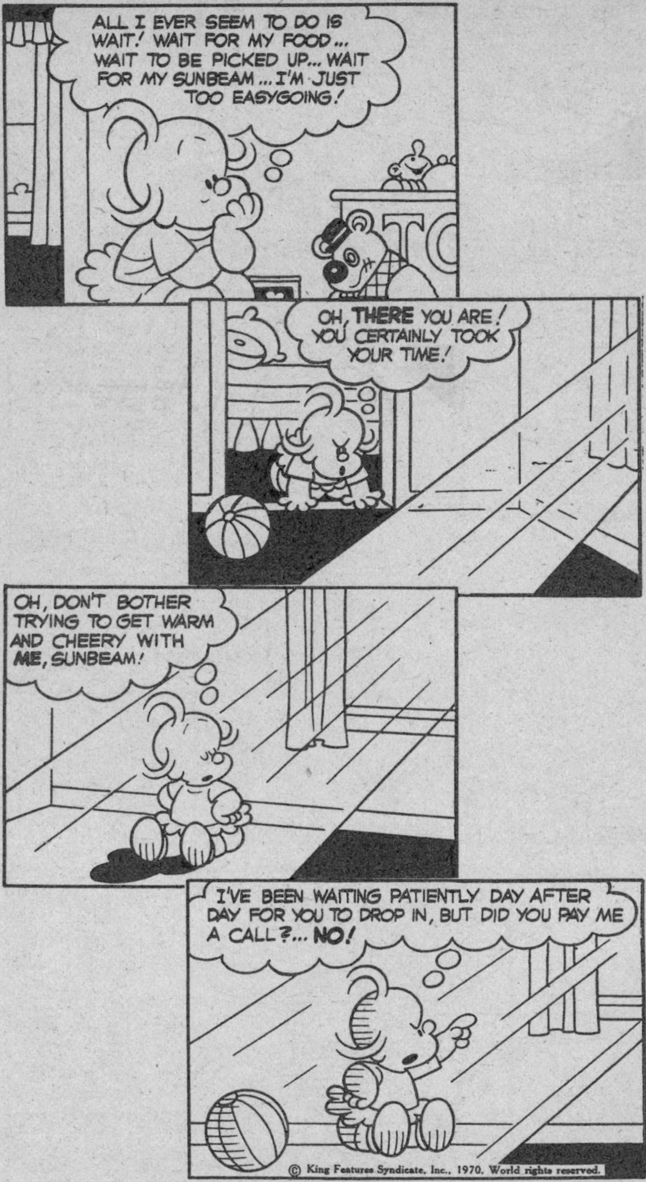
ALL I EVER SEEM TO DO IS WAIT! WAIT FOR MY FOOD... WAIT TO BE PICKED UP... WAIT FOR MY SUNBEAM... I'M JUST TOO EASYGOING!
OH, THERE YOU ARE! YOU CERTAINLY TOOK YOUR TIME!
OH, DON'T BOTHER TRYING TO GET WARM AND CHEERY WITH ME, SUNBEAM!
I'VE BEEN WAITING PATIENTLY DAY AFTER DAY FOR YOU TO DROP IN, BUT DID YOU PAY ME A CALL?... NO!
© King Features Syndicate, Inc., 1970. World rights reserved.

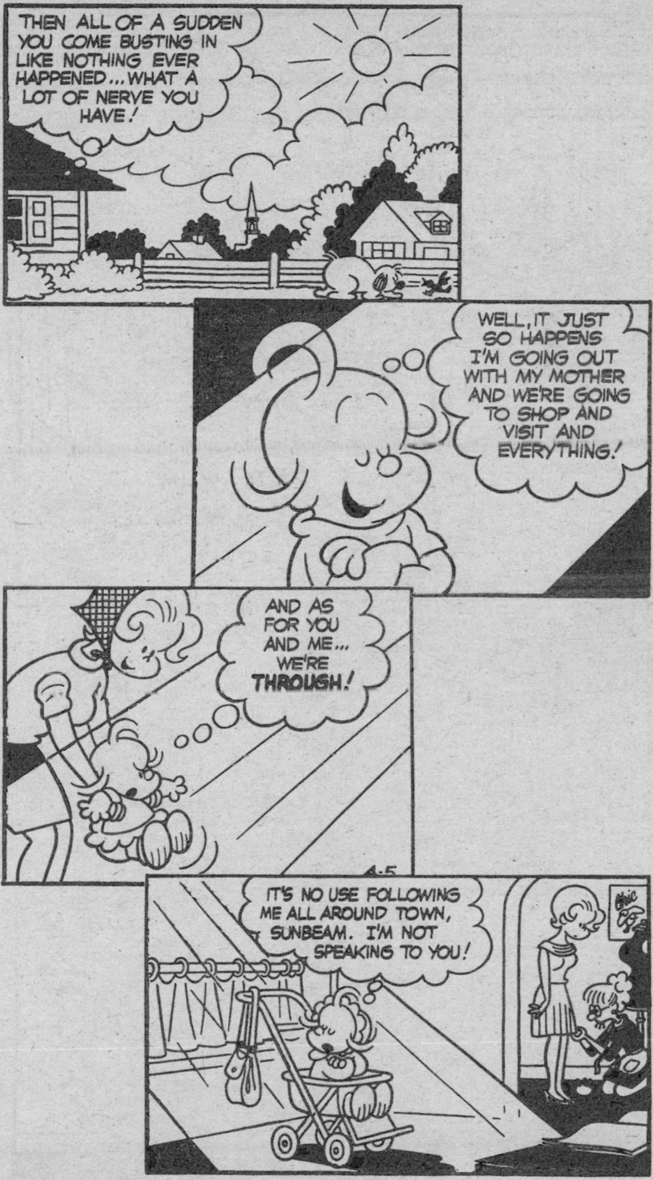
THEN ALL OF A SUDDEN YOU COME BUSTING IN LIKE NOTHING EVER HAPPENED... WHAT A LOT OF NERVE YOU HAVE!
WELL, IT JUST SO HAPPENS I'M GOING OUT WITH MY MOTHER AND WE'RE GOING TO SHOP AND VISIT AND EVERYTHING!
AND AS FOR YOU AND ME... WE'RE **THROUGH!**
IT'S NO USE FOLLOWING ME ALL AROUND TOWN, SUNBEAM. I'M NOT SPEAKING TO YOU!

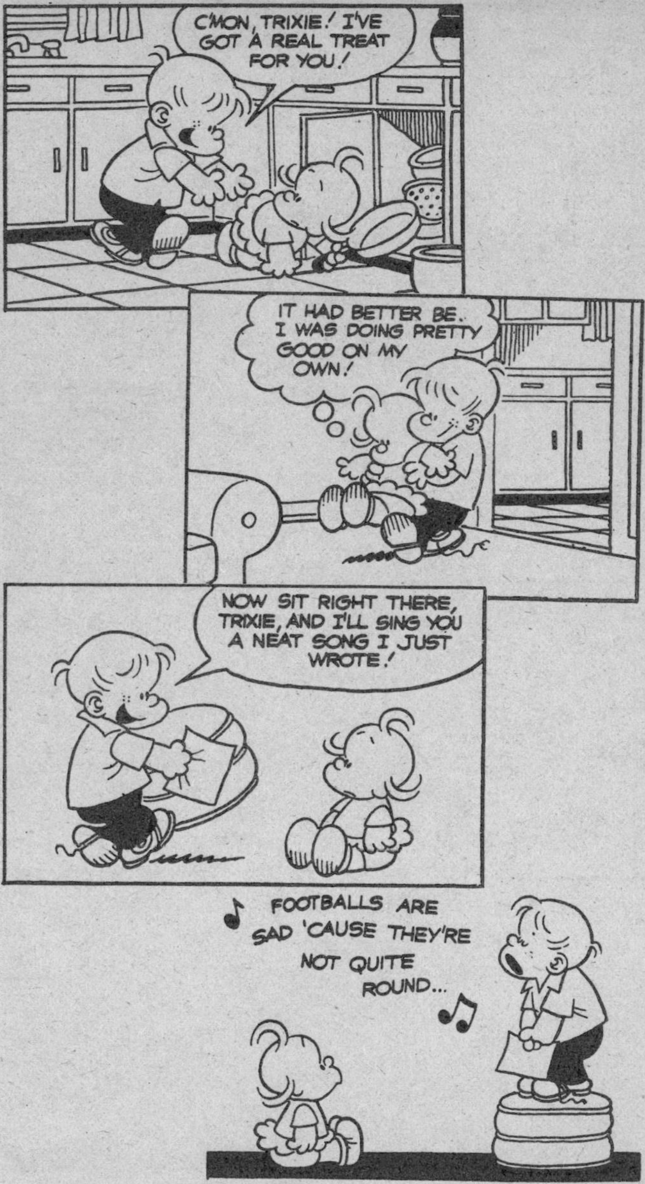
C'MON, TRIXIE! I'VE GOT A REAL TREAT FOR YOU!
IT HAD BETTER BE. I WAS DOING PRETTY GOOD ON MY OWN!
NOW SIT RIGHT THERE, TRIXIE, AND I'LL SING YOU A NEAT SONG I JUST WROTE!
FOOTBALLS ARE SAD 'CAUSE THEY'RE NOT QUITE ROUND...

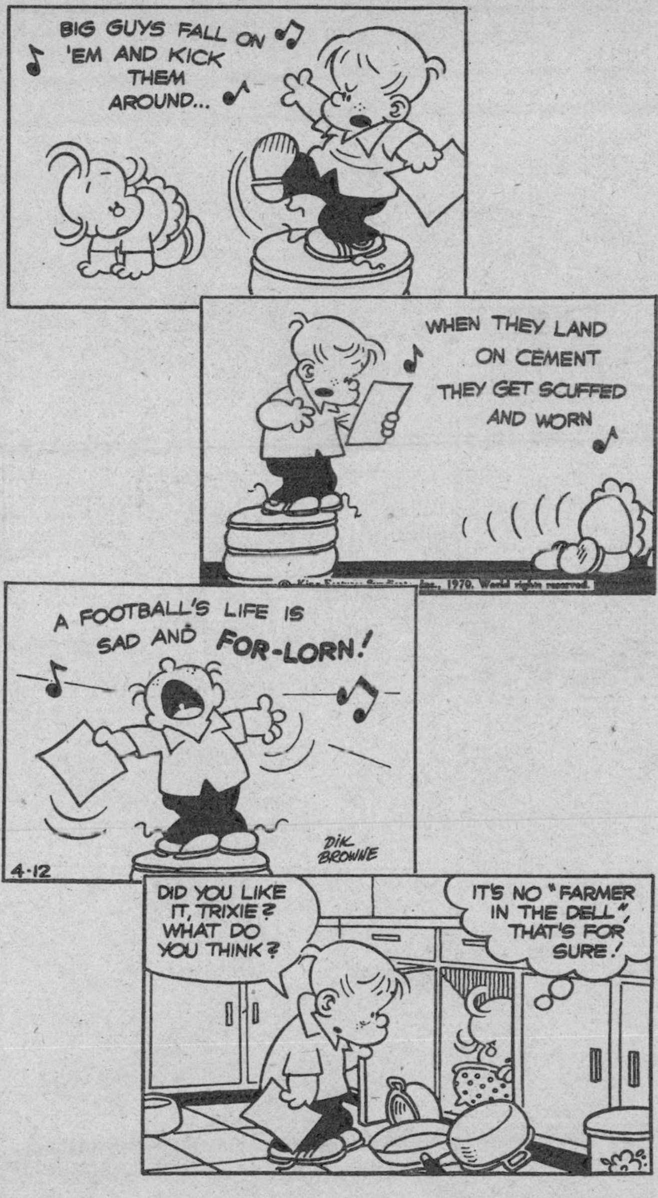
BIG GUYS FALL ON 'EM AND KICK THEM AROUND...
WHEN THEY LAND ON CEMENT THEY GET SCUFFED AND WORN
Inc., 1970. World rights reserved.
A FOOTBALL'S LIFE IS SAD AND FOR-LORN!
DIK BROWNE
4-12
DID YOU LIKE IT, TRIXIE? WHAT DO YOU THINK?
IT'S NO "FARMER IN THE DELL", THAT'S FOR SURE!

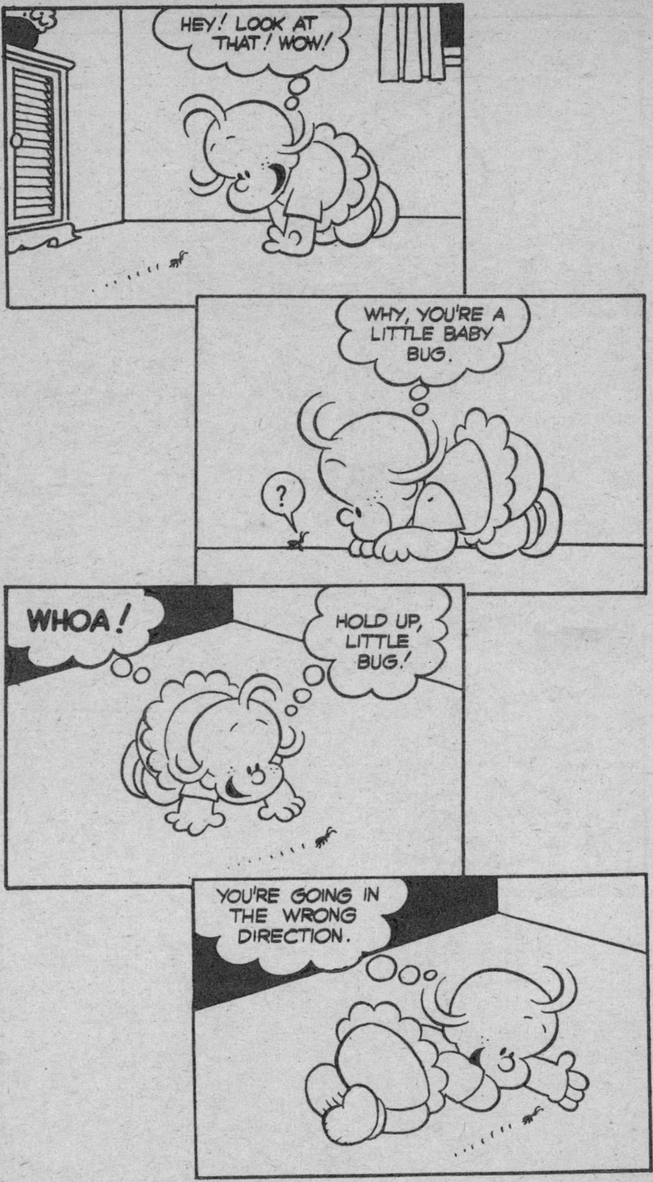
HEY! LOOK AT THAT! WOW!
WHY, YOU'RE A LITTLE BABY BUG.
?
WHOA!
HOLD UP, LITTLE BUG!
YOU'RE GOING IN THE WRONG DIRECTION.

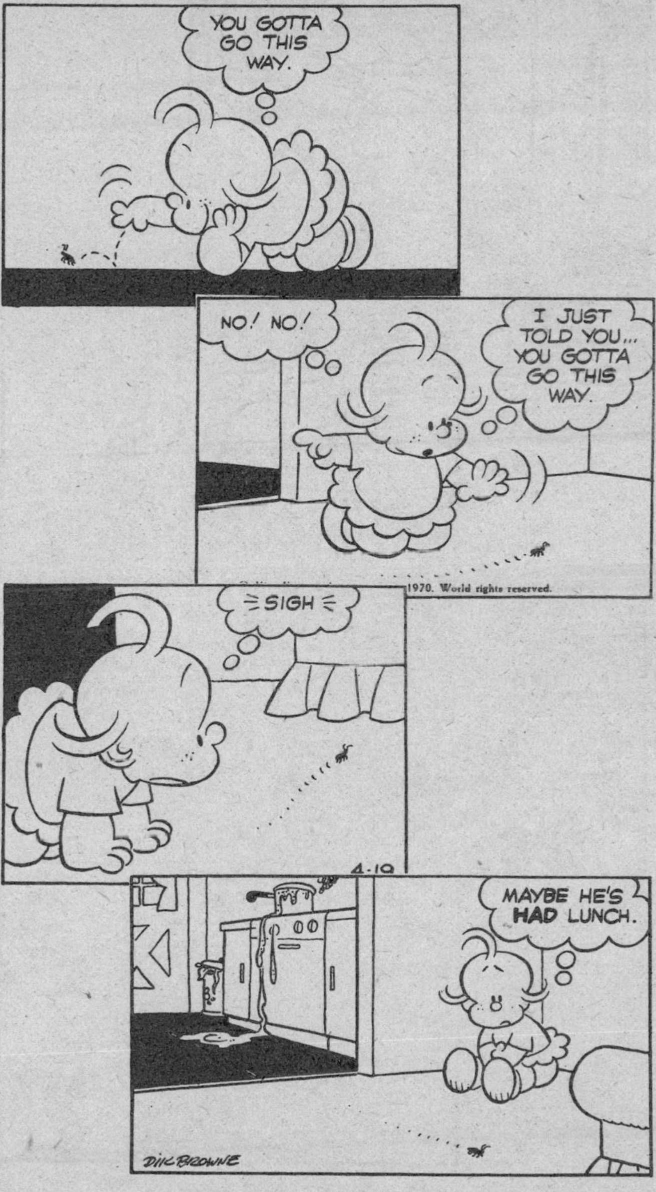
YOU GOTTA GO THIS WAY.
NO! NO!
I JUST TOLD YOU... YOU GOTTA GO THIS WAY.
1970. World rights reserved.
SIGH
4-19
MAYBE HE'S **HAD** LUNCH.
DIK BROWNE

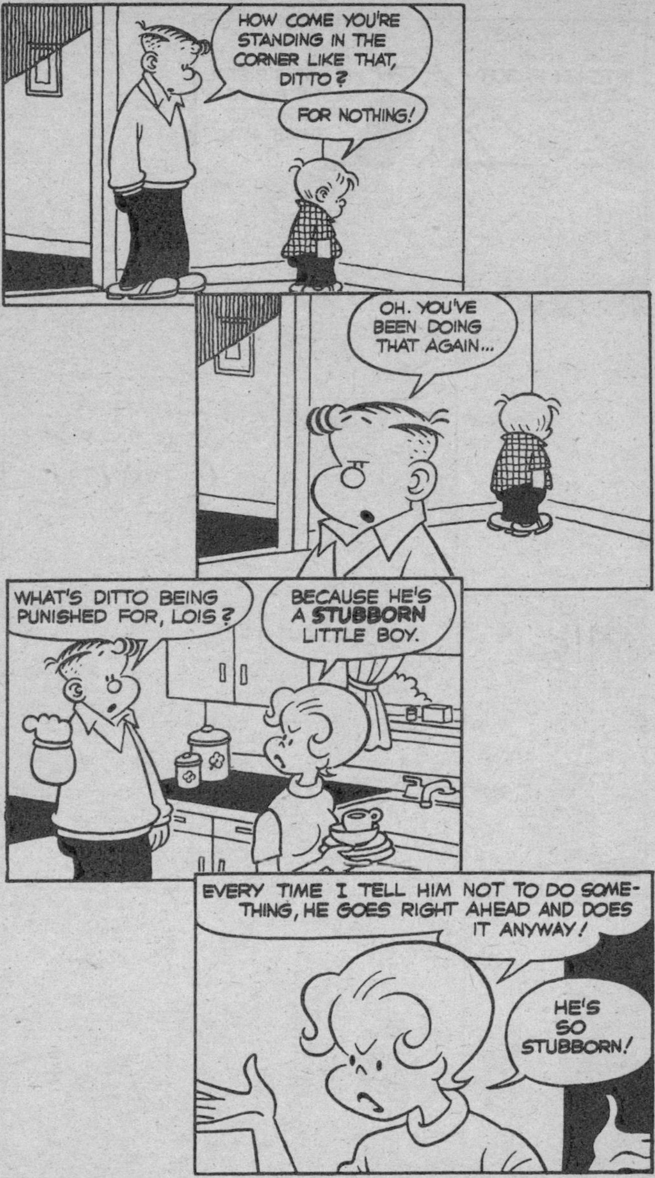
HOW COME YOU'RE STANDING IN THE CORNER LIKE THAT, DITTO?
FOR NOTHING!
OH. YOU'VE BEEN DOING THAT AGAIN...
WHAT'S DITTO BEING PUNISHED FOR, LOIS?
BECAUSE HE'S A STUBBORN LITTLE BOY.
EVERY TIME I TELL HIM NOT TO DO SOMETHING, HE GOES RIGHT AHEAD AND DOES IT ANYWAY!
HE'S SO STUBBORN!

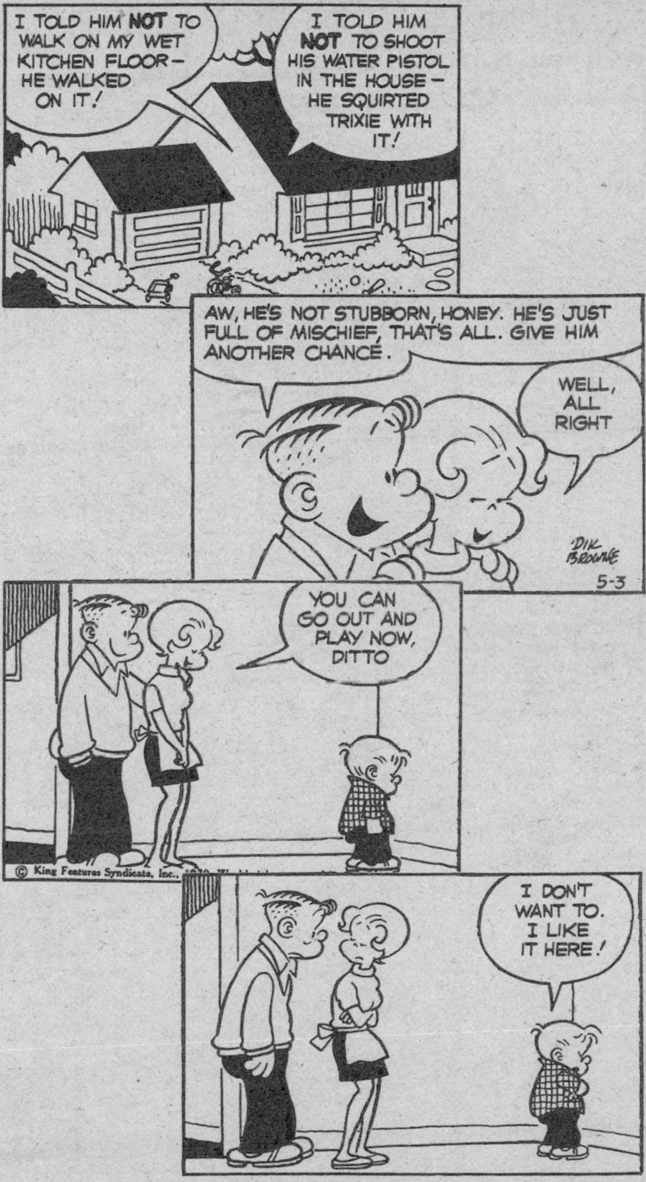
I TOLD HIM NOT TO WALK ON MY WET KITCHEN FLOOR– HE WALKED ON IT!
I TOLD HIM NOT TO SHOOT HIS WATER PISTOL IN THE HOUSE– HE SQUIRTED TRIXIE WITH IT!
AW, HE'S NOT STUBBORN, HONEY. HE'S JUST FULL OF MISCHIEF, THAT'S ALL. GIVE HIM ANOTHER CHANCE.
WELL, ALL RIGHT
DIK BROWNE
5-3
YOU CAN GO OUT AND PLAY NOW, DITTO
© King Features Syndicate, Inc.,
I DON'T WANT TO. I LIKE IT HERE!

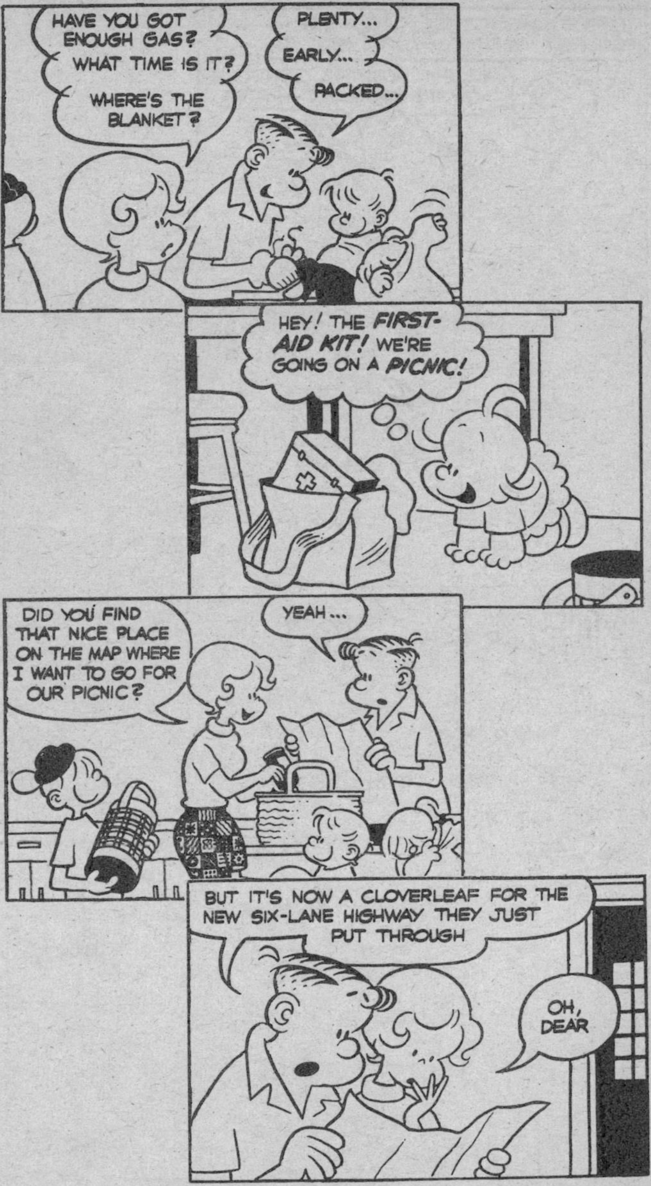
HAVE YOU GOT ENOUGH GAS?
PLENTY...
WHAT TIME IS IT?
EARLY...
WHERE'S THE BLANKET?
PACKED...
HEY! THE FIRST-AID KIT! WE'RE GOING ON A PICNIC!
DID YOU FIND THAT NICE PLACE ON THE MAP WHERE I WANT TO GO FOR OUR PICNIC?
YEAH...
BUT IT'S NOW A CLOVERLEAF FOR THE NEW SIX-LANE HIGHWAY THEY JUST PUT THROUGH
OH, DEAR

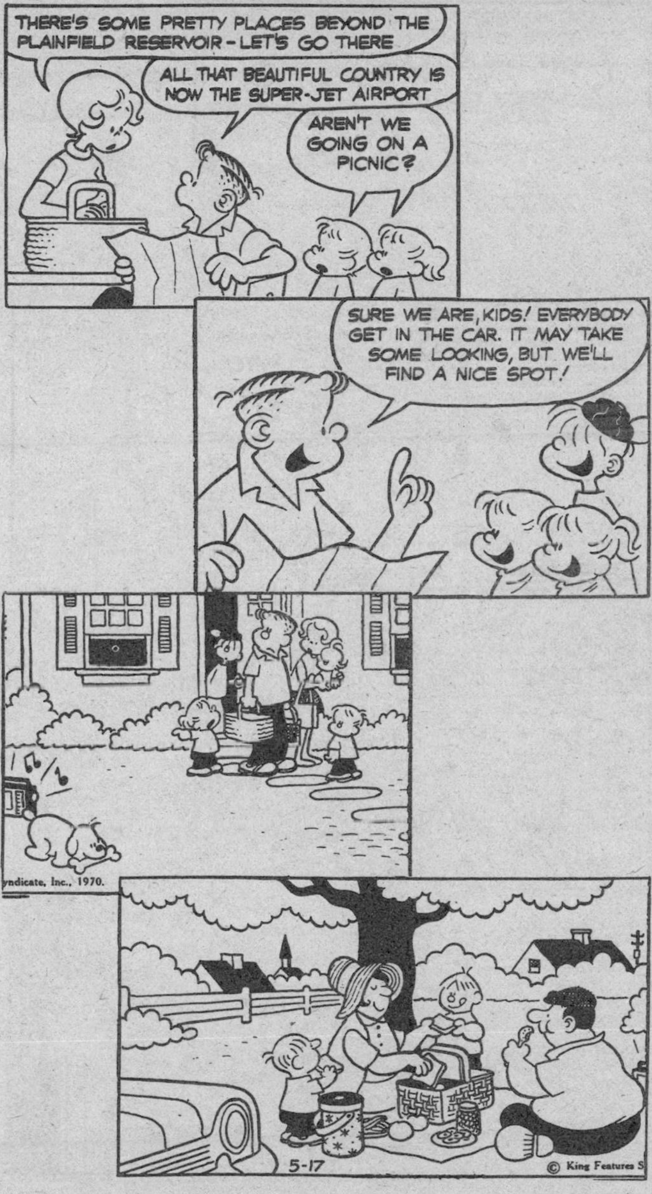

THERE'S SOME PRETTY PLACES BEYOND THE PLAINFIELD RESERVOIR - LET'S GO THERE
ALL THAT BEAUTIFUL COUNTRY IS NOW THE SUPER-JET AIRPORT
AREN'T WE GOING ON A PICNIC?
SURE WE ARE, KIDS! EVERYBODY GET IN THE CAR. IT MAY TAKE SOME LOOKING, BUT WE'LL FIND A NICE SPOT!
yndicate, Inc., 1970.
5-17
© King Features S

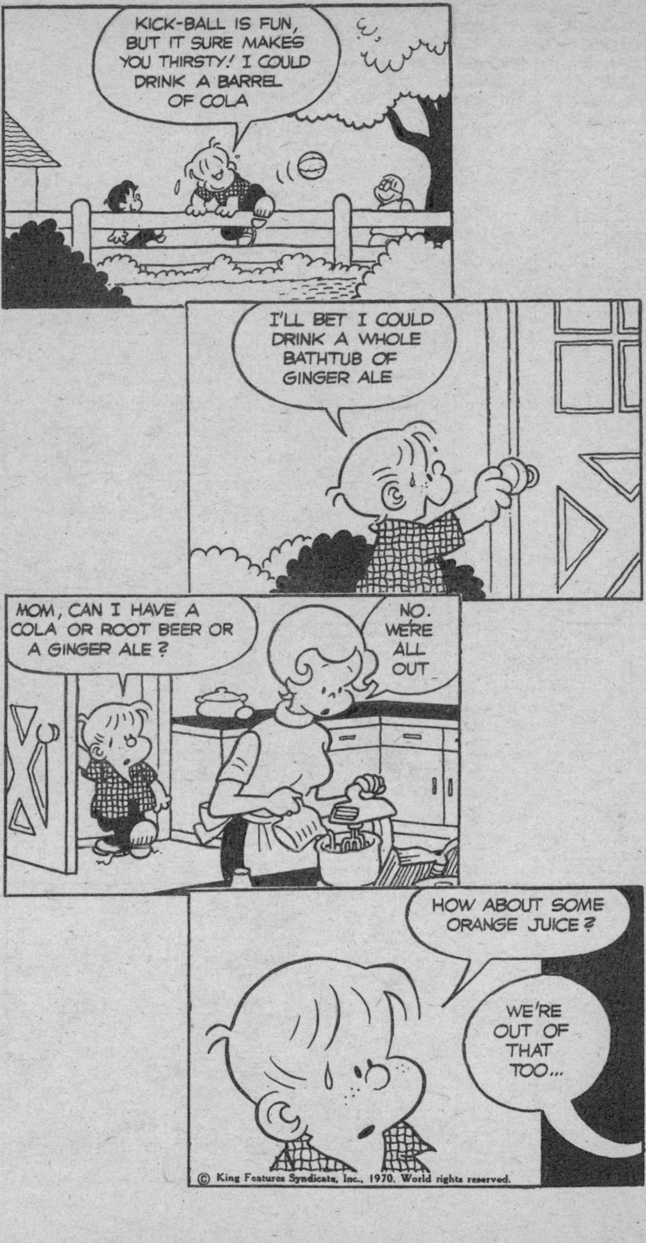
KICK-BALL IS FUN, BUT IT SURE MAKES YOU THIRSTY! I COULD DRINK A BARREL OF COLA
I'LL BET I COULD DRINK A WHOLE BATHTUB OF GINGER ALE
MOM, CAN I HAVE A COLA OR ROOT BEER OR A GINGER ALE?
NO. WE'RE ALL OUT
HOW ABOUT SOME ORANGE JUICE?
WE'RE OUT OF THAT TOO...

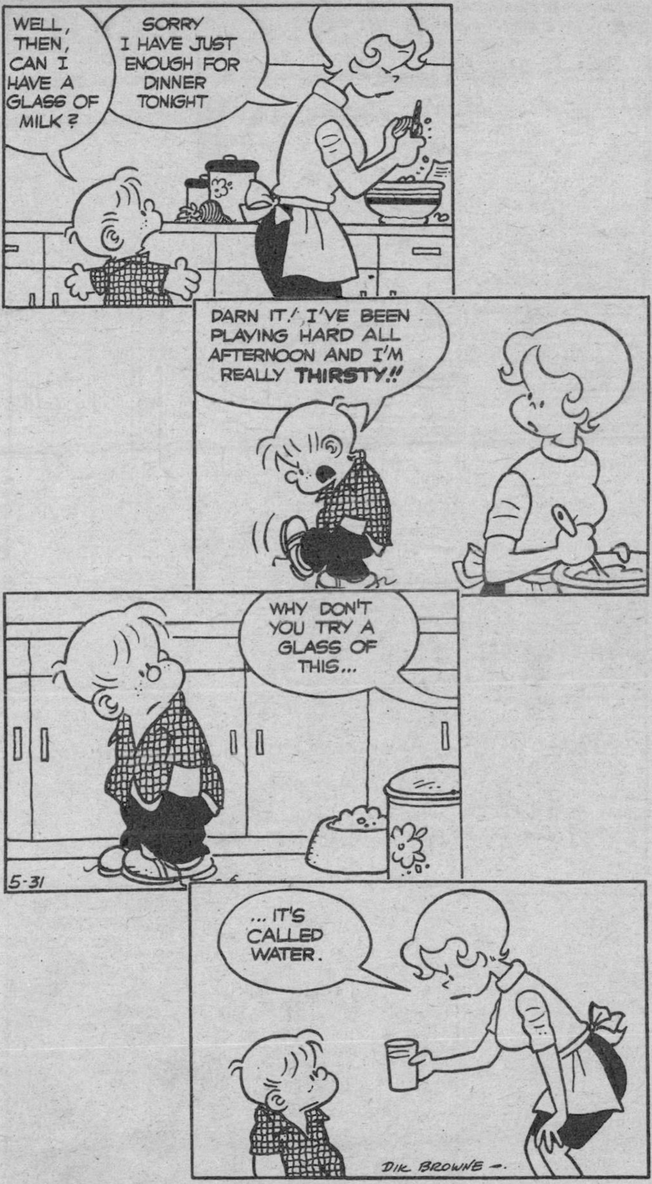
WELL, THEN, CAN I HAVE A GLASS OF MILK?
SORRY I HAVE JUST ENOUGH FOR DINNER TONIGHT
DARN IT! I'VE BEEN PLAYING HARD ALL AFTERNOON AND I'M REALLY THIRSTY!!
WHY DON'T YOU TRY A GLASS OF THIS...
5-31
... IT'S CALLED WATER.
DIK BROWNE

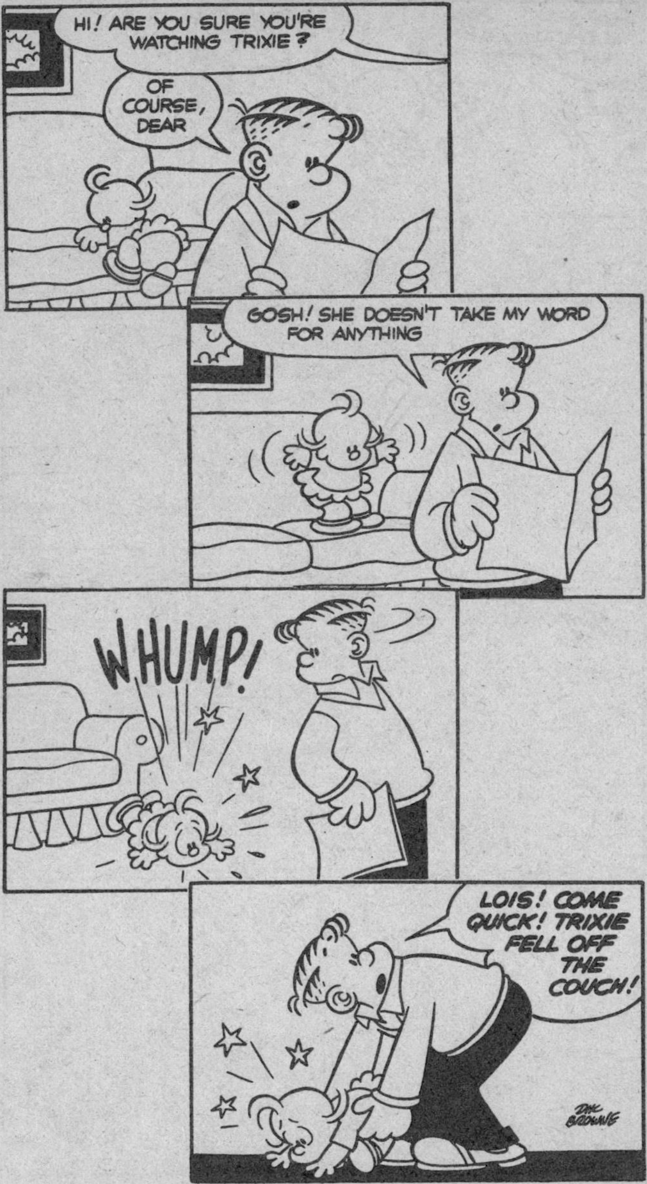
HI! ARE YOU SURE YOU'RE WATCHING TRIXIE?
OF COURSE, DEAR
GOSH! SHE DOESN'T TAKE MY WORD FOR ANYTHING
WHUMP!
LOIS! COME QUICK! TRIXIE FELL OFF THE COUCH!
DIK BROWNE

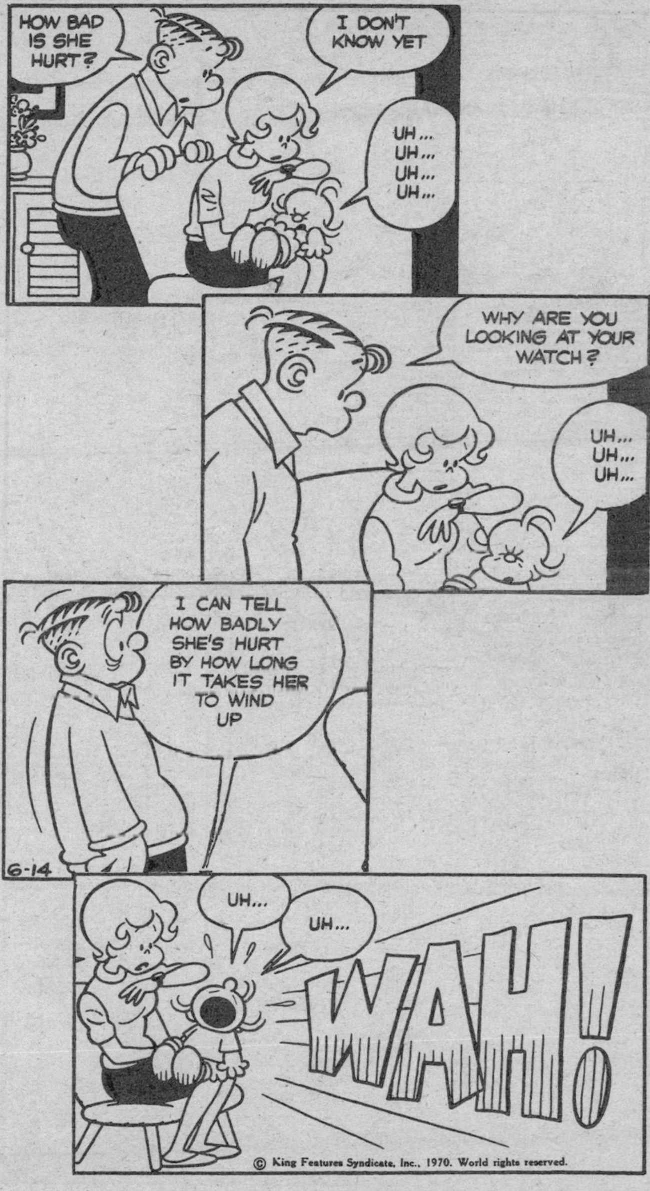
HOW BAD IS SHE HURT?
I DON'T KNOW YET
UH... UH... UH... UH...
WHY ARE YOU LOOKING AT YOUR WATCH?
UH... UH... UH...
I CAN TELL HOW BADLY SHE'S HURT BY HOW LONG IT TAKES HER TO WIND UP
6-14
UH...
UH...
WAH!

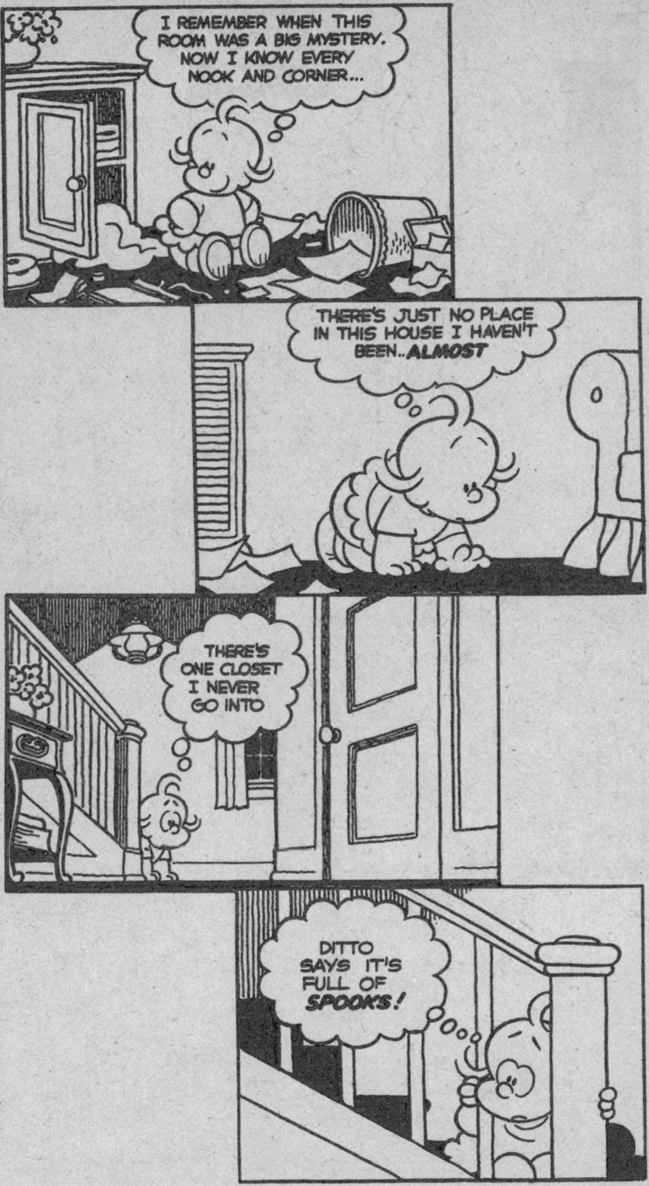
I REMEMBER WHEN THIS ROOM WAS A BIG MYSTERY. NOW I KNOW EVERY NOOK AND CORNER...
THERE'S JUST NO PLACE IN THIS HOUSE I HAVEN'T BEEN..ALMOST
THERE'S ONE CLOSET I NEVER GO INTO
DITTO SAYS IT'S FULL OF SPOOKS!

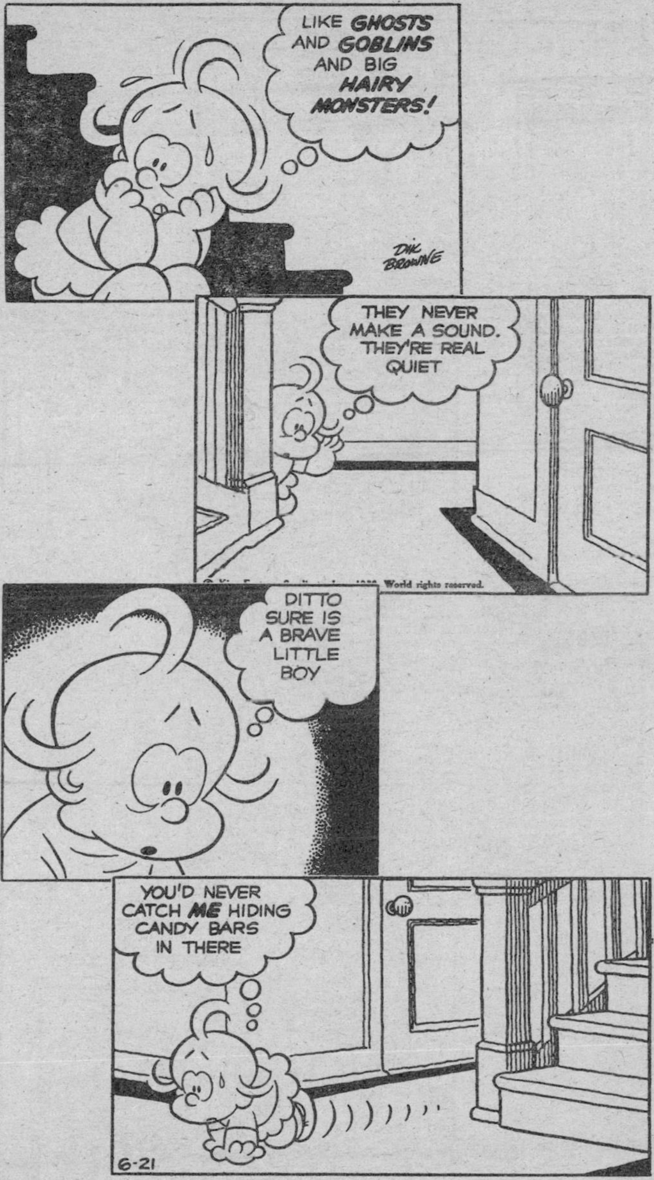

LIKE GHOSTS AND GOBLINS AND BIG HAIRY MONSTERS!
DIK BROWNE
THEY NEVER MAKE A SOUND. THEY'RE REAL QUIET
World rights reserved.
DITTO SURE IS A BRAVE LITTLE BOY
YOU'D NEVER CATCH ME HIDING CANDY BARS IN THERE
6-21

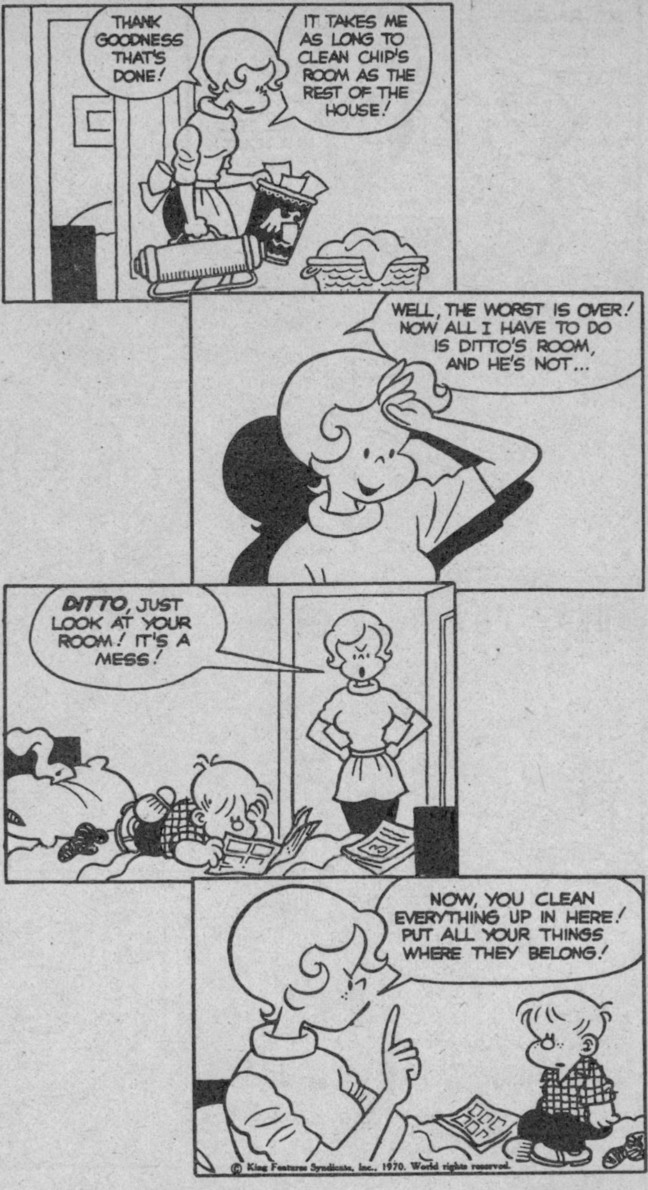
THANK GOODNESS THAT'S DONE!
IT TAKES ME AS LONG TO CLEAN CHIP'S ROOM AS THE REST OF THE HOUSE!
WELL, THE WORST IS OVER! NOW ALL I HAVE TO DO IS DITTO'S ROOM, AND HE'S NOT...
DITTO, JUST LOOK AT YOUR ROOM! IT'S A MESS!
NOW, YOU CLEAN EVERYTHING UP IN HERE! PUT ALL YOUR THINGS WHERE THEY BELONG!

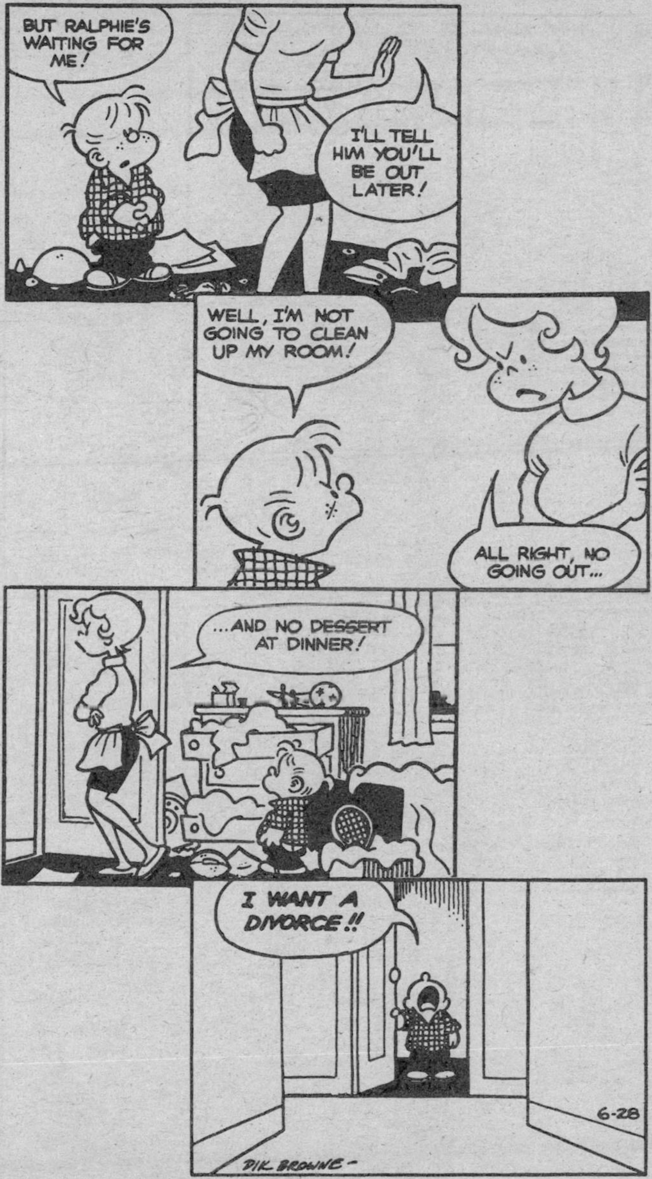
BUT RALPHIE'S WAITING FOR ME!
I'LL TELL HIM YOU'LL BE OUT LATER!
WELL, I'M NOT GOING TO CLEAN UP MY ROOM!
ALL RIGHT, NO GOING OUT...
...AND NO DESSERT AT DINNER!
I WANT A DIVORCE!!
6-28
DIK BROWNE

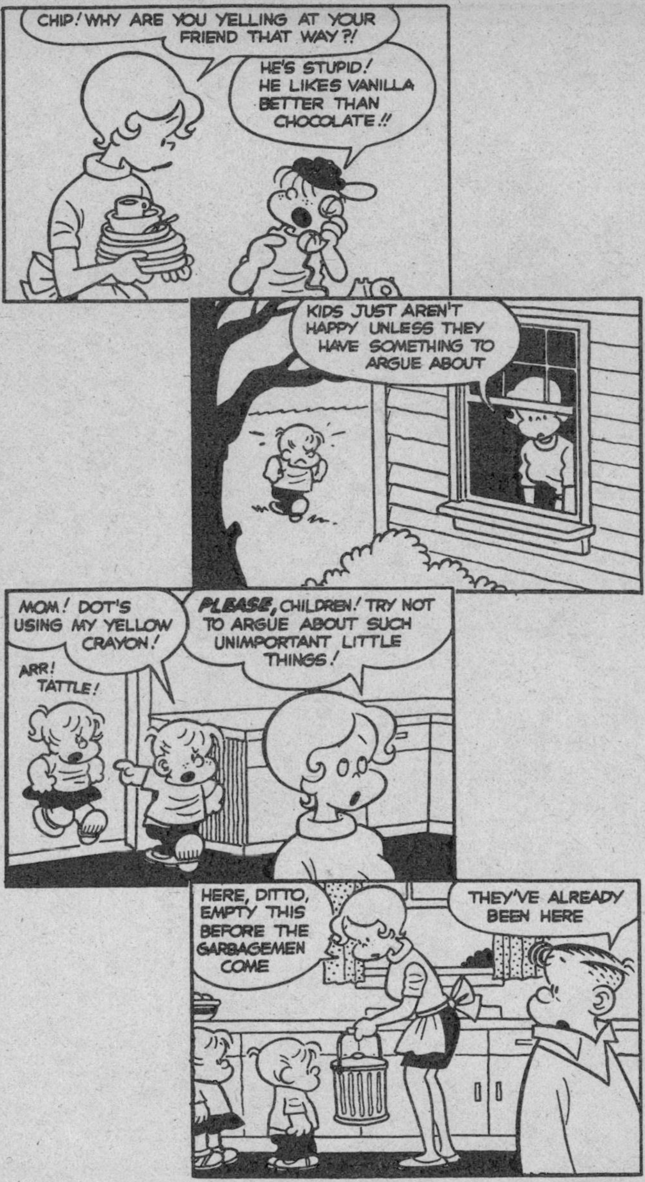
CHIP! WHY ARE YOU YELLING AT YOUR FRIEND THAT WAY?!
HE'S STUPID! HE LIKES VANILLA BETTER THAN CHOCOLATE!!
KIDS JUST AREN'T HAPPY UNLESS THEY HAVE SOMETHING TO ARGUE ABOUT
MOM! DOT'S USING MY YELLOW CRAYON!
ARR! TATTLE!
PLEASE, CHILDREN! TRY NOT TO ARGUE ABOUT SUCH UNIMPORTANT LITTLE THINGS!
HERE, DITTO, EMPTY THIS BEFORE THE GARBAGEMEN COME
THEY'VE ALREADY BEEN HERE

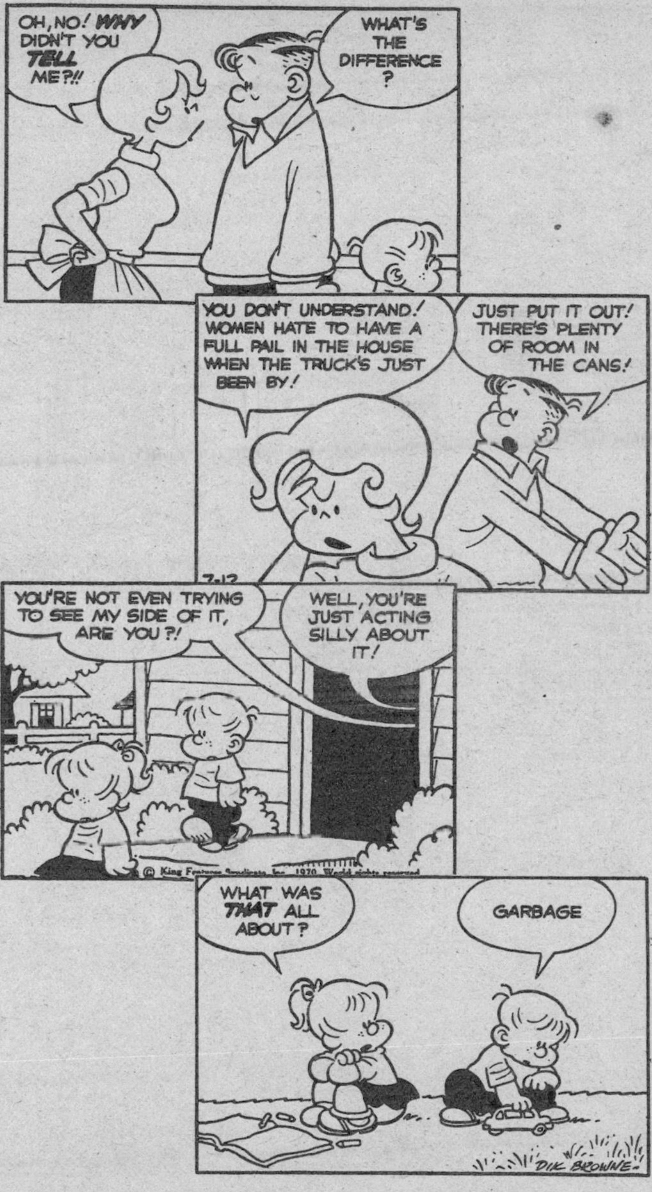

OH, NO! WHY DIDN'T YOU TELL ME?!!
WHAT'S THE DIFFERENCE ?
YOU DON'T UNDERSTAND! WOMEN HATE TO HAVE A FULL PAIL IN THE HOUSE WHEN THE TRUCK'S JUST BEEN BY!
JUST PUT IT OUT! THERE'S PLENTY OF ROOM IN THE CANS!
YOU'RE NOT EVEN TRYING TO SEE MY SIDE OF IT, ARE YOU ?!
WELL, YOU'RE JUST ACTING SILLY ABOUT IT!
© King Features Syndicate, Inc. 1970 World rights reserved
WHAT WAS THAT ALL ABOUT ?
GARBAGE
DIK BROWNE

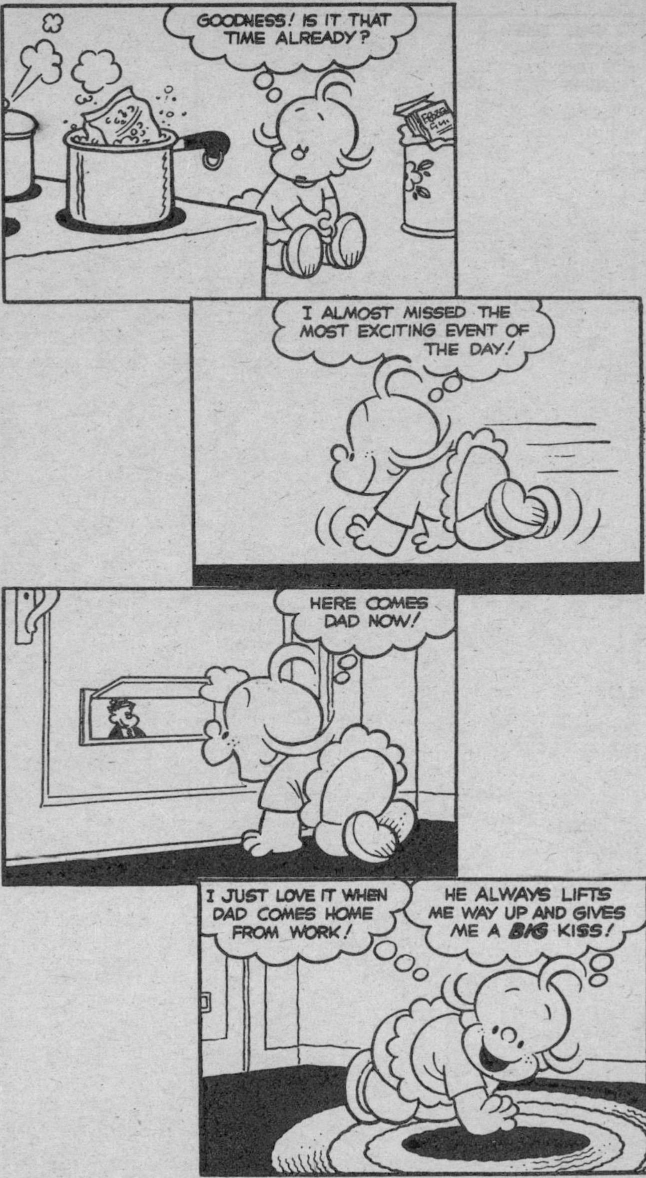
GOODNESS! IS IT THAT TIME ALREADY?
I ALMOST MISSED THE MOST EXCITING EVENT OF THE DAY!
HERE COMES DAD NOW!
I JUST LOVE IT WHEN DAD COMES HOME FROM WORK!
HE ALWAYS LIFTS ME WAY UP AND GIVES ME A BIG KISS!

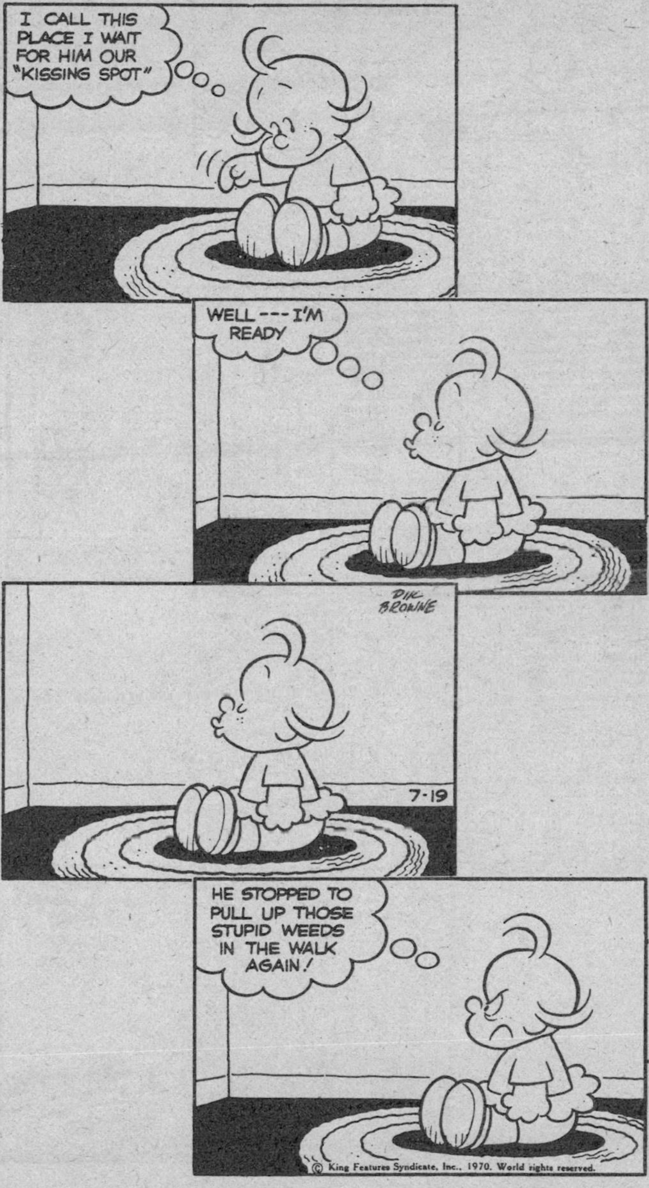
I CALL THIS PLACE I WAIT FOR HIM OUR "KISSING SPOT"
WELL --- I'M READY
DIK BROWNE
7-19
HE STOPPED TO PULL UP THOSE STUPID WEEDS IN THE WALK AGAIN!
© King Features Syndicate, Inc., 1970. World rights reserved.

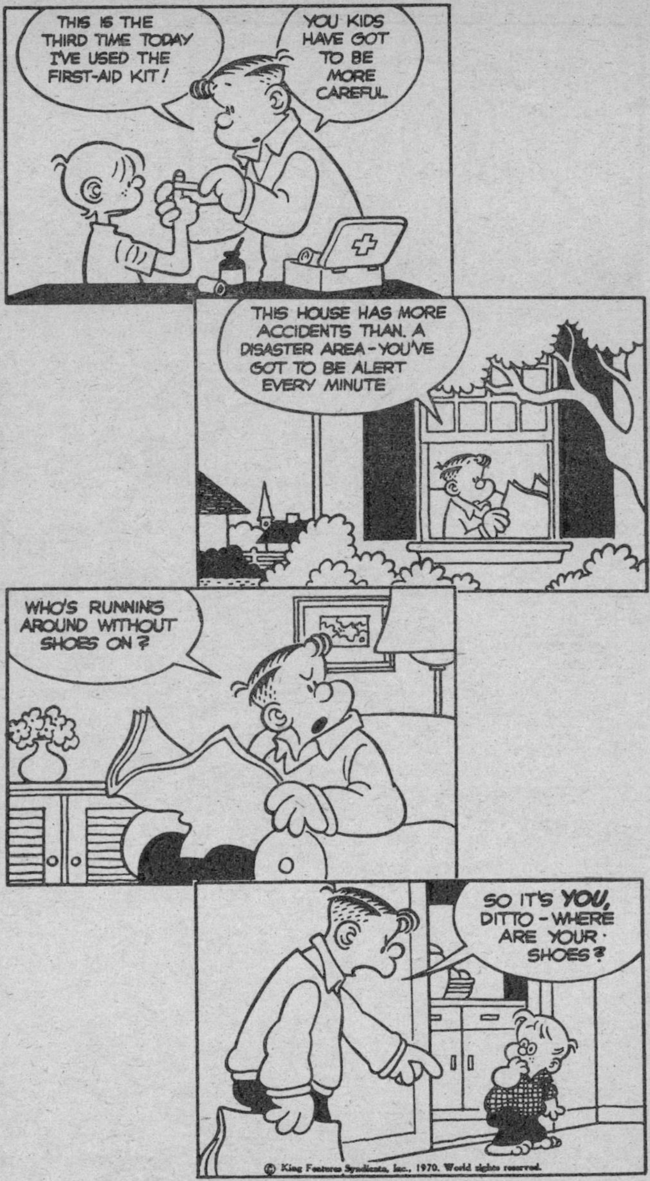
THIS IS THE THIRD TIME TODAY I'VE USED THE FIRST-AID KIT!
YOU KIDS HAVE GOT TO BE MORE CAREFUL
THIS HOUSE HAS MORE ACCIDENTS THAN. A DISASTER AREA - YOU'VE GOT TO BE ALERT EVERY MINUTE
WHO'S RUNNING AROUND WITHOUT SHOES ON?
SO IT'S **YOU,** DITTO - WHERE ARE YOUR SHOES?

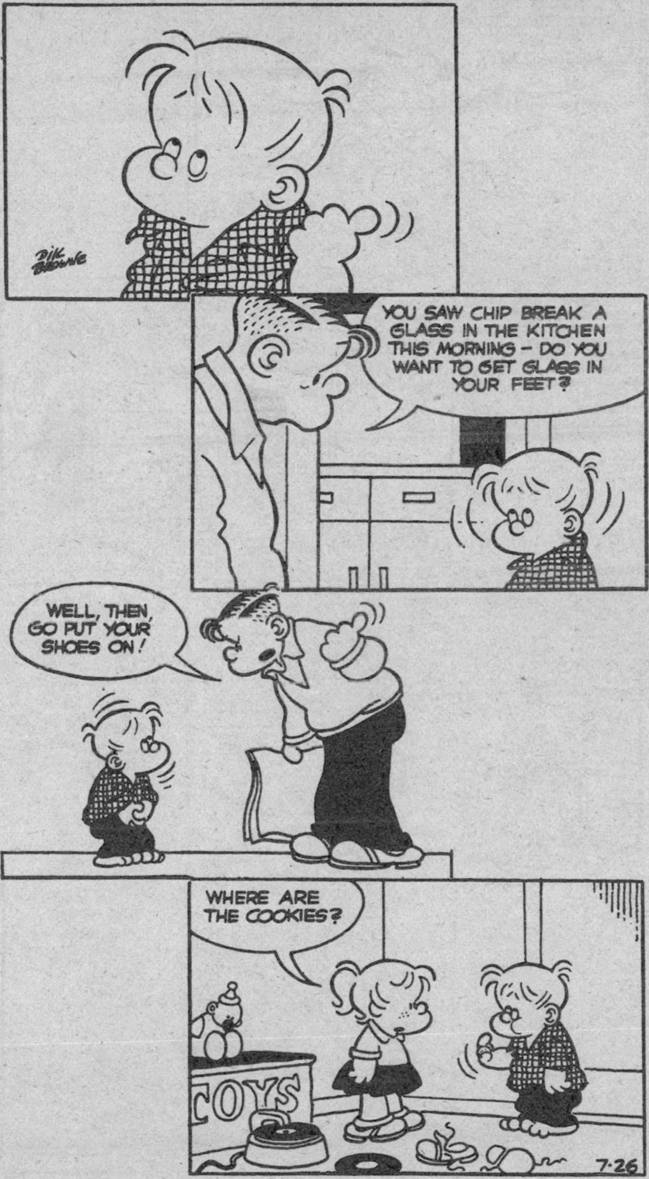
DIK BROWNE
YOU SAW CHIP BREAK A GLASS IN THE KITCHEN THIS MORNING – DO YOU WANT TO GET GLASS IN YOUR FEET?
WELL, THEN, GO PUT YOUR SHOES ON!
WHERE ARE THE COOKIES?
TOYS
7·26

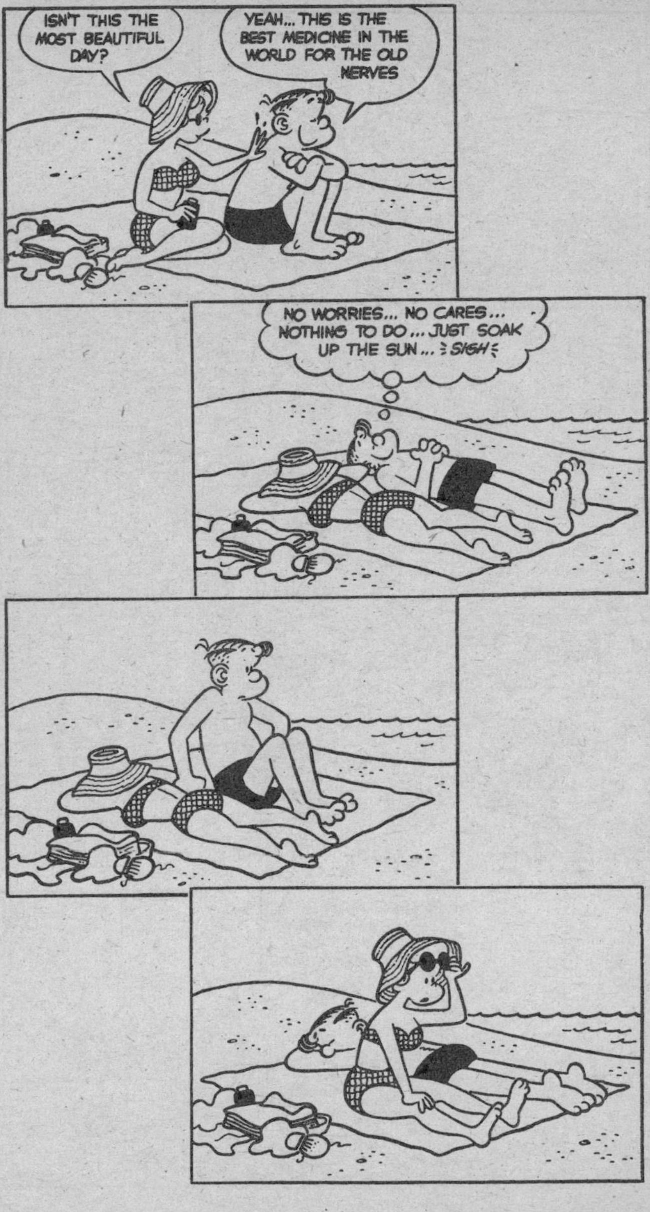
ISN'T THIS THE MOST BEAUTIFUL DAY?
YEAH... THIS IS THE BEST MEDICINE IN THE WORLD FOR THE OLD NERVES
NO WORRIES... NO CARES... NOTHING TO DO ... JUST SOAK UP THE SUN ... SIGH

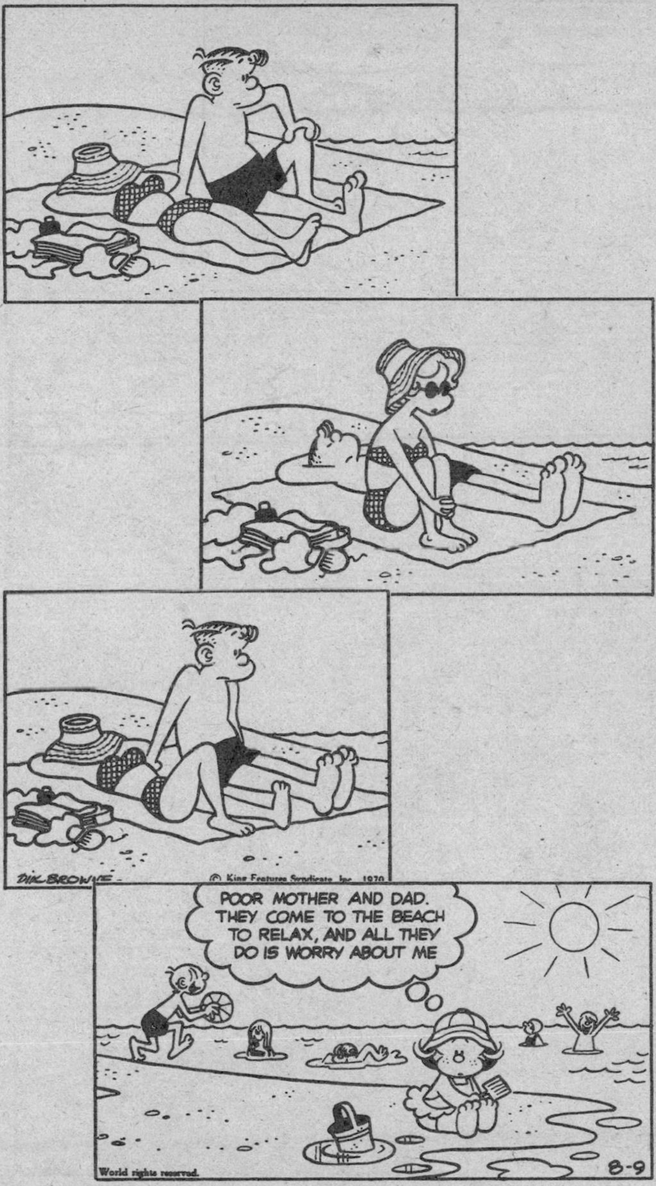
DIK BROWNE
© King Features Syndicate, Inc., 1970
POOR MOTHER AND DAD. THEY COME TO THE BEACH TO RELAX, AND ALL THEY DO IS WORRY ABOUT ME
World rights reserved.
8-9

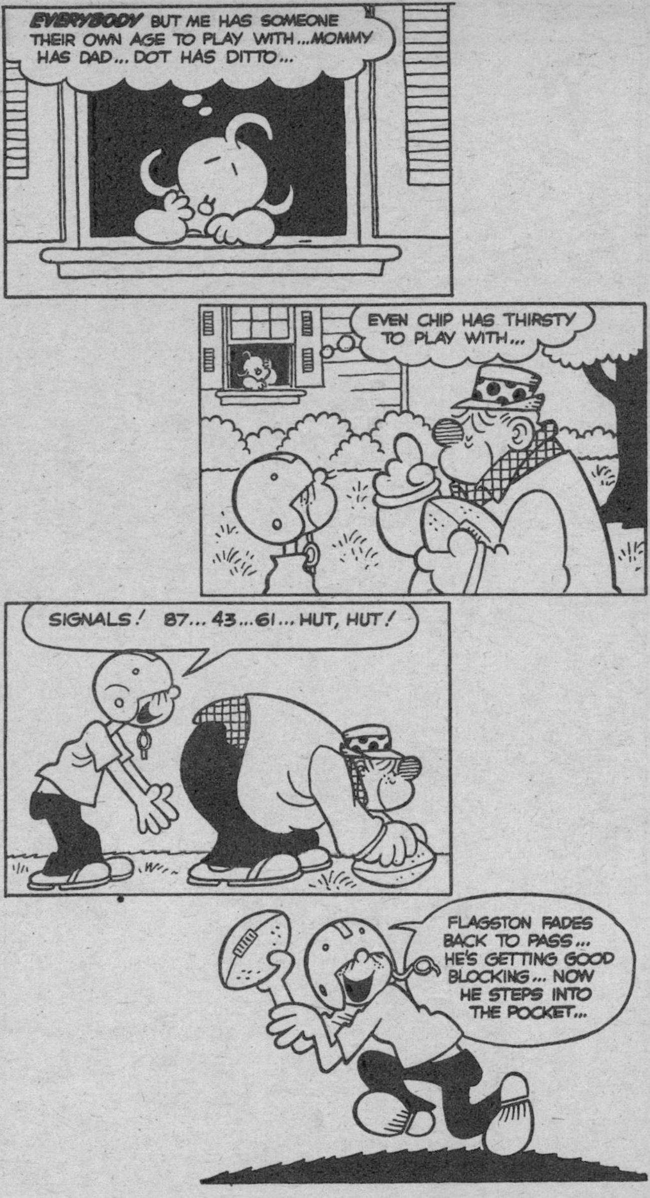
EVERYBODY BUT ME HAS SOMEONE THEIR OWN AGE TO PLAY WITH...MOMMY HAS DAD... DOT HAS DITTO...
EVEN CHIP HAS THIRSTY TO PLAY WITH...
SIGNALS! 87... 43...61... HUT, HUT!
FLAGSTON FADES BACK TO PASS... HE'S GETTING GOOD BLOCKING... NOW HE STEPS INTO THE POCKET...

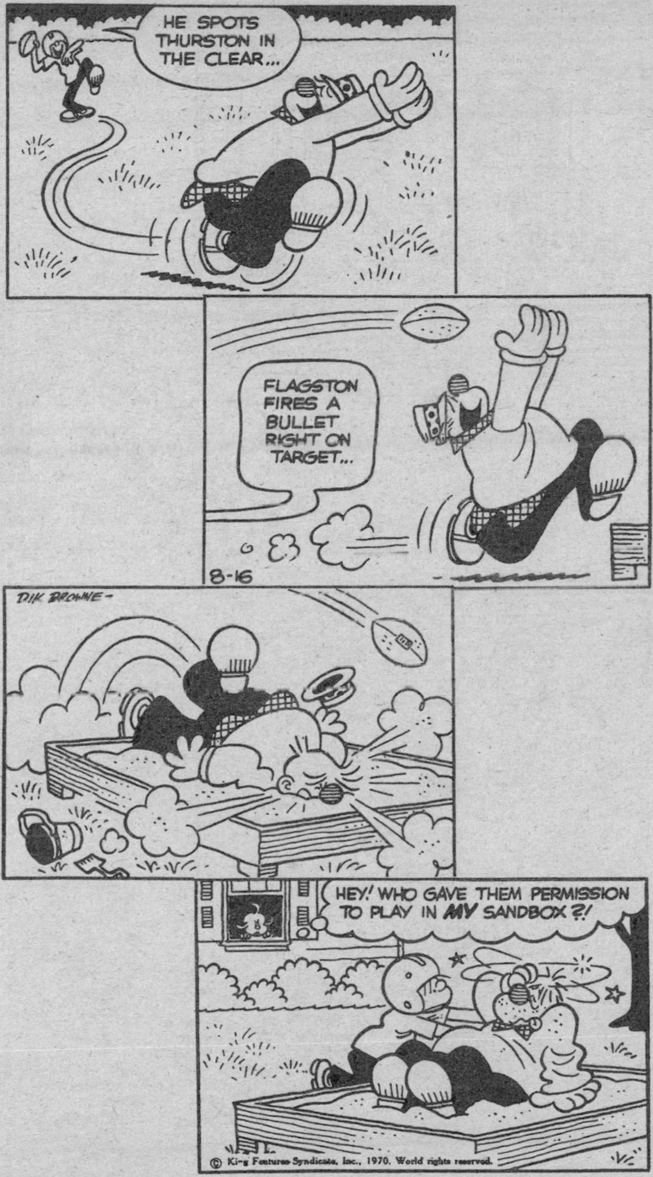
HE SPOTS THURSTON IN THE CLEAR...
FLAGSTON FIRES A BULLET RIGHT ON TARGET...
8-16
DIK BROWNE
HEY! WHO GAVE THEM PERMISSION TO PLAY IN *MY* SANDBOX ?!

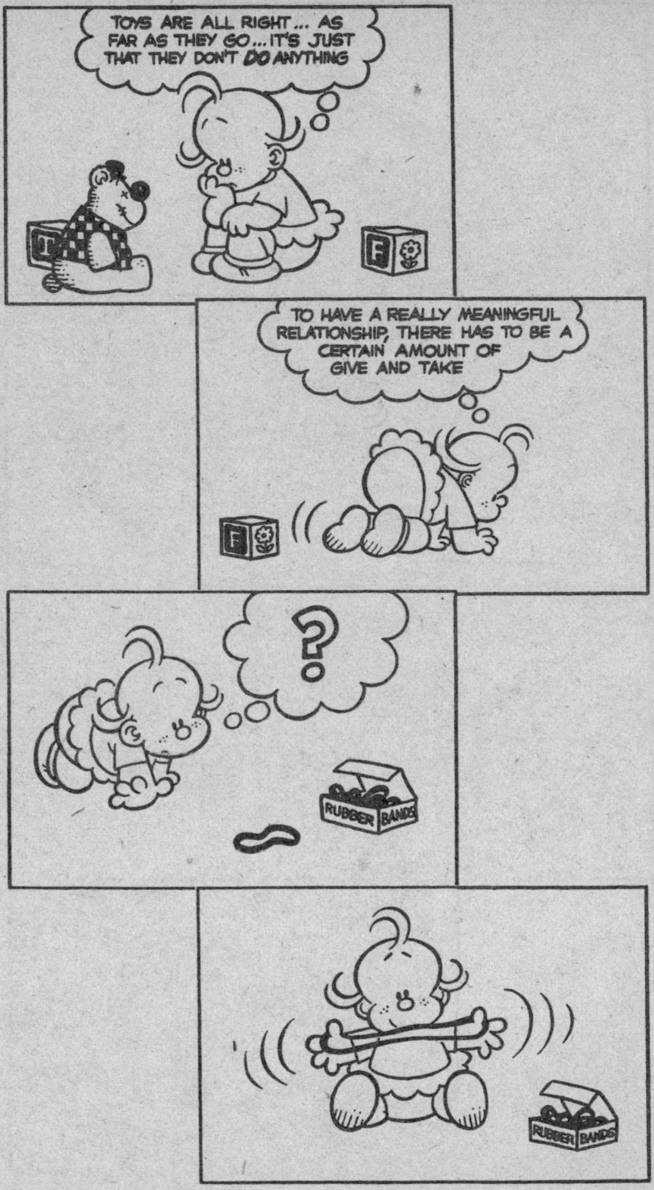
TOYS ARE ALL RIGHT... AS FAR AS THEY GO... IT'S JUST THAT THEY DON'T DO ANYTHING
TO HAVE A REALLY MEANINGFUL RELATIONSHIP, THERE HAS TO BE A CERTAIN AMOUNT OF GIVE AND TAKE
?
RUBBER BANDS
RUBBER BANDS

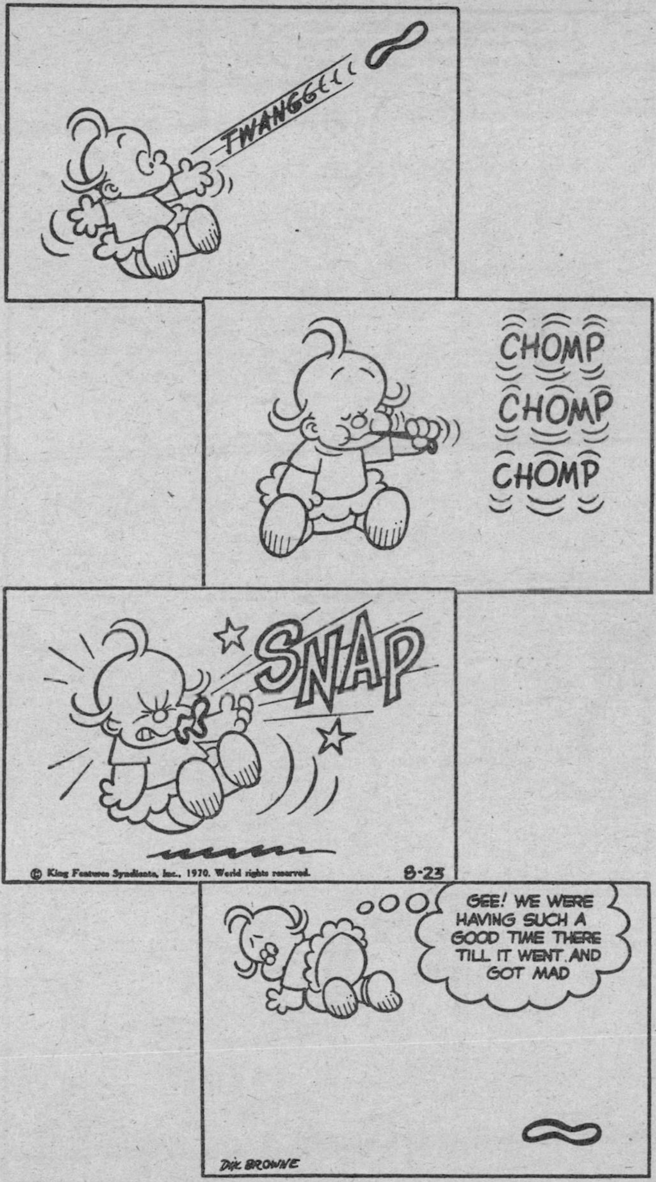
TWANGG
CHOMP
CHOMP
CHOMP
SNAP
© King Features Syndicate, Inc., 1970. World rights reserved.
8-23
GEE! WE WERE HAVING SUCH A GOOD TIME THERE TILL IT WENT AND GOT MAD
DIK BROWNE

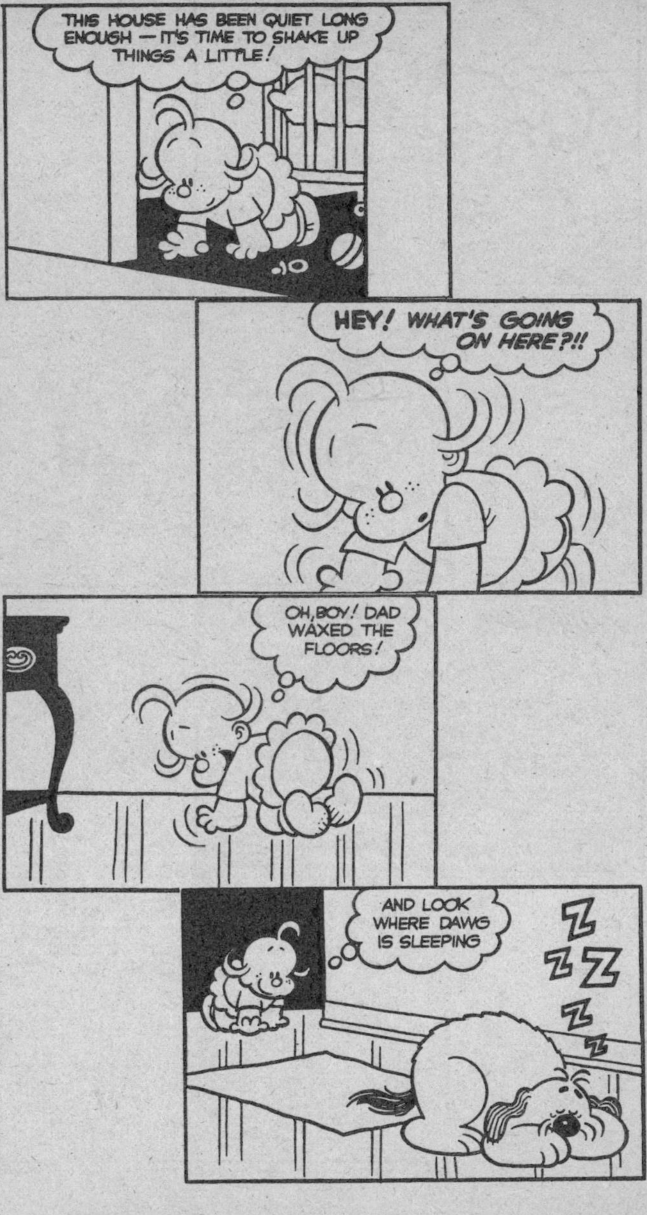
THIS HOUSE HAS BEEN QUIET LONG ENOUGH — IT'S TIME TO SHAKE UP THINGS A LITTLE!
HEY! WHAT'S GOING ON HERE?!!
OH, BOY! DAD WAXED THE FLOORS!
AND LOOK WHERE DAWG IS SLEEPING
Z Z Z Z Z

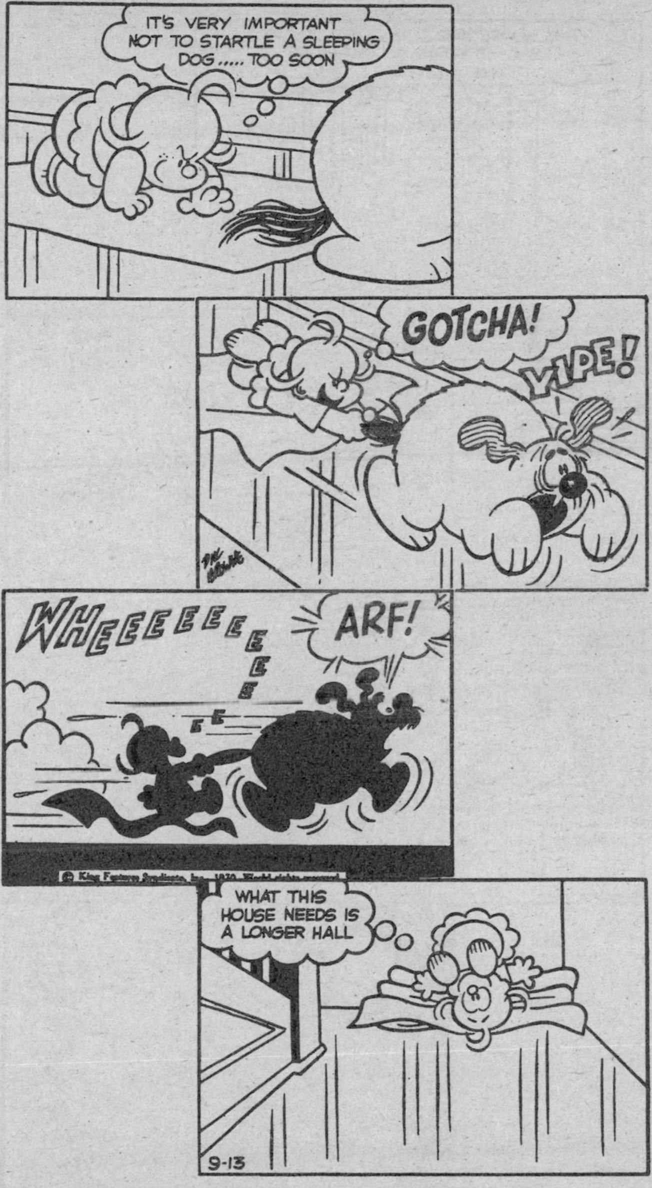
IT'S VERY IMPORTANT NOT TO STARTLE A SLEEPING DOG..... TOO SOON
GOTCHA!
YIPE!
WHEEEEEEEEEEEEE
ARF!
© King Features Syndicate, Inc., 1970
WHAT THIS HOUSE NEEDS IS A LONGER HALL
9-13

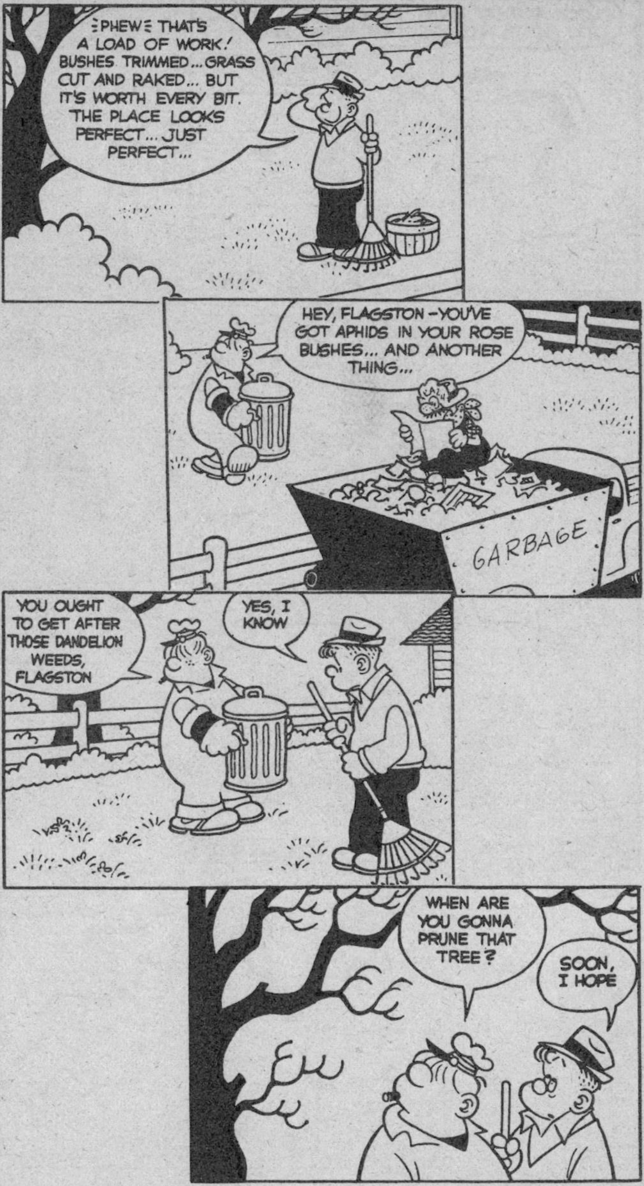
PHEW THAT'S A LOAD OF WORK! BUSHES TRIMMED... GRASS CUT AND RAKED... BUT IT'S WORTH EVERY BIT. THE PLACE LOOKS PERFECT... JUST PERFECT...
HEY, FLAGSTON -YOU'VE GOT APHIDS IN YOUR ROSE BUSHES... AND ANOTHER THING...
GARBAGE
YOU OUGHT TO GET AFTER THOSE DANDELION WEEDS, FLAGSTON
YES, I KNOW
WHEN ARE YOU GONNA PRUNE THAT TREE?
SOON, I HOPE

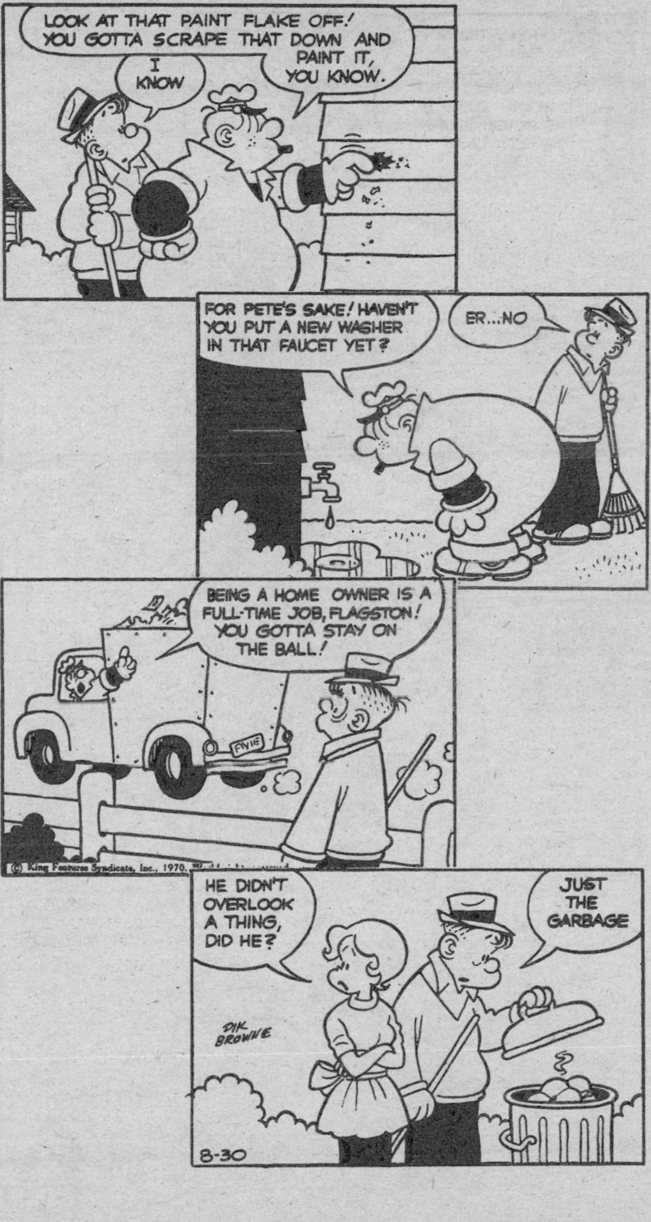
LOOK AT THAT PAINT FLAKE OFF! YOU GOTTA SCRAPE THAT DOWN AND PAINT IT, YOU KNOW.
I KNOW
FOR PETE'S SAKE! HAVEN'T YOU PUT A NEW WASHER IN THAT FAUCET YET?
ER...NO
BEING A HOME OWNER IS A FULL-TIME JOB, FLAGSTON! YOU GOTTA STAY ON THE BALL!
© King Features Syndicate, Inc., 1970.
HE DIDN'T OVERLOOK A THING, DID HE?
JUST THE GARBAGE
DIK BROWNE
8-30

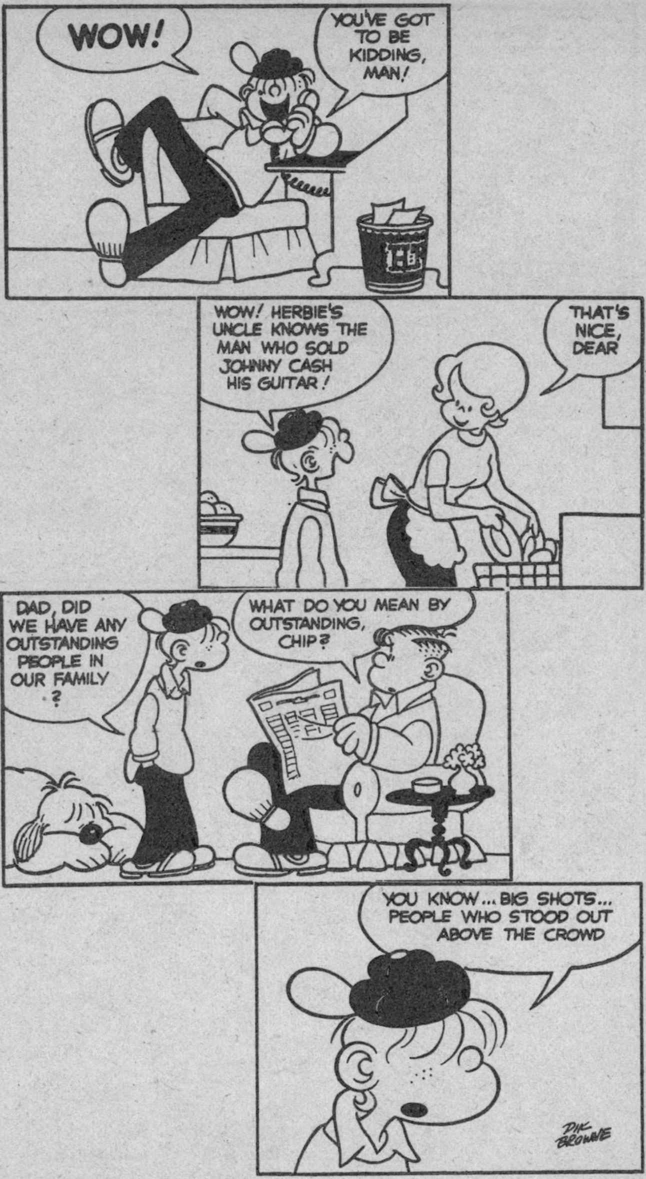
WOW!
YOU'VE GOT TO BE KIDDING, MAN!
WOW! HERBIE'S UNCLE KNOWS THE MAN WHO SOLD JOHNNY CASH HIS GUITAR!
THAT'S NICE, DEAR
DAD, DID WE HAVE ANY OUTSTANDING PEOPLE IN OUR FAMILY ?
WHAT DO YOU MEAN BY OUTSTANDING, CHIP?
YOU KNOW... BIG SHOTS... PEOPLE WHO STOOD OUT ABOVE THE CROWD
DIK BROWNE

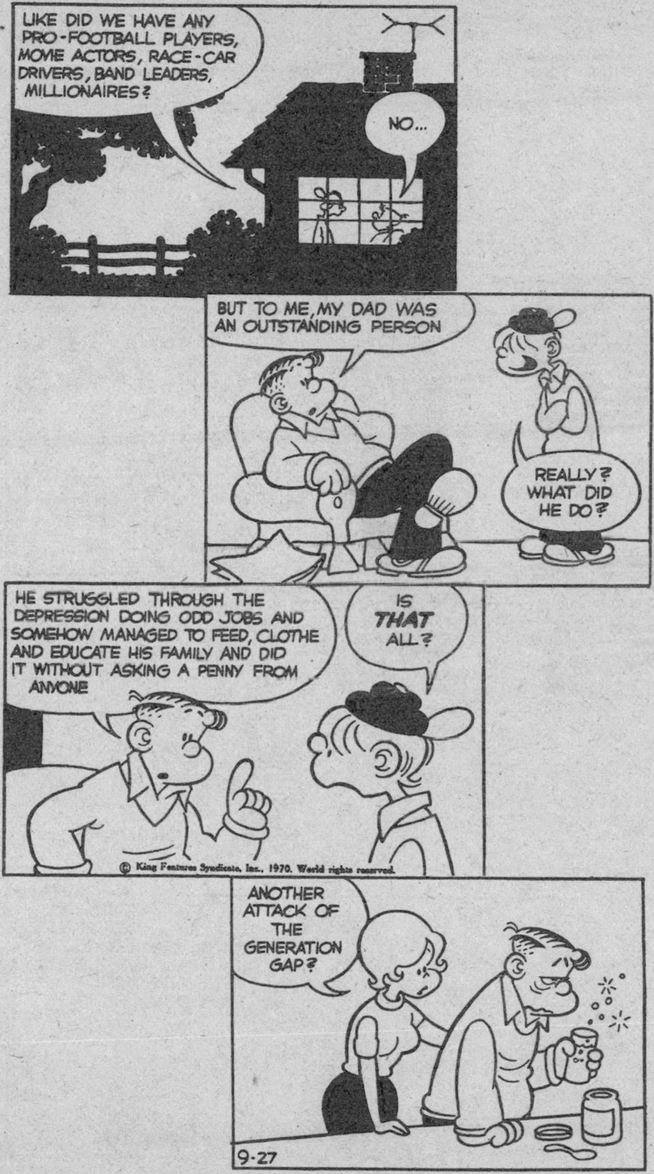
LIKE DID WE HAVE ANY PRO-FOOTBALL PLAYERS, MOVIE ACTORS, RACE-CAR DRIVERS, BAND LEADERS, MILLIONAIRES?
NO...
BUT TO ME, MY DAD WAS AN OUTSTANDING PERSON
REALLY? WHAT DID HE DO?
HE STRUGGLED THROUGH THE DEPRESSION DOING ODD JOBS AND SOMEHOW MANAGED TO FEED, CLOTHE AND EDUCATE HIS FAMILY AND DID IT WITHOUT ASKING A PENNY FROM ANYONE
IS *THAT* ALL?
© King Features Syndicate, Inc., 1970. World rights reserved.
ANOTHER ATTACK OF THE GENERATION GAP?
9-27

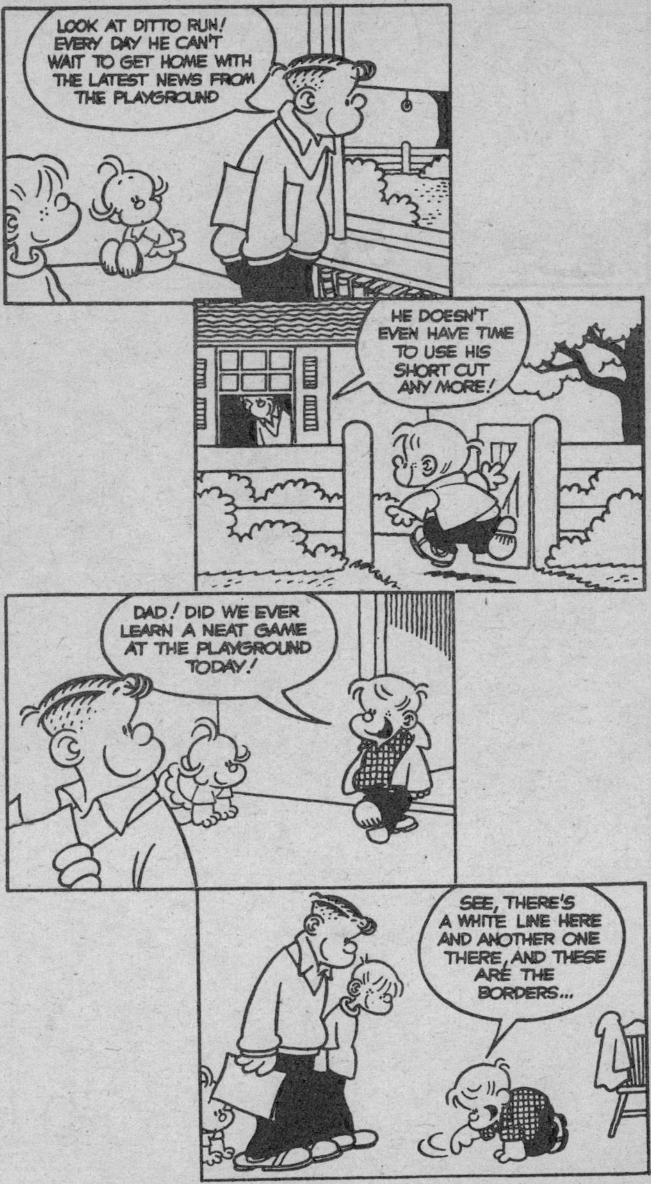
LOOK AT DITTO RUN! EVERY DAY HE CAN'T WAIT TO GET HOME WITH THE LATEST NEWS FROM THE PLAYGROUND
HE DOESN'T EVEN HAVE TIME TO USE HIS SHORT CUT ANY MORE!
DAD! DID WE EVER LEARN A NEAT GAME AT THE PLAYGROUND TODAY!
SEE, THERE'S A WHITE LINE HERE AND ANOTHER ONE THERE, AND THESE ARE THE BORDERS...

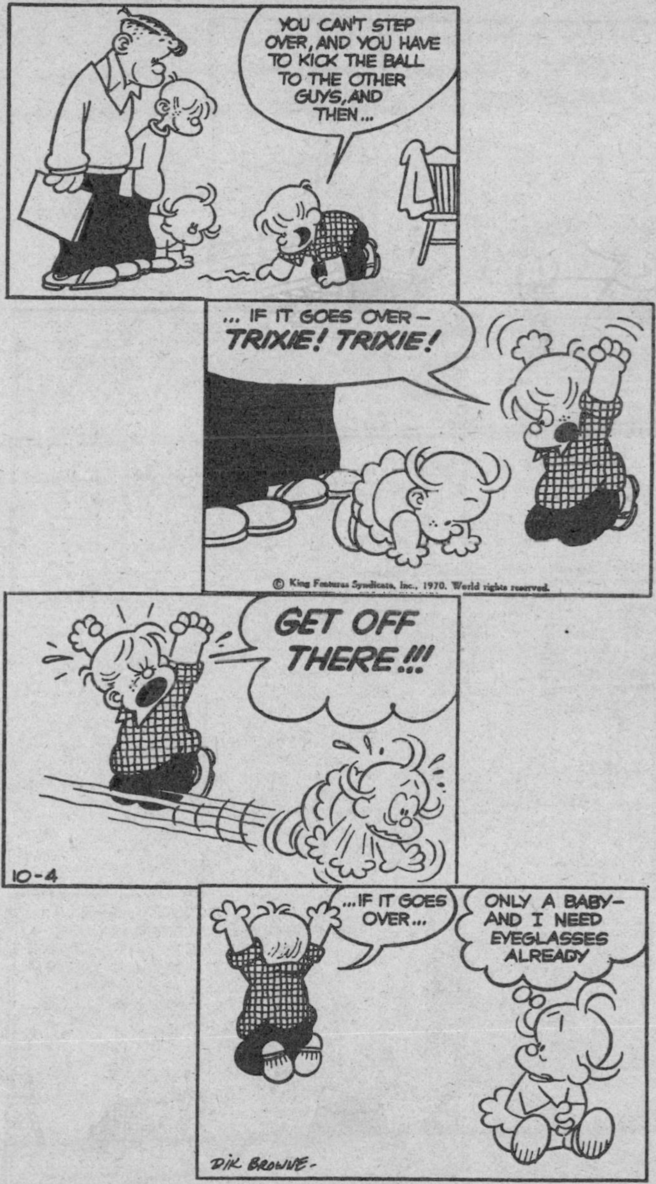
YOU CAN'T STEP OVER, AND YOU HAVE TO KICK THE BALL TO THE OTHER GUYS, AND THEN ...
... IF IT GOES OVER — TRIXIE! TRIXIE!
© King Features Syndicate, Inc., 1970. World rights reserved.
GET OFF THERE!!!
10-4
...IF IT GOES OVER...
ONLY A BABY— AND I NEED EYEGLASSES ALREADY
DIK BROWNE

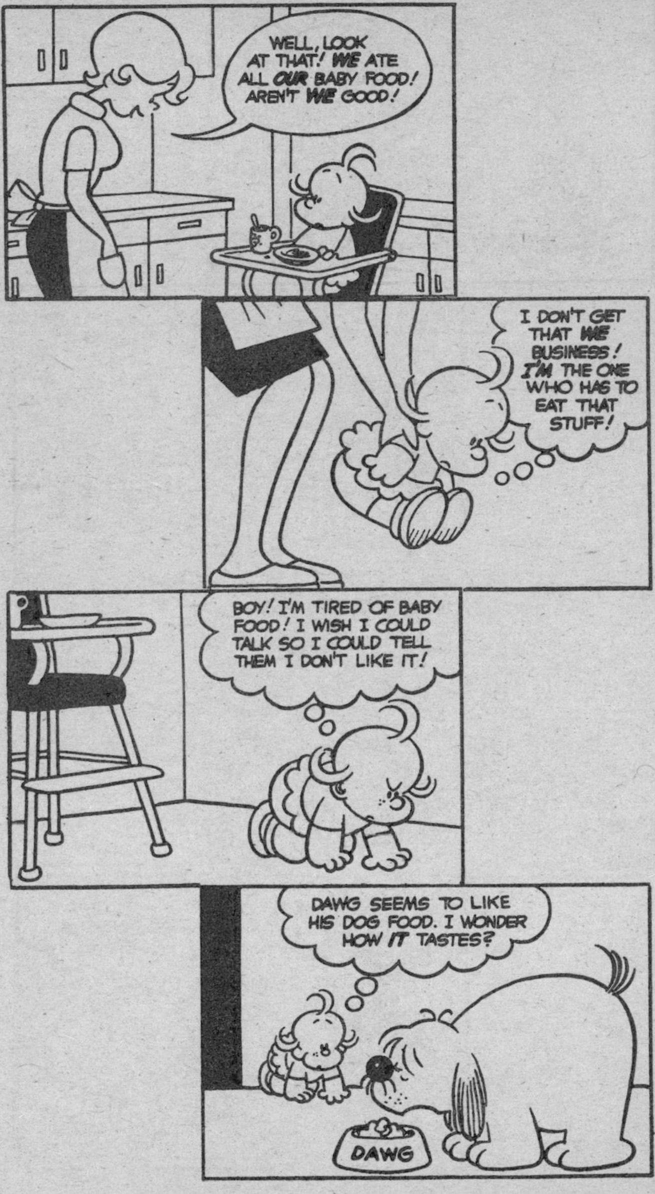

WELL, LOOK AT THAT! WE ATE ALL OUR BABY FOOD! AREN'T WE GOOD!
I DON'T GET THAT WE BUSINESS! I'M THE ONE WHO HAS TO EAT THAT STUFF!
BOY! I'M TIRED OF BABY FOOD! I WISH I COULD TALK SO I COULD TELL THEM I DON'T LIKE IT!
DAWG SEEMS TO LIKE HIS DOG FOOD. I WONDER HOW IT TASTES?
DAWG

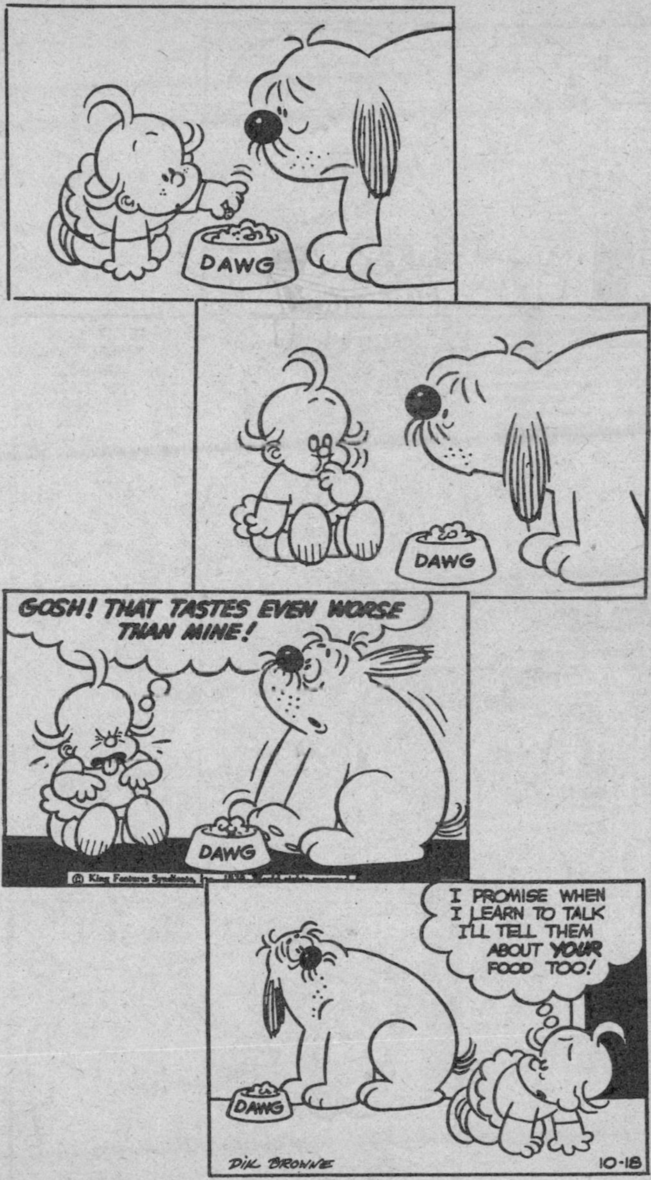
DAWG
DAWG
GOSH! THAT TASTES EVEN WORSE THAN MINE!
DAWG
© King Features Syndicate, Inc.
I PROMISE WHEN I LEARN TO TALK I'LL TELL THEM ABOUT YOUR FOOD TOO!
DAWG
DIK BROWNE
10-18

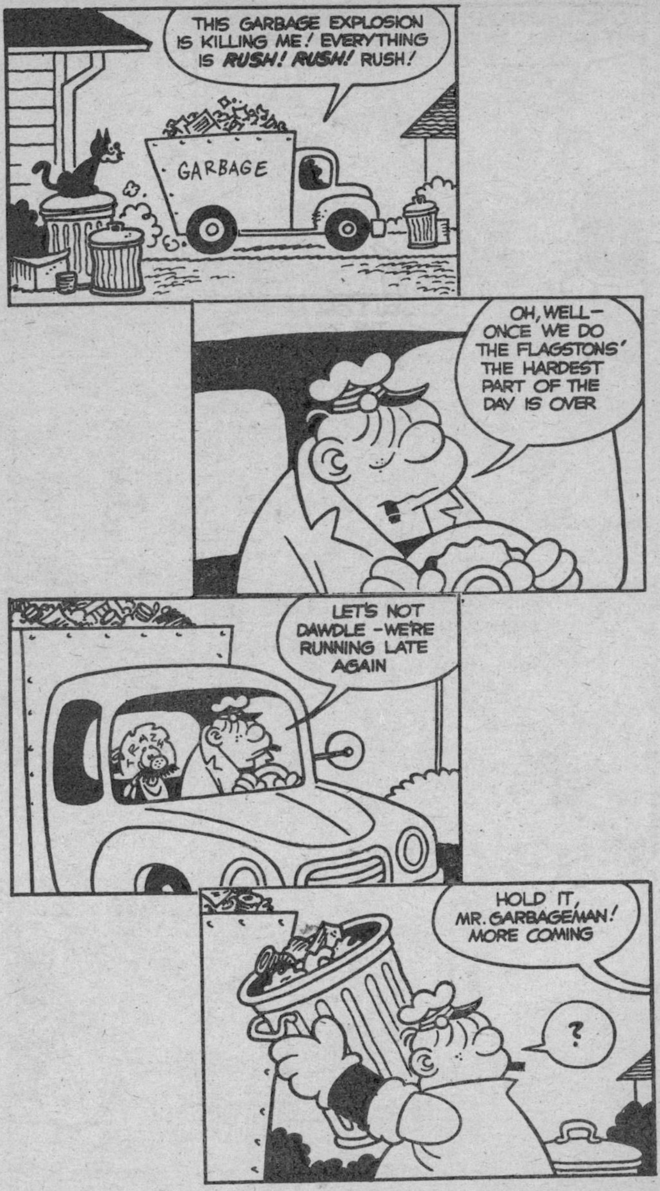
THIS GARBAGE EXPLOSION IS KILLING ME! EVERYTHING IS RUSH! RUSH! RUSH!
GARBAGE
OH, WELL— ONCE WE DO THE FLAGSTONS' THE HARDEST PART OF THE DAY IS OVER
LET'S NOT DAWDLE —WE'RE RUNNING LATE AGAIN
TRAZH
HOLD IT, MR. GARBAGEMAN! MORE COMING
?

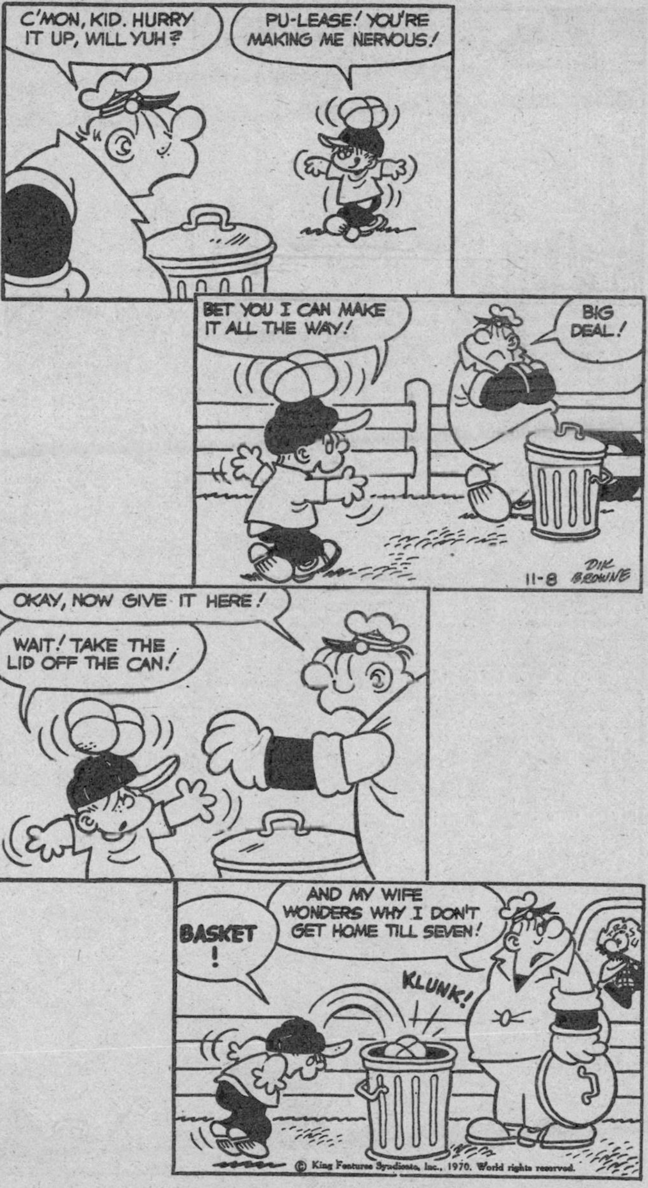
C'MON, KID. HURRY IT UP, WILL YUH?
PU-LEASE! YOU'RE MAKING ME NERVOUS!
BET YOU I CAN MAKE IT ALL THE WAY!
BIG DEAL!
DIK BROWNE
11-8
OKAY, NOW GIVE IT HERE!
WAIT! TAKE THE LID OFF THE CAN!
BASKET!
AND MY WIFE WONDERS WHY I DON'T GET HOME TILL SEVEN!
KLUNK!
© King Features Syndicate, Inc., 1970. World rights reserved.

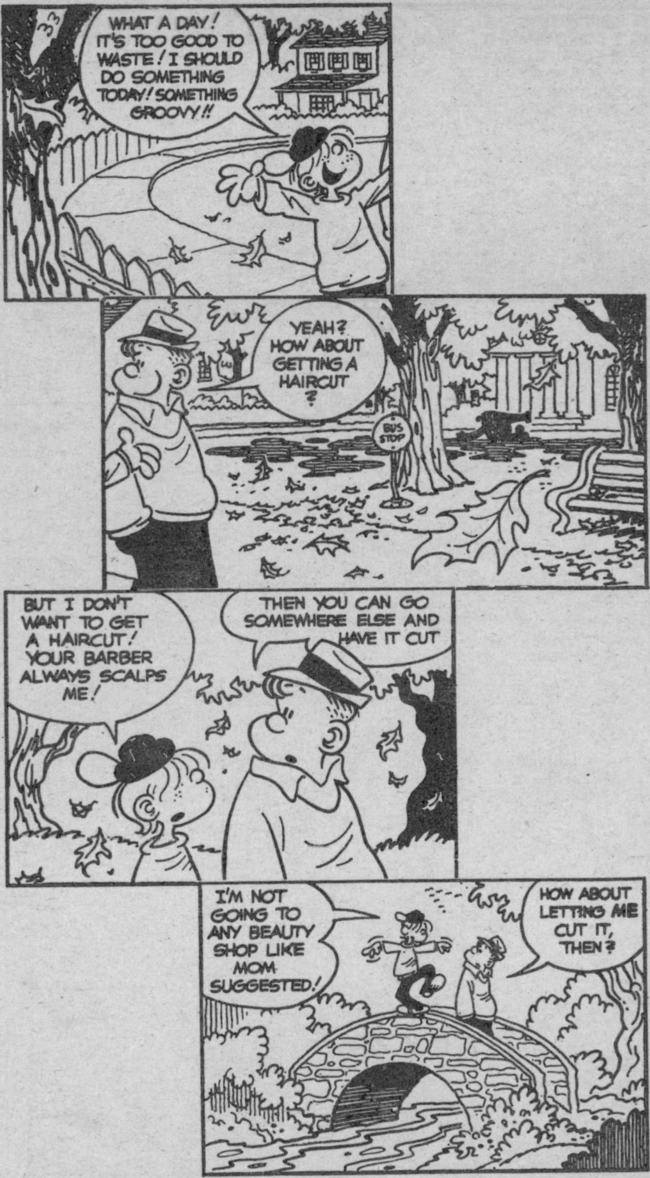
WHAT A DAY! IT'S TOO GOOD TO WASTE! I SHOULD DO SOMETHING TODAY! SOMETHING GROOVY!!
YEAH? HOW ABOUT GETTING A HAIRCUT?
BUS STOP
BUT I DON'T WANT TO GET A HAIRCUT! YOUR BARBER ALWAYS SCALPS ME!
THEN YOU CAN GO SOMEWHERE ELSE AND HAVE IT CUT
I'M NOT GOING TO ANY BEAUTY SHOP LIKE MOM SUGGESTED!
HOW ABOUT LETTING ME CUT IT, THEN?

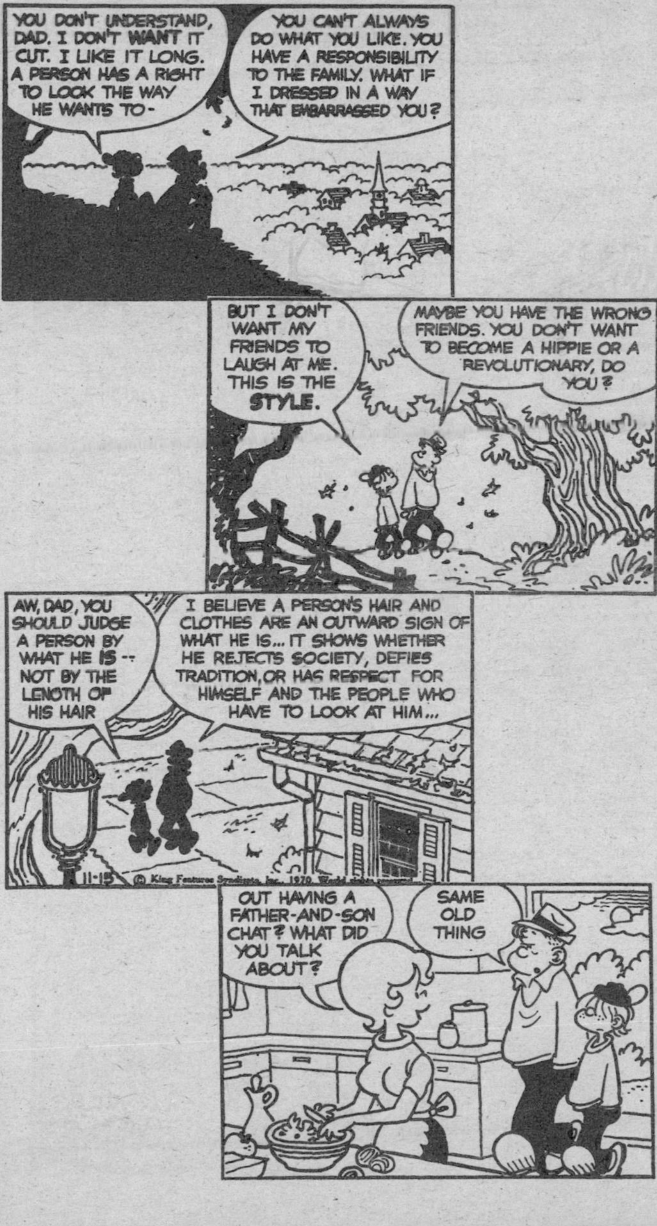
YOU DON'T UNDERSTAND, DAD. I DON'T **WANT** IT CUT. I LIKE IT LONG. A PERSON HAS A RIGHT TO LOOK THE WAY HE WANTS TO-
YOU CAN'T ALWAYS DO WHAT YOU LIKE. YOU HAVE A RESPONSIBILITY TO THE FAMILY. WHAT IF I DRESSED IN A WAY THAT EMBARRASSED YOU?
BUT I DON'T WANT MY FRIENDS TO LAUGH AT ME. THIS IS THE **STYLE.**
MAYBE YOU HAVE THE WRONG FRIENDS. YOU DON'T WANT TO BECOME A HIPPIE OR A REVOLUTIONARY, DO YOU?
AW, DAD, YOU SHOULD JUDGE A PERSON BY WHAT HE **IS** -- NOT BY THE LENGTH OF HIS HAIR
I BELIEVE A PERSON'S HAIR AND CLOTHES ARE AN OUTWARD SIGN OF WHAT HE IS... IT SHOWS WHETHER HE REJECTS SOCIETY, DEFIES TRADITION, OR HAS RESPECT FOR HIMSELF AND THE PEOPLE WHO HAVE TO LOOK AT HIM...
11-15 © King Features Syndicate, Inc., 1970. World rights reserved
OUT HAVING A FATHER-AND-SON CHAT? WHAT DID YOU TALK ABOUT?
SAME OLD THING

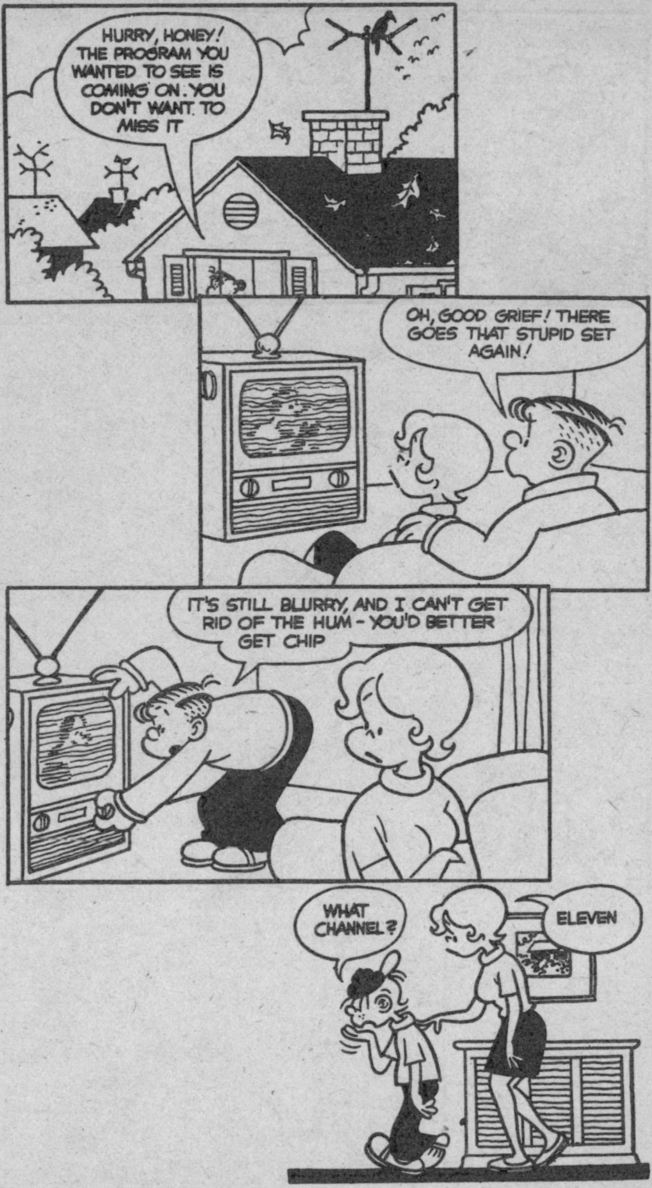
HURRY, HONEY! THE PROGRAM YOU WANTED TO SEE IS COMING ON. YOU DON'T WANT TO MISS IT
OH, GOOD GRIEF! THERE GOES THAT STUPID SET AGAIN!
IT'S STILL BLURRY, AND I CAN'T GET RID OF THE HUM - YOU'D BETTER GET CHIP
WHAT CHANNEL?
ELEVEN

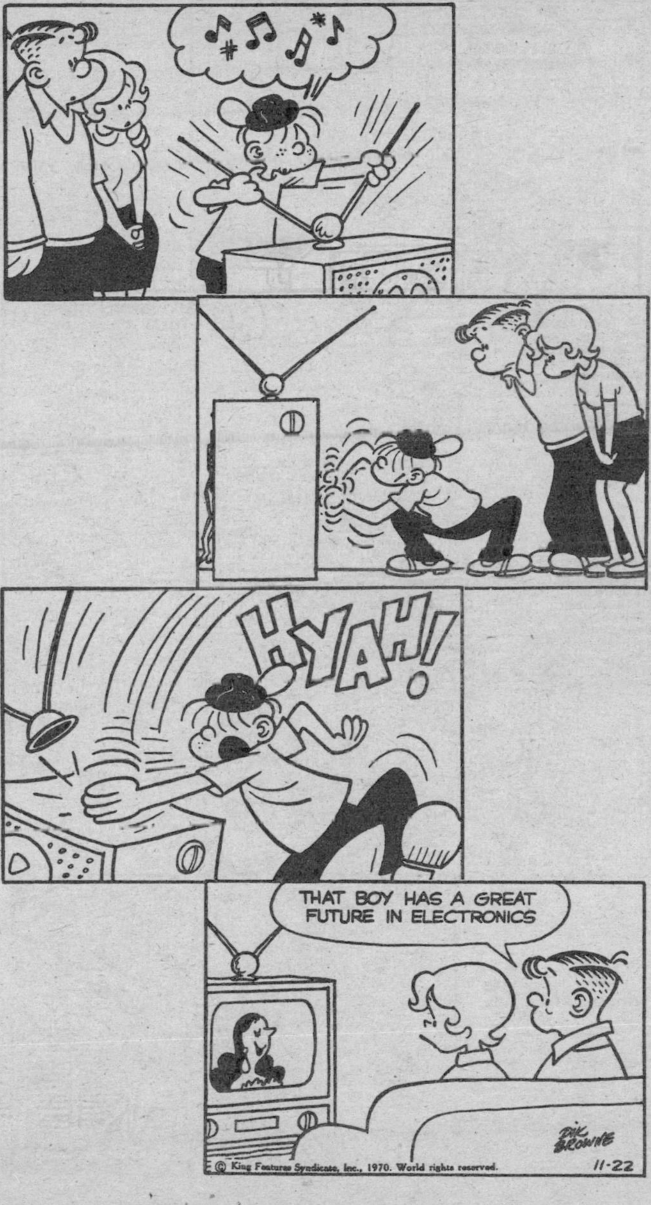
HYAH!
THAT BOY HAS A GREAT FUTURE IN ELECTRONICS
DIK BROWNE
© King Features Syndicate, Inc., 1970. World rights reserved.
11-22

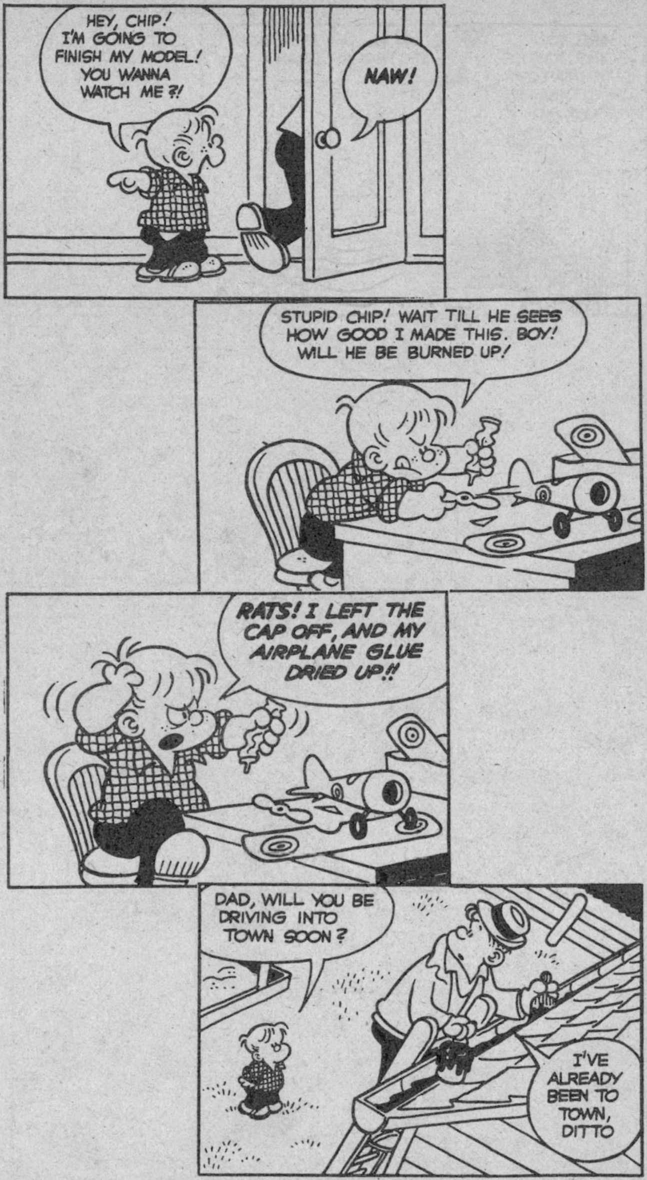
HEY, CHIP! I'M GOING TO FINISH MY MODEL! YOU WANNA WATCH ME ?!
NAW!
STUPID CHIP! WAIT TILL HE SEES HOW GOOD I MADE THIS. BOY! WILL HE BE BURNED UP!
RATS! I LEFT THE CAP OFF, AND MY AIRPLANE GLUE DRIED UP!!
DAD, WILL YOU BE DRIVING INTO TOWN SOON?
I'VE ALREADY BEEN TO TOWN, DITTO

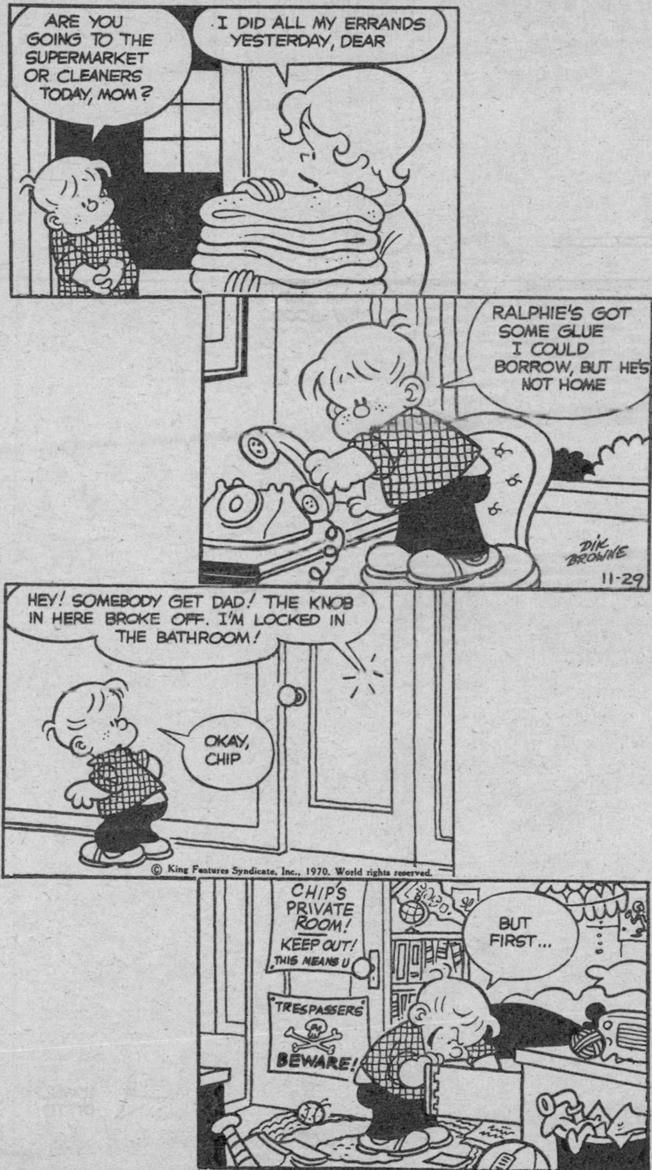
ARE YOU GOING TO THE SUPERMARKET OR CLEANERS TODAY, MOM?
I DID ALL MY ERRANDS YESTERDAY, DEAR
RALPHIE'S GOT SOME GLUE I COULD BORROW, BUT HE'S NOT HOME
DIK BROWNE
11-29
HEY! SOMEBODY GET DAD! THE KNOB IN HERE BROKE OFF. I'M LOCKED IN THE BATHROOM!
OKAY, CHIP
CHIP'S PRIVATE ROOM! KEEP OUT! THIS MEANS U
TRESPASSERS BEWARE!
BUT FIRST...

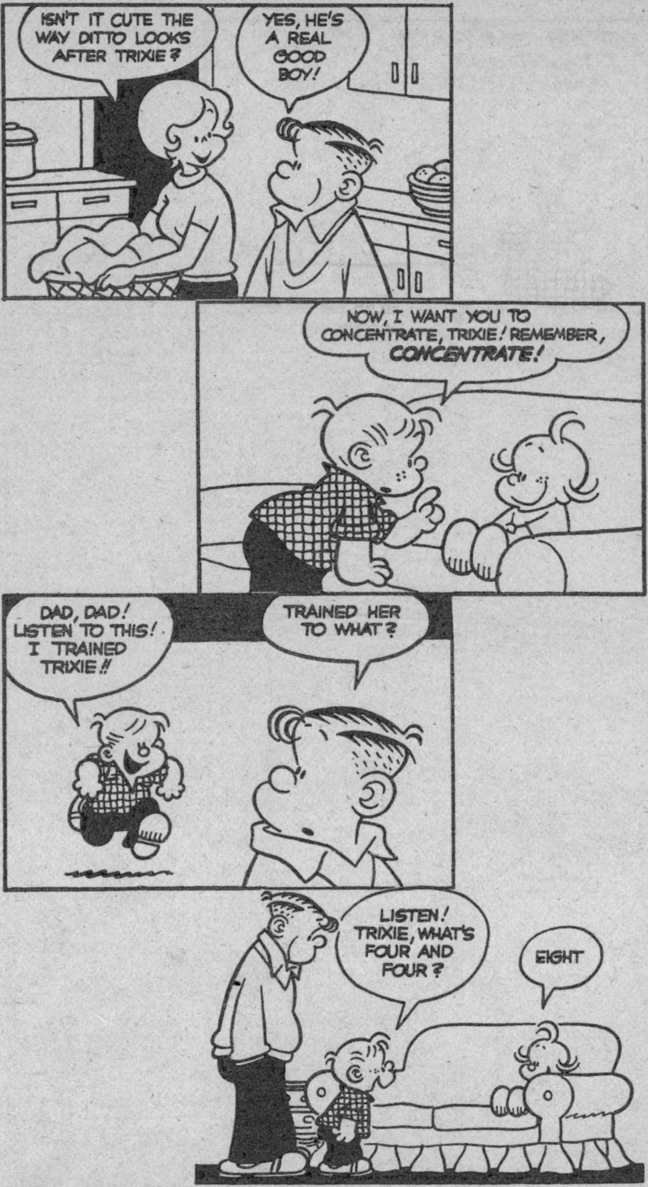
ISN'T IT CUTE THE WAY DITTO LOOKS AFTER TRIXIE?
YES, HE'S A REAL GOOD BOY!
NOW, I WANT YOU TO CONCENTRATE, TRIXIE! REMEMBER, CONCENTRATE!
DAD, DAD! LISTEN TO THIS! I TRAINED TRIXIE!!
TRAINED HER TO WHAT?
LISTEN! TRIXIE, WHAT'S FOUR AND FOUR?
EIGHT

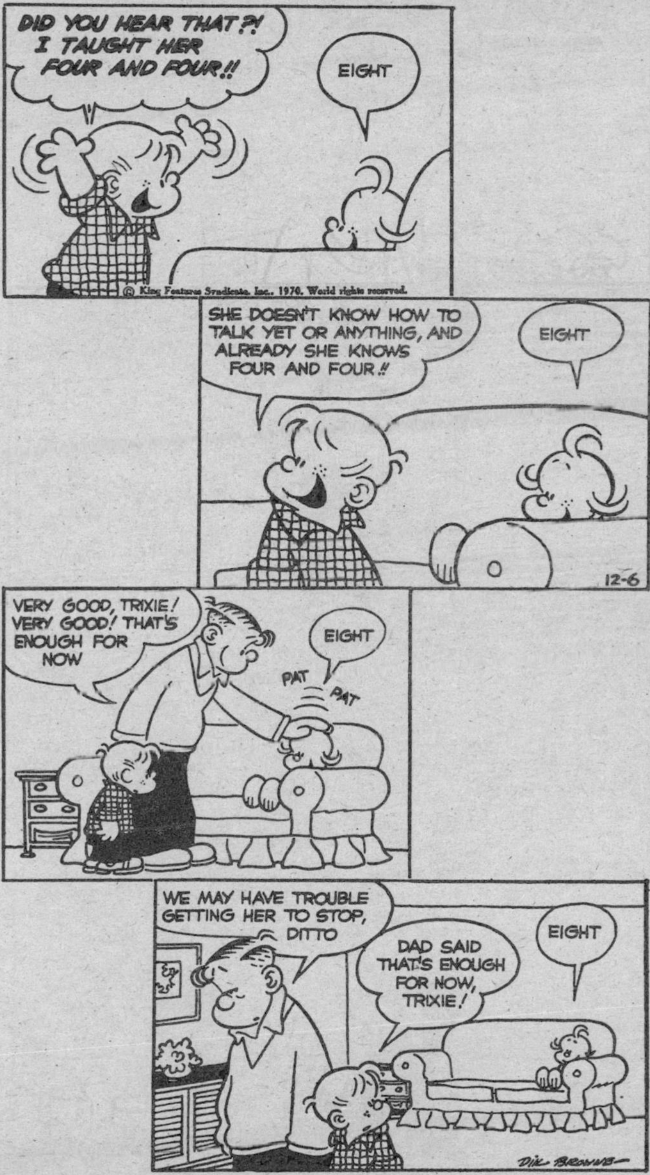

DID YOU HEAR THAT?! I TAUGHT HER FOUR AND FOUR!!
EIGHT
© King Features Syndicate, Inc., 1970. World rights reserved.
SHE DOESN'T KNOW HOW TO TALK YET OR ANYTHING, AND ALREADY SHE KNOWS FOUR AND FOUR!!
EIGHT
12-6
VERY GOOD, TRIXIE! VERY GOOD! THAT'S ENOUGH FOR NOW
EIGHT
PAT
PAT
WE MAY HAVE TROUBLE GETTING HER TO STOP, DITTO
DAD SAID THAT'S ENOUGH FOR NOW, TRIXIE!
EIGHT
DIK BROWNE

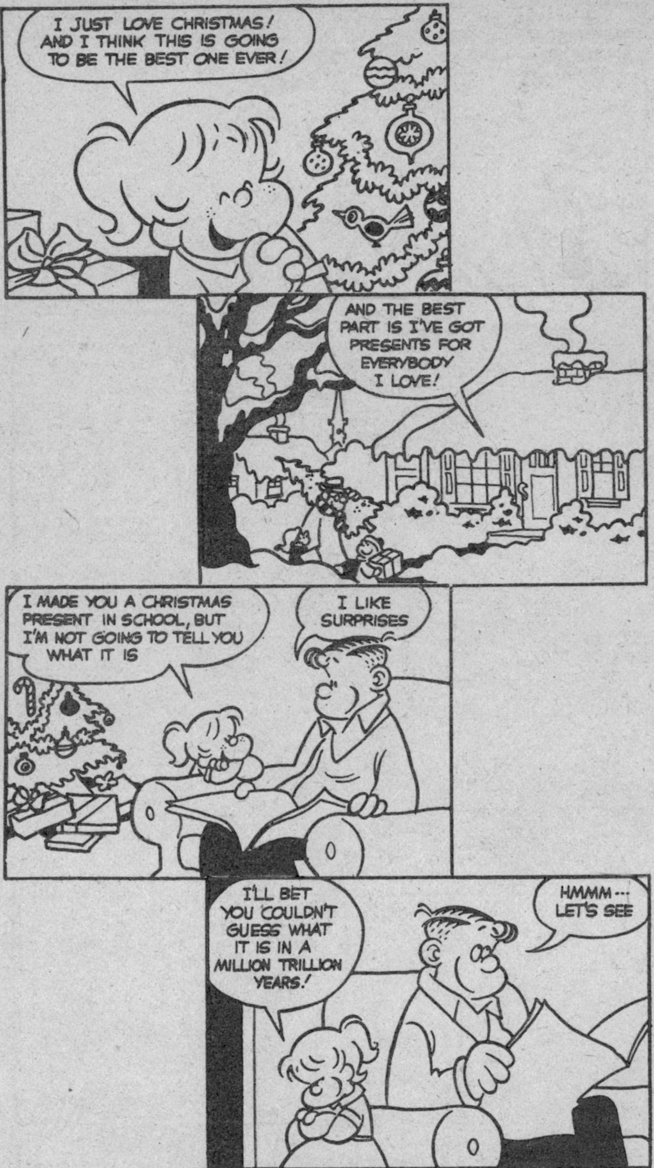
I JUST LOVE CHRISTMAS! AND I THINK THIS IS GOING TO BE THE BEST ONE EVER!
AND THE BEST PART IS I'VE GOT PRESENTS FOR EVERYBODY I LOVE!
I MADE YOU A CHRISTMAS PRESENT IN SCHOOL, BUT I'M NOT GOING TO TELL YOU WHAT IT IS
I LIKE SURPRISES
I'LL BET YOU COULDN'T GUESS WHAT IT IS IN A MILLION TRILLION YEARS!
HMMM--- LET'S SEE

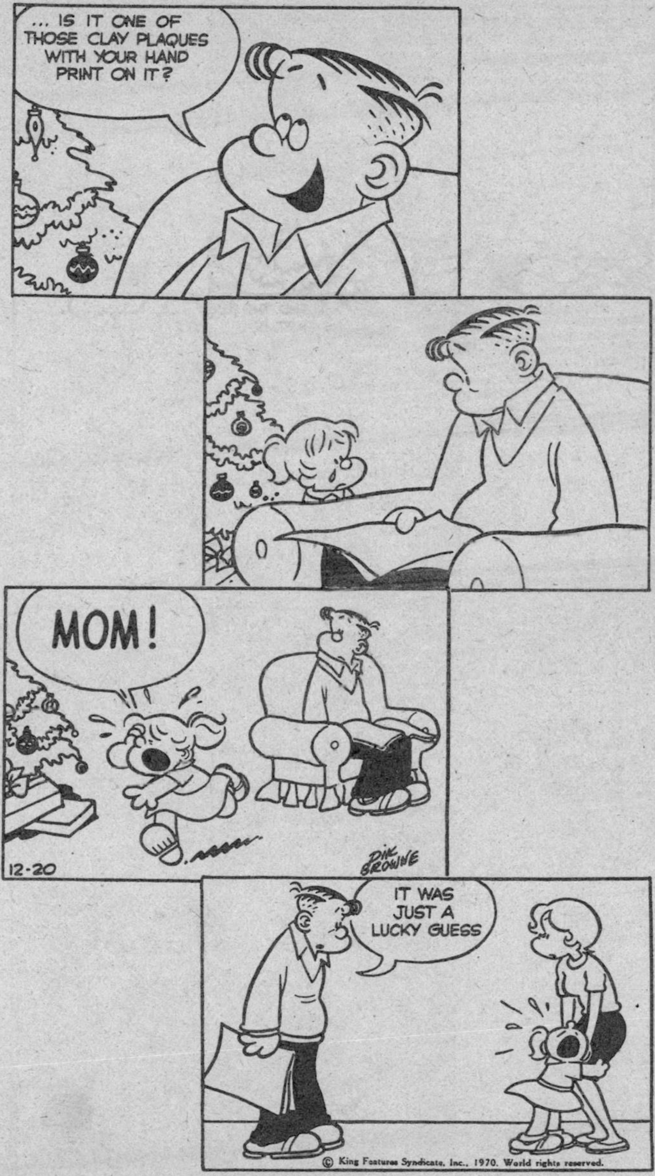

... IS IT ONE OF THOSE CLAY PLAQUES WITH YOUR HAND PRINT ON IT?
MOM!
12-20
DIK BROWNE
IT WAS JUST A LUCKY GUESS

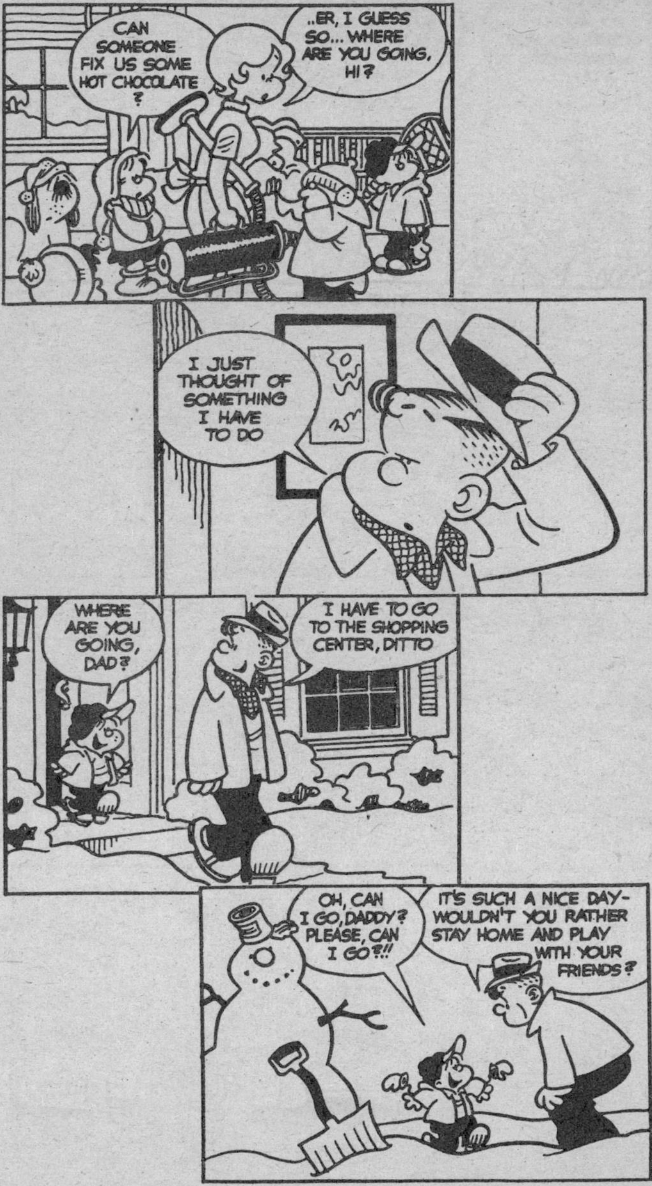
CAN SOMEONE FIX US SOME HOT CHOCOLATE ?
..ER, I GUESS SO... WHERE ARE YOU GOING, HI?
I JUST THOUGHT OF SOMETHING I HAVE TO DO
WHERE ARE YOU GOING, DAD?
I HAVE TO GO TO THE SHOPPING CENTER, DITTO
OH, CAN I GO, DADDY? PLEASE, CAN I GO?!!
IT'S SUCH A NICE DAY- WOULDN'T YOU RATHER STAY HOME AND PLAY WITH YOUR FRIENDS?

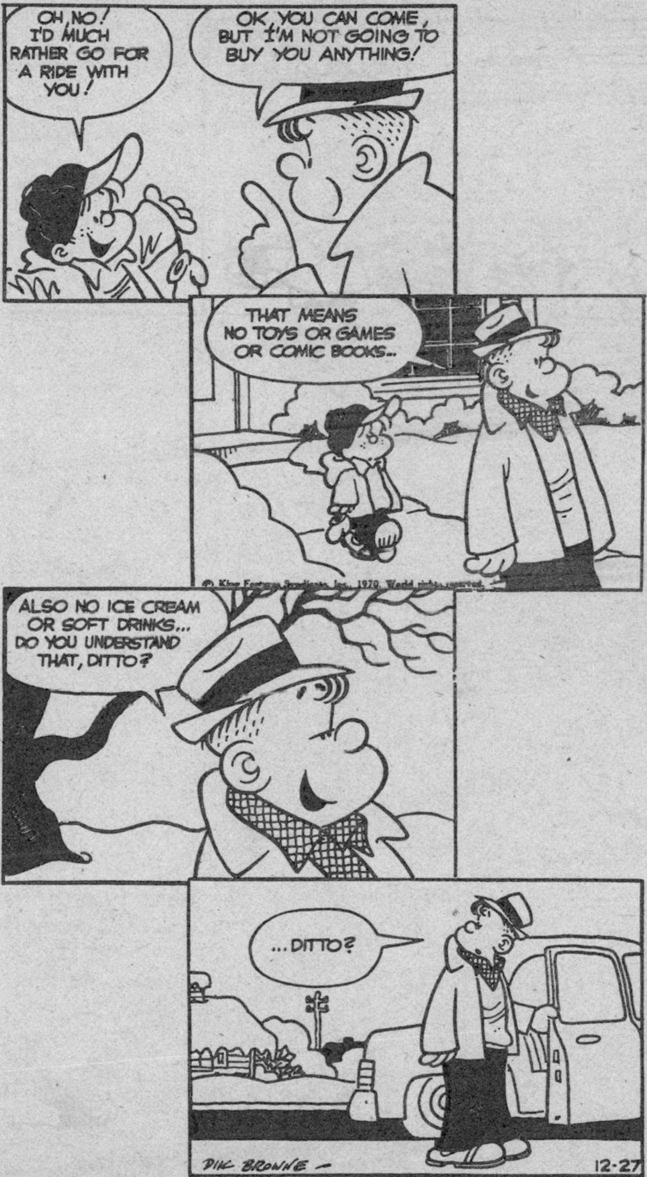
OH, NO! I'D MUCH RATHER GO FOR A RIDE WITH YOU!
OK, YOU CAN COME, BUT I'M NOT GOING TO BUY YOU ANYTHING!
THAT MEANS NO TOYS OR GAMES OR COMIC BOOKS...
© King Features Syndicate, Inc., 1970. World rights reserved.
ALSO NO ICE CREAM OR SOFT DRINKS... DO YOU UNDERSTAND THAT, DITTO?
...DITTO?
DIK BROWNE
12-27

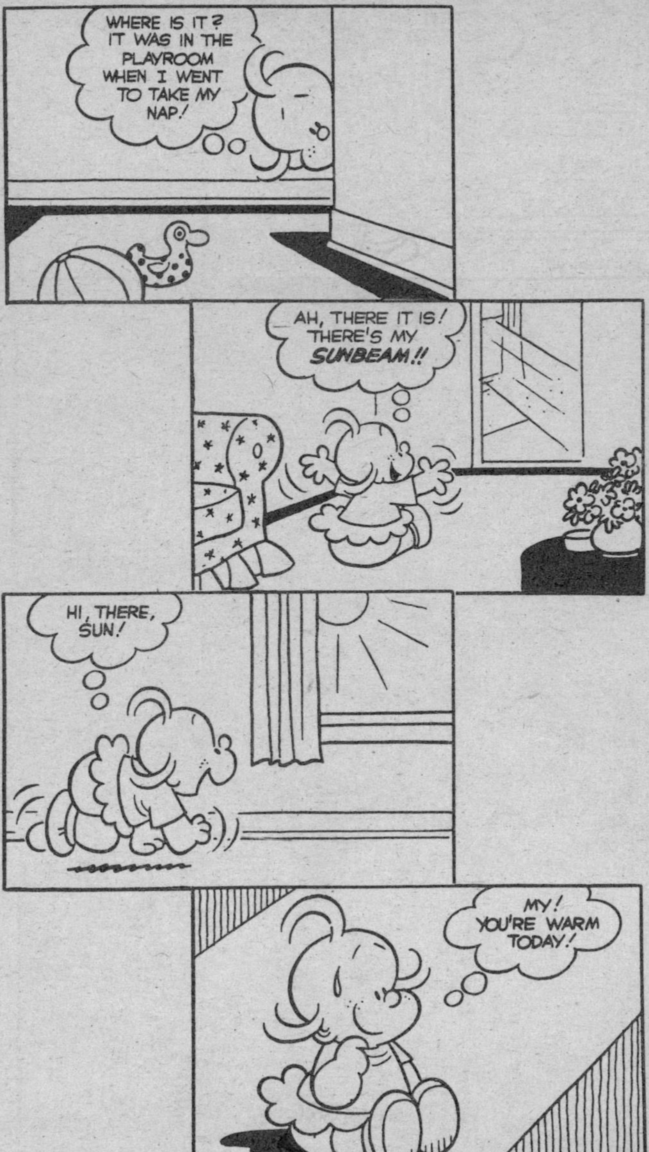
WHERE IS IT? IT WAS IN THE PLAYROOM WHEN I WENT TO TAKE MY NAP!
AH, THERE IT IS! THERE'S MY SUNBEAM!!
HI, THERE, SUN!
MY! YOU'RE WARM TODAY!

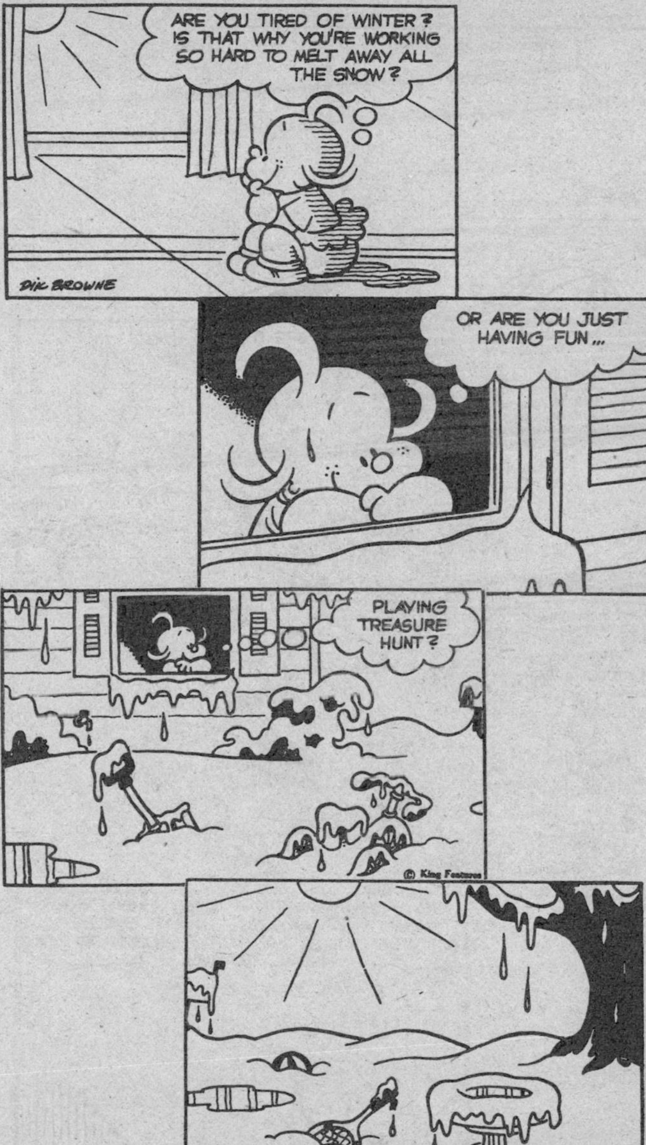
ARE YOU TIRED OF WINTER? IS THAT WHY YOU'RE WORKING SO HARD TO MELT AWAY ALL THE SNOW?
DIK BROWNE
OR ARE YOU JUST HAVING FUN...
PLAYING TREASURE HUNT?
© King Features
Syndicate, Inc., 1970. World rights reserved.
1-3

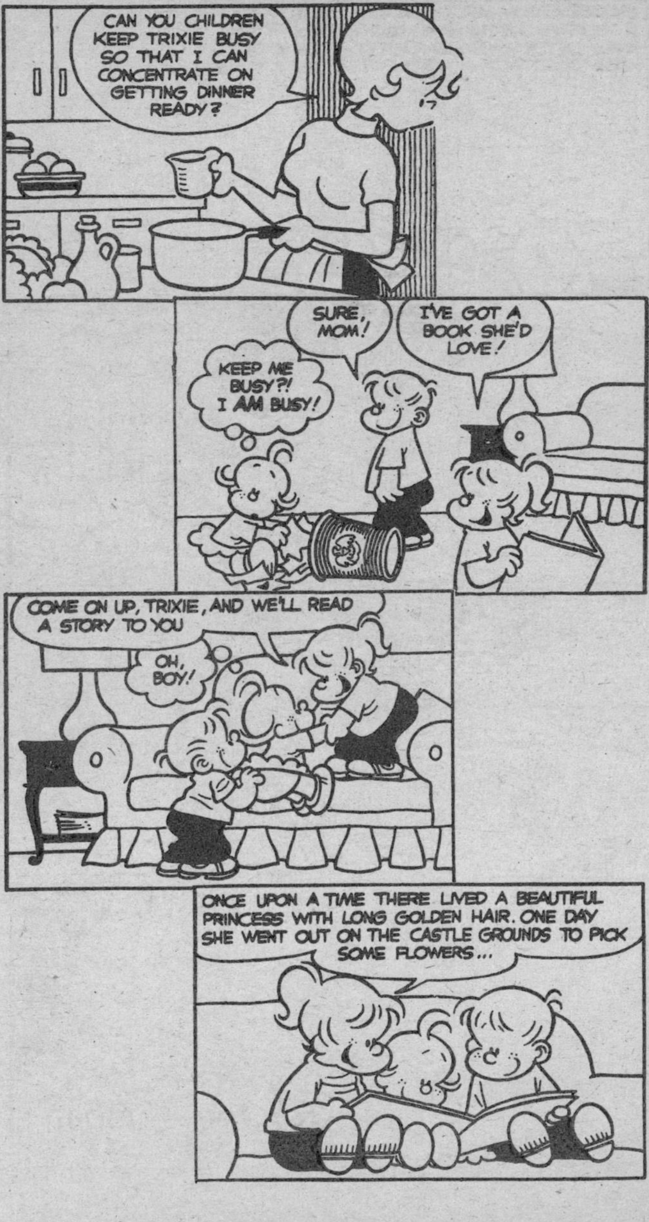
CAN YOU CHILDREN KEEP TRIXIE BUSY SO THAT I CAN CONCENTRATE ON GETTING DINNER READY?
SURE, MOM!
I'VE GOT A BOOK SHE'D LOVE!
KEEP ME BUSY?! I AM BUSY!
COME ON UP, TRIXIE, AND WE'LL READ A STORY TO YOU
OH, BOY!
ONCE UPON A TIME THERE LIVED A BEAUTIFUL PRINCESS WITH LONG GOLDEN HAIR. ONE DAY SHE WENT OUT ON THE CASTLE GROUNDS TO PICK SOME FLOWERS...

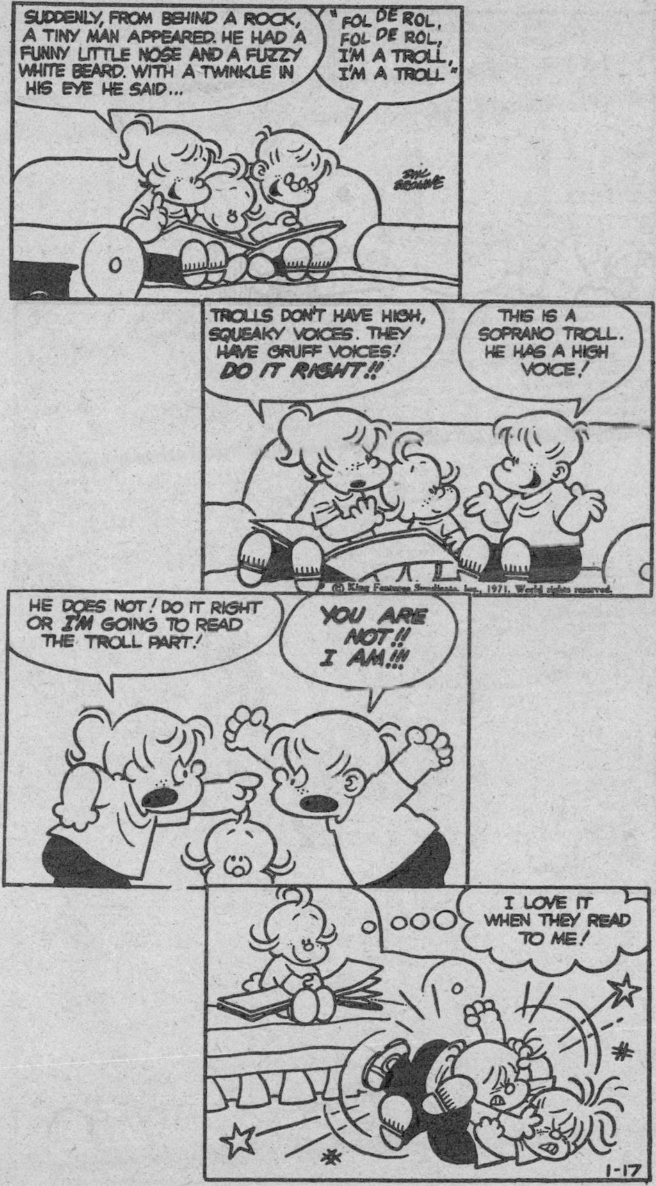
SUDDENLY, FROM BEHIND A ROCK, A TINY MAN APPEARED. HE HAD A FUNNY LITTLE NOSE AND A FUZZY WHITE BEARD. WITH A TWINKLE IN HIS EYE HE SAID...
"FOL DE ROL, FOL DE ROL, I'M A TROLL, I'M A TROLL."
TROLLS DON'T HAVE HIGH, SQUEAKY VOICES. THEY HAVE GRUFF VOICES! DO IT RIGHT!!
THIS IS A SOPRANO TROLL. HE HAS A HIGH VOICE!
HE DOES NOT! DO IT RIGHT OR I'M GOING TO READ THE TROLL PART!
YOU ARE NOT!! I AM!!!
I LOVE IT WHEN THEY READ TO ME!
1-17

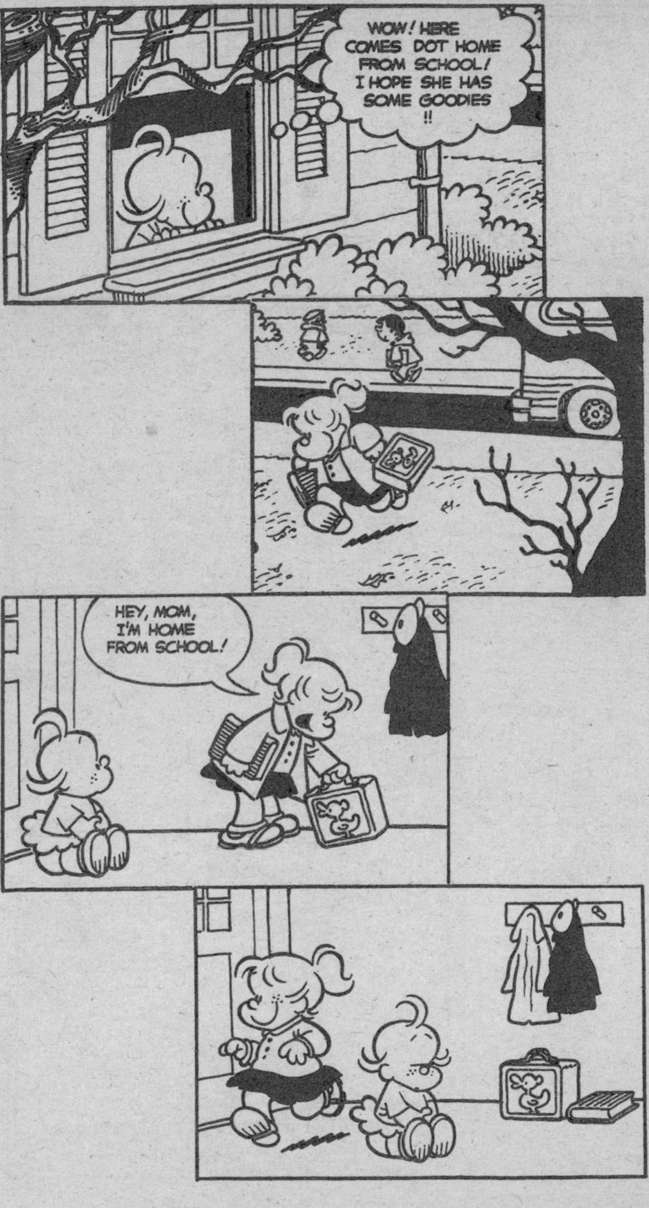
WOW! HERE COMES DOT HOME FROM SCHOOL! I HOPE SHE HAS SOME GOODIES !!
HEY, MOM, I'M HOME FROM SCHOOL!

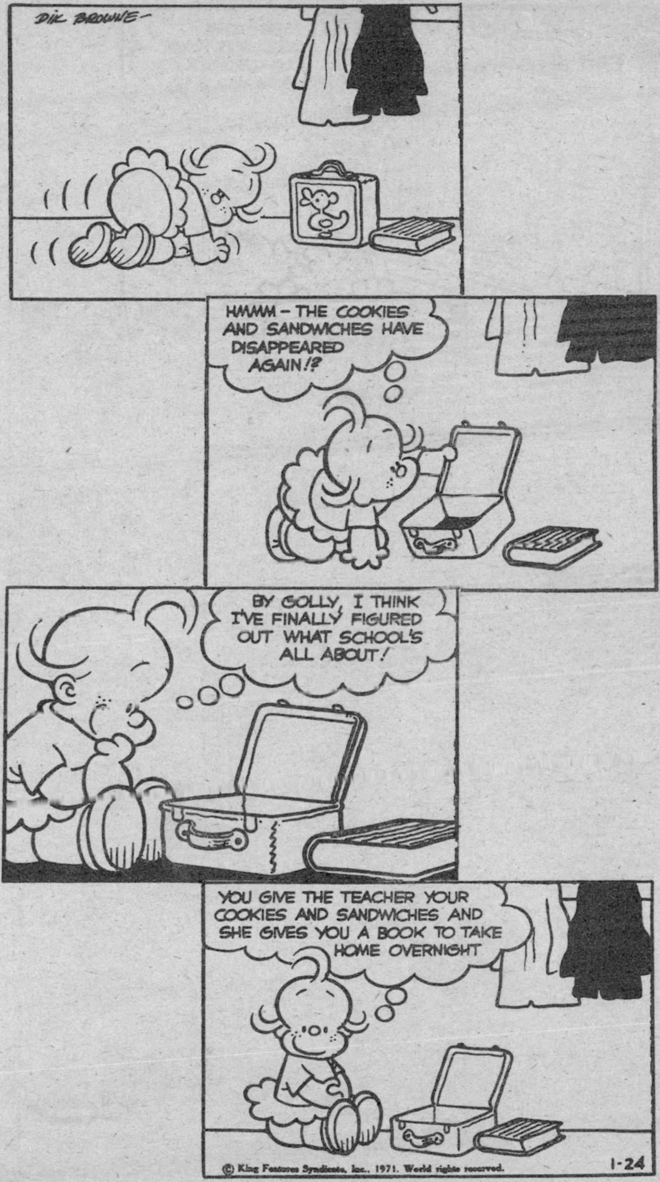
DIK BROWNE
HMMM – THE COOKIES AND SANDWICHES HAVE DISAPPEARED AGAIN!?
BY GOLLY, I THINK I'VE FINALLY FIGURED OUT WHAT SCHOOL'S ALL ABOUT!
YOU GIVE THE TEACHER YOUR COOKIES AND SANDWICHES AND SHE GIVES YOU A BOOK TO TAKE HOME OVERNIGHT
1-24

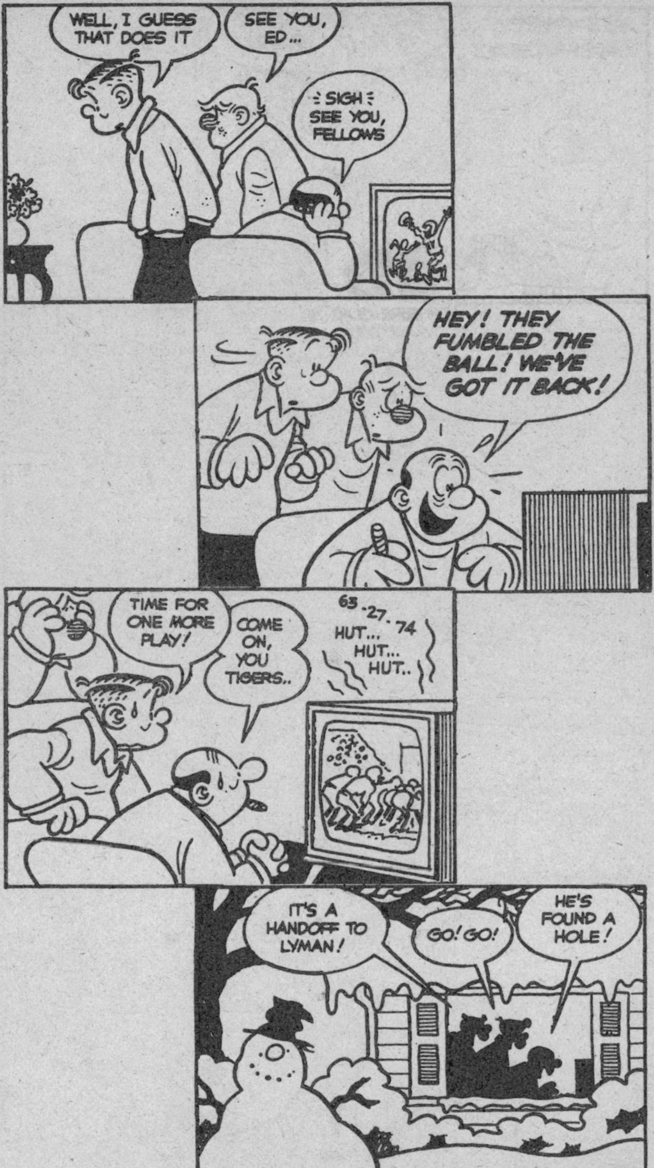
WELL, I GUESS THAT DOES IT
SEE YOU, ED...
SIGH SEE YOU, FELLOWS
HEY! THEY FUMBLED THE BALL! WE'VE GOT IT BACK!
TIME FOR ONE MORE PLAY!
COME ON, YOU TIGERS..
63 - 27 - 74 HUT... HUT... HUT..
IT'S A HANDOFF TO LYMAN!
GO! GO!
HE'S FOUND A HOLE!

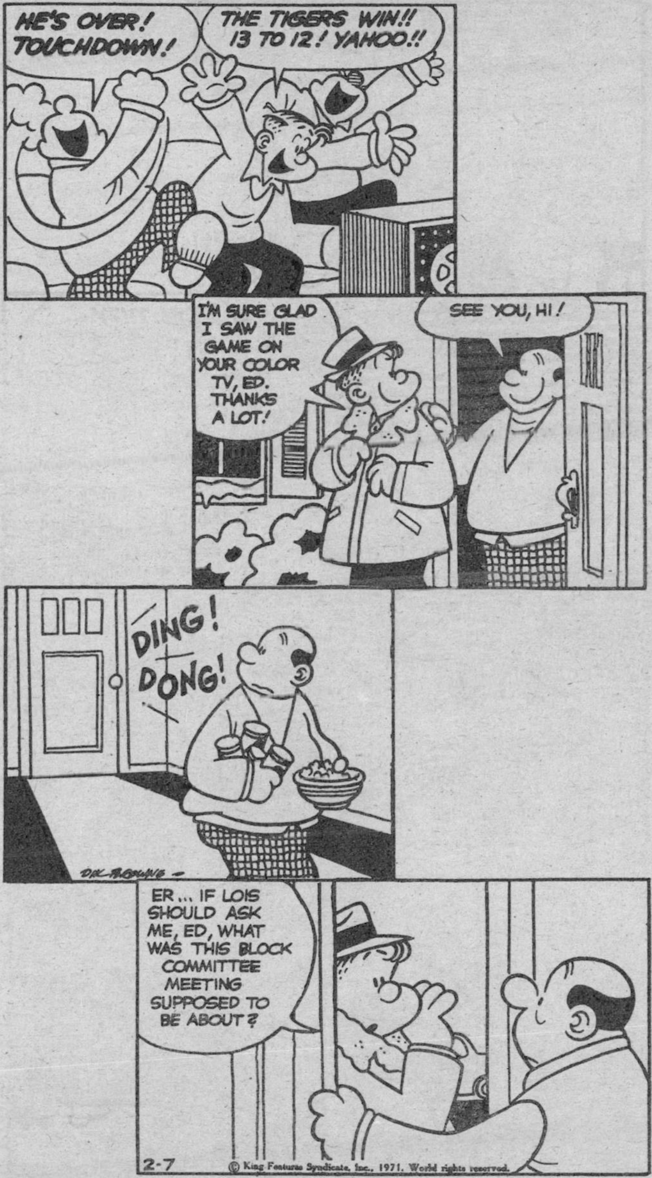
HE'S OVER! TOUCHDOWN!
THE TIGERS WIN!! 13 TO 12! YAHOO!!
I'M SURE GLAD I SAW THE GAME ON YOUR COLOR TV, ED. THANKS A LOT!
SEE YOU, HI!
DING! DONG!
ER... IF LOIS SHOULD ASK ME, ED, WHAT WAS THIS BLOCK COMMITTEE MEETING SUPPOSED TO BE ABOUT?
2-7
© King Features Syndicate, Inc., 1971. World rights reserved.

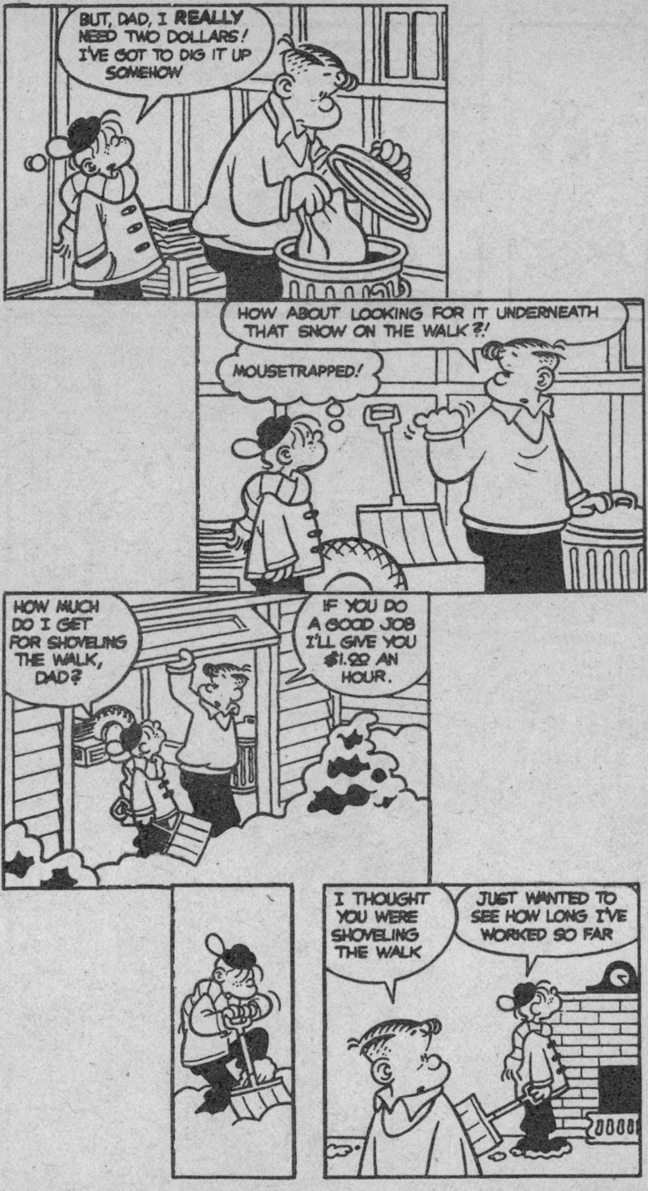
BUT, DAD, I REALLY NEED TWO DOLLARS! I'VE GOT TO DIG IT UP SOMEHOW
HOW ABOUT LOOKING FOR IT UNDERNEATH THAT SNOW ON THE WALK?!
MOUSETRAPPED!
HOW MUCH DO I GET FOR SHOVELING THE WALK, DAD?
IF YOU DO A GOOD JOB I'LL GIVE YOU $1.00 AN HOUR.
I THOUGHT YOU WERE SHOVELING THE WALK
JUST WANTED TO SEE HOW LONG I'VE WORKED SO FAR

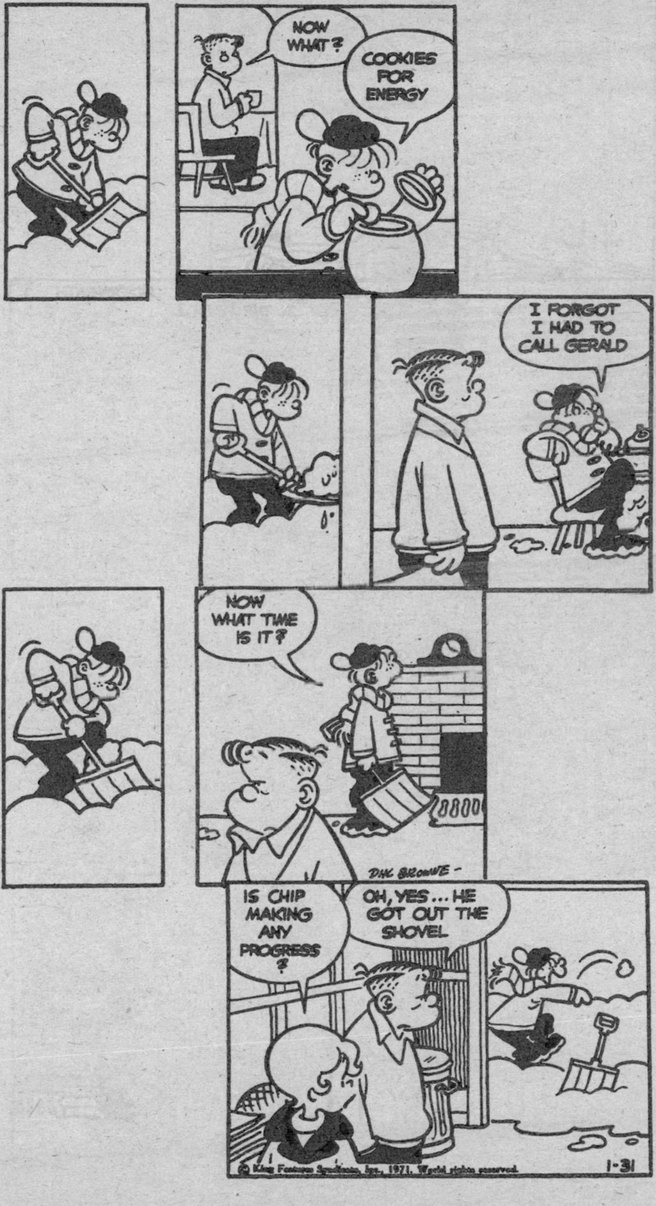
NOW WHAT?
COOKIES FOR ENERGY
I FORGOT I HAD TO CALL GERALD
NOW WHAT TIME IS IT?
DIK BROWNE
IS CHIP MAKING ANY PROGRESS?
OH, YES... HE GOT OUT THE SHOVEL
© King Features Syndicate, Inc., 1971. World rights reserved.
1-31

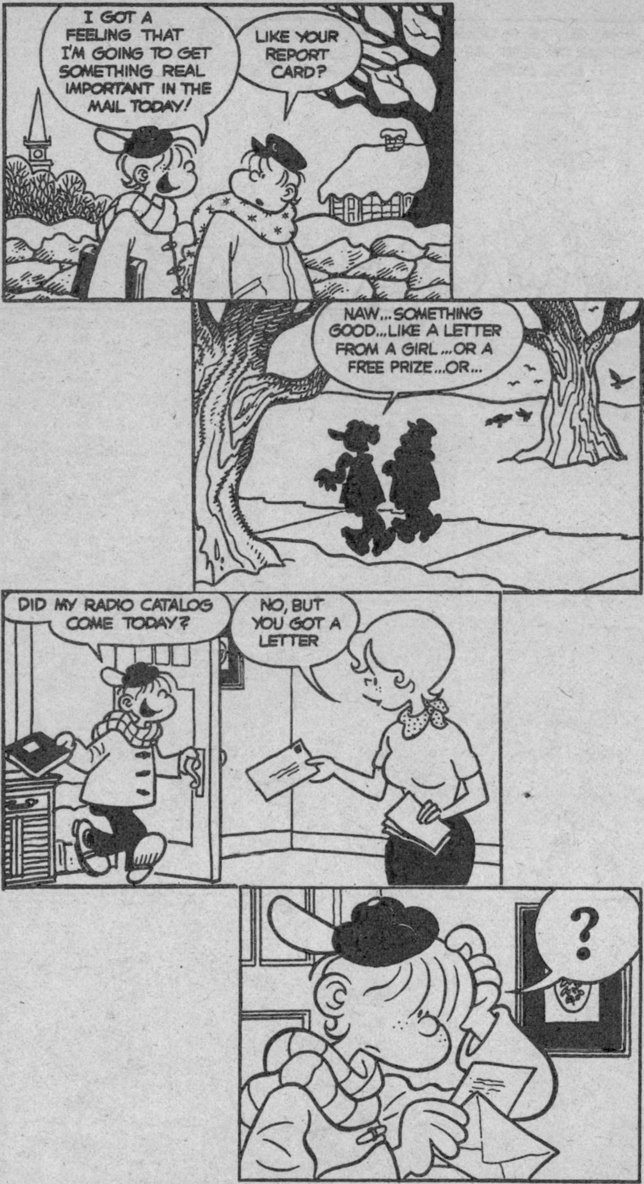
I GOT A FEELING THAT I'M GOING TO GET SOMETHING REAL IMPORTANT IN THE MAIL TODAY!
LIKE YOUR REPORT CARD?
NAW...SOMETHING GOOD...LIKE A LETTER FROM A GIRL...OR A FREE PRIZE...OR...
DID MY RADIO CATALOG COME TODAY?
NO, BUT YOU GOT A LETTER
?

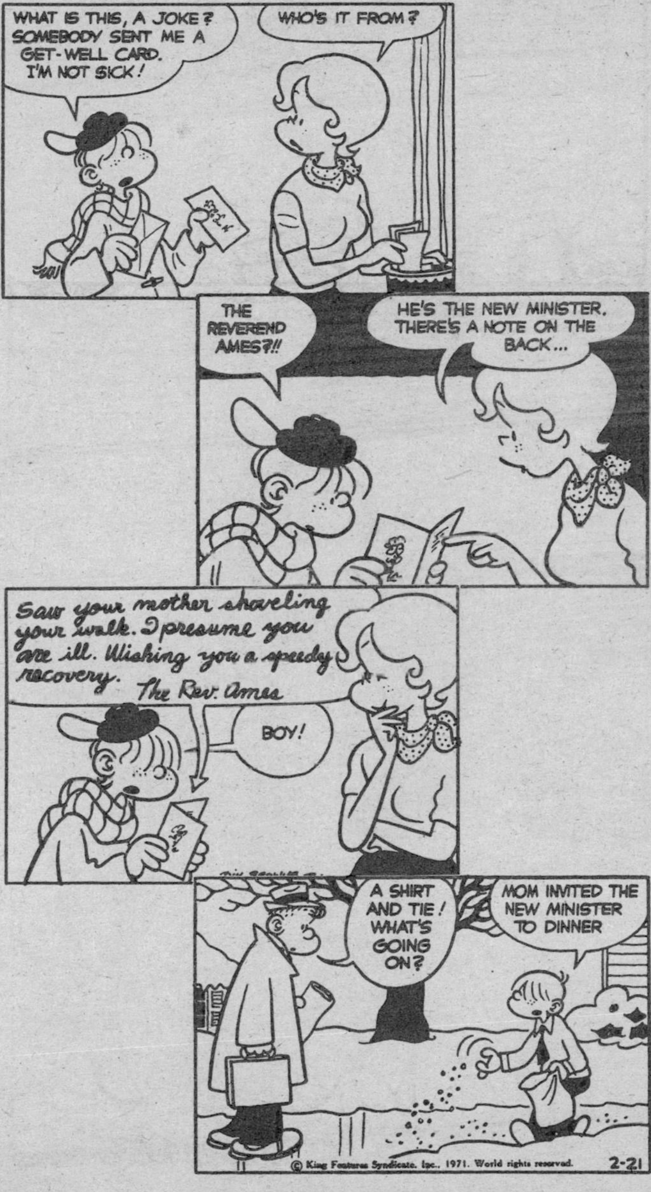
WHAT IS THIS, A JOKE? SOMEBODY SENT ME A GET-WELL CARD. I'M NOT SICK!
WHO'S IT FROM?
THE REVEREND AMES?!!
HE'S THE NEW MINISTER. THERE'S A NOTE ON THE BACK...
Saw your mother shoveling your walk. I presume you are ill. Wishing you a speedy recovery. The Rev. Ames
BOY!
A SHIRT AND TIE! WHAT'S GOING ON?
MOM INVITED THE NEW MINISTER TO DINNER
© King Features Syndicate, Inc., 1971. World rights reserved.
2-21

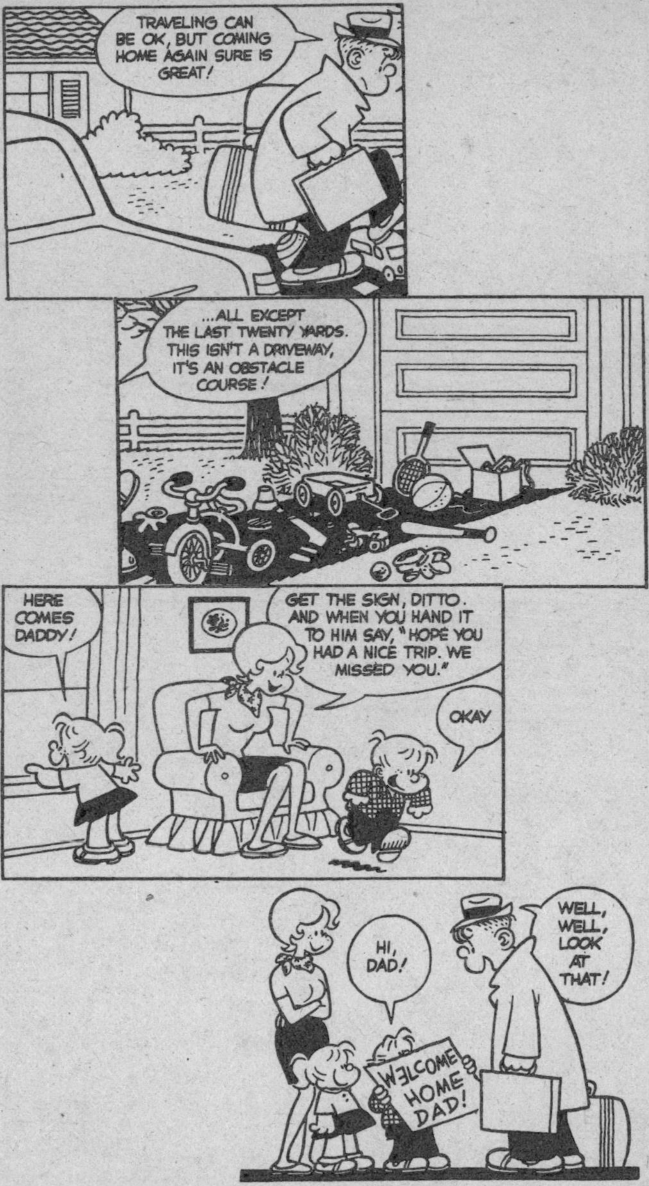
TRAVELING CAN BE OK, BUT COMING HOME AGAIN SURE IS GREAT!
...ALL EXCEPT THE LAST TWENTY YARDS. THIS ISN'T A DRIVEWAY, IT'S AN OBSTACLE COURSE!
HERE COMES DADDY!
GET THE SIGN, DITTO. AND WHEN YOU HAND IT TO HIM SAY, "HOPE YOU HAD A NICE TRIP. WE MISSED YOU."
OKAY
HI, DAD!
WELL, WELL, LOOK AT THAT!
WELCOME HOME DAD!

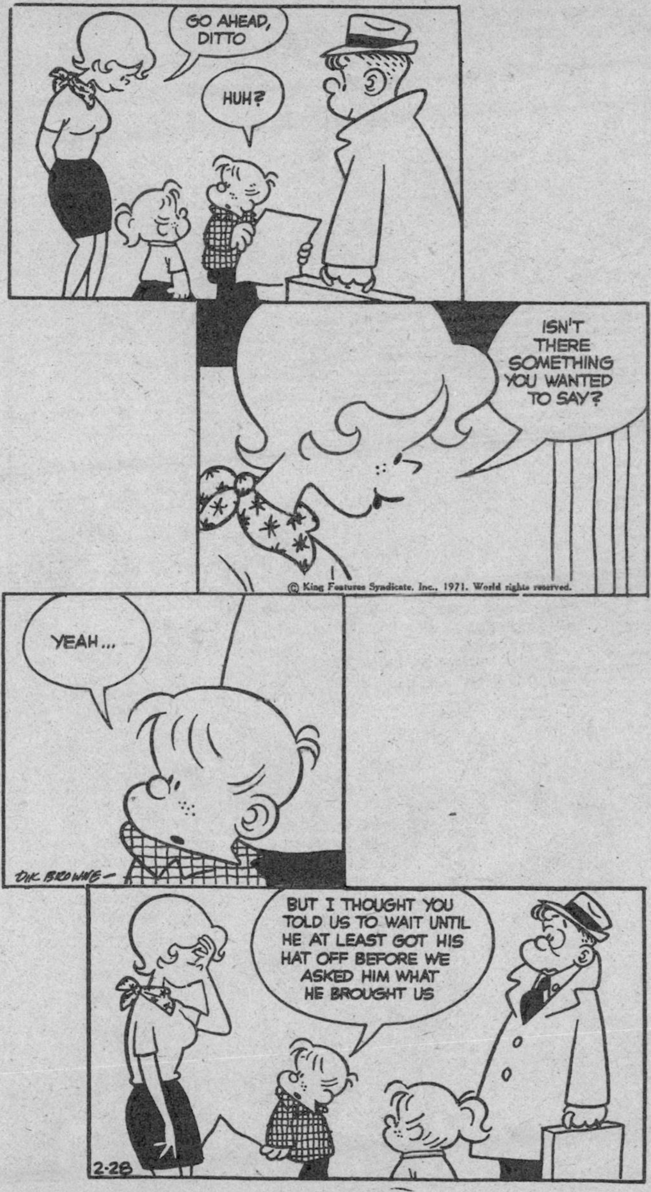
GO AHEAD, DITTO
HUH?
ISN'T THERE SOMETHING YOU WANTED TO SAY?
© King Features Syndicate, Inc., 1971. World rights reserved.
YEAH...
DIK BROWNE
BUT I THOUGHT YOU TOLD US TO WAIT UNTIL HE AT LEAST GOT HIS HAT OFF BEFORE WE ASKED HIM WHAT HE BROUGHT US
2-28

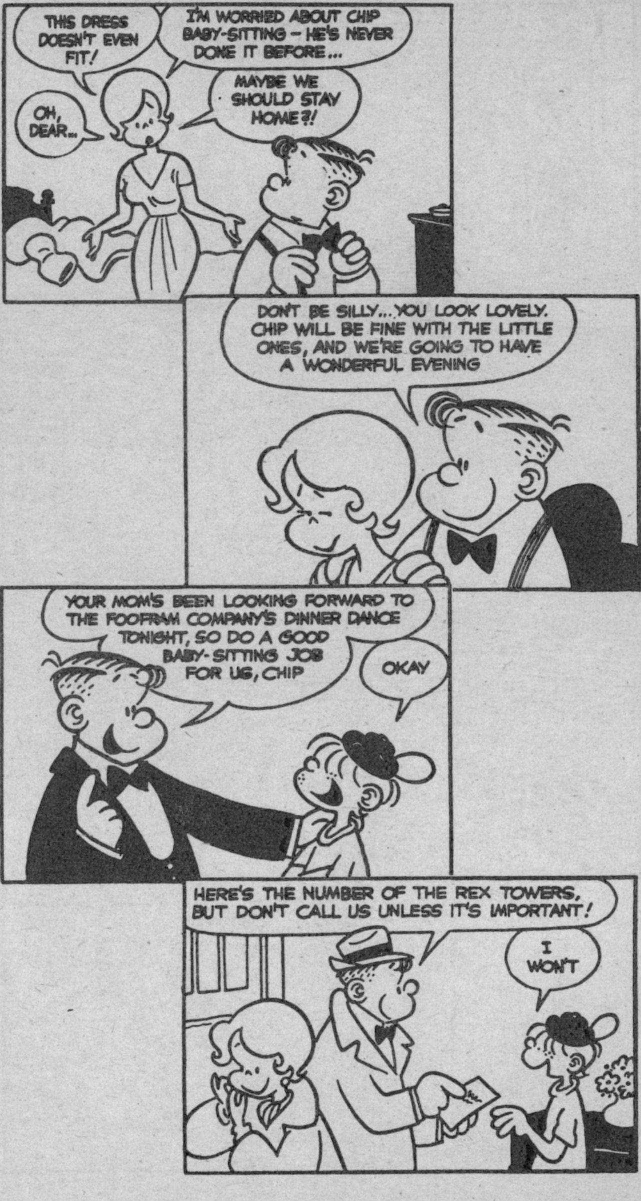
THIS DRESS DOESN'T EVEN FIT!
I'M WORRIED ABOUT CHIP BABY-SITTING – HE'S NEVER DONE IT BEFORE...
OH, DEAR...
MAYBE WE SHOULD STAY HOME?!
DON'T BE SILLY... YOU LOOK LOVELY. CHIP WILL BE FINE WITH THE LITTLE ONES, AND WE'RE GOING TO HAVE A WONDERFUL EVENING
YOUR MOM'S BEEN LOOKING FORWARD TO THE FOOFRAM COMPANY'S DINNER DANCE TONIGHT, SO DO A GOOD BABY-SITTING JOB FOR US, CHIP
OKAY
HERE'S THE NUMBER OF THE REX TOWERS, BUT DON'T CALL US UNLESS IT'S IMPORTANT!
I WON'T

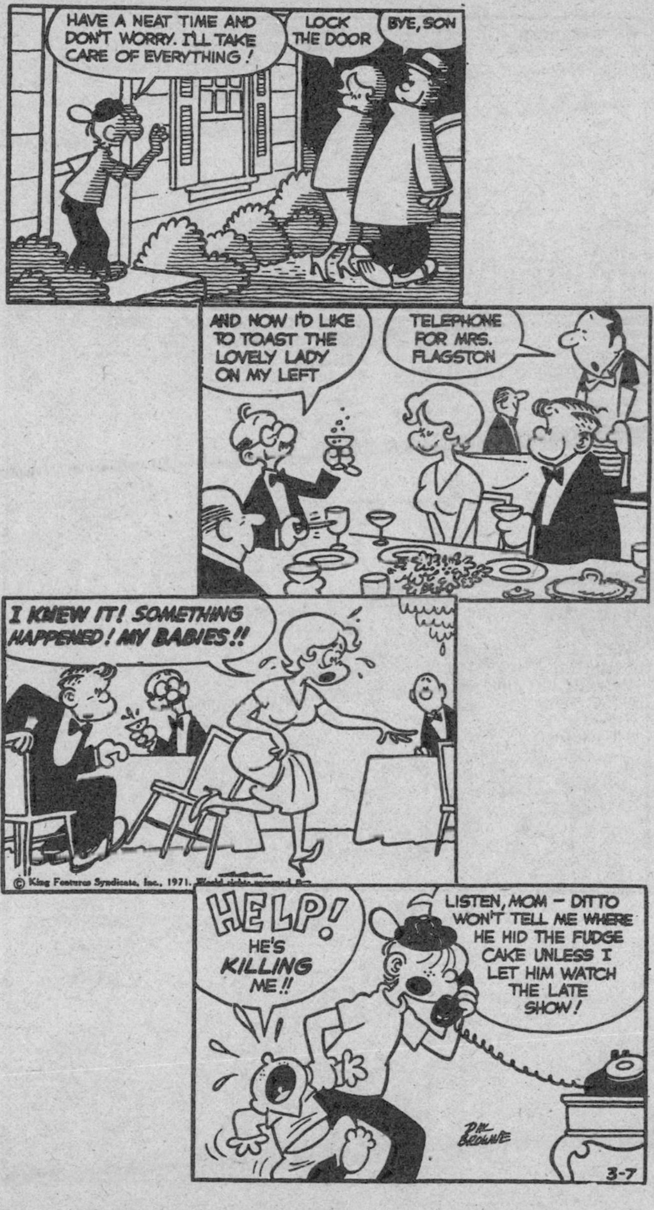
HAVE A NEAT TIME AND DON'T WORRY. I'LL TAKE CARE OF EVERYTHING!
LOCK THE DOOR
BYE, SON
AND NOW I'D LIKE TO TOAST THE LOVELY LADY ON MY LEFT
TELEPHONE FOR MRS. FLAGSTON
I KNEW IT! SOMETHING HAPPENED! MY BABIES!!
HELP! HE'S KILLING ME!!
LISTEN, MOM – DITTO WON'T TELL ME WHERE HE HID THE FUDGE CAKE UNLESS I LET HIM WATCH THE LATE SHOW!
DIK BROWNE
3-7

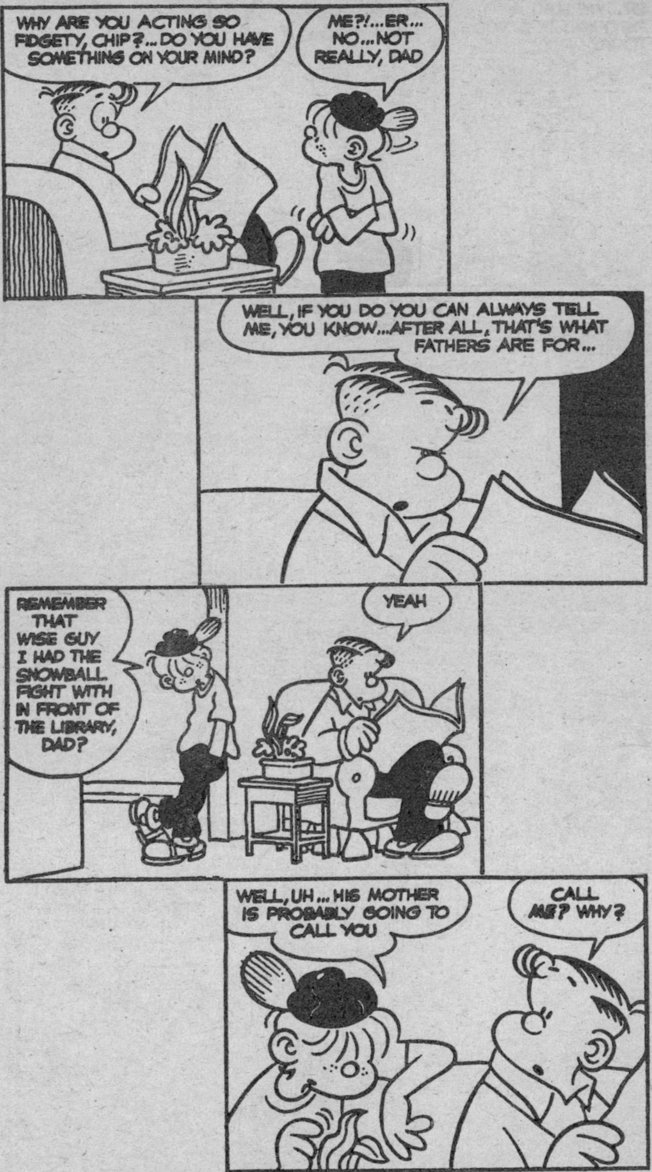
WHY ARE YOU ACTING SO FIDGETY, CHIP?...DO YOU HAVE SOMETHING ON YOUR MIND?
ME?!...ER... NO...NOT REALLY, DAD
WELL, IF YOU DO YOU CAN ALWAYS TELL ME, YOU KNOW...AFTER ALL, THAT'S WHAT FATHERS ARE FOR...
REMEMBER THAT WISE GUY I HAD THE SNOWBALL FIGHT WITH IN FRONT OF THE LIBRARY, DAD?
YEAH
WELL, UH... HIS MOTHER IS PROBABLY GOING TO CALL YOU
CALL ME? WHY?

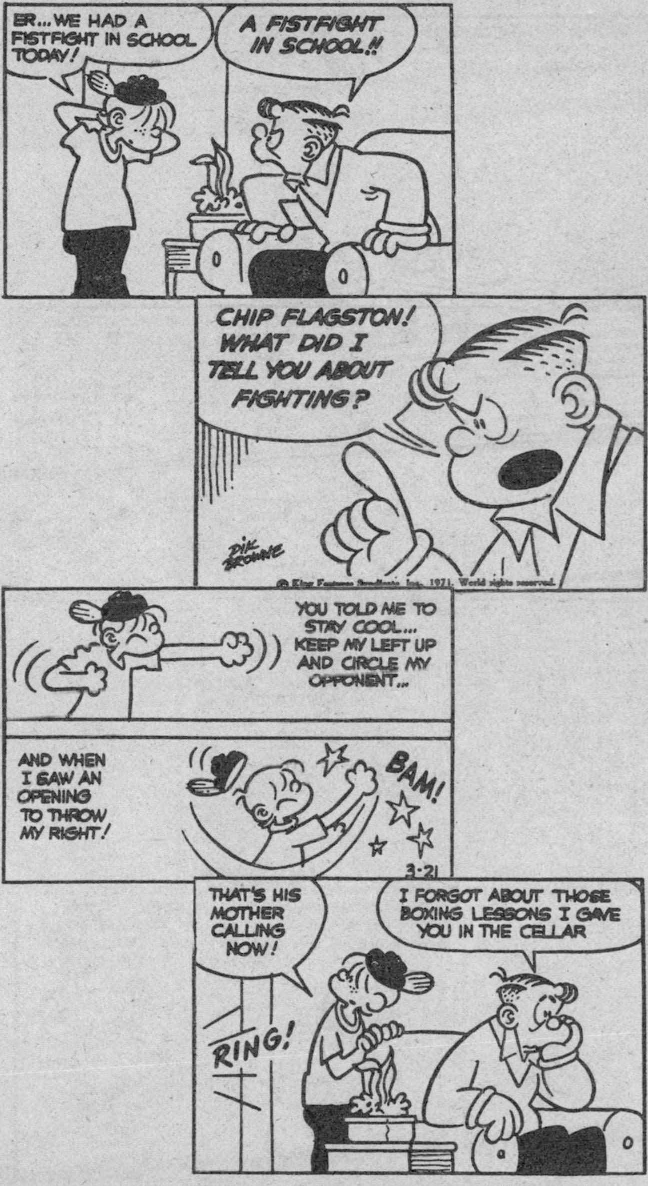
ER...WE HAD A FISTFIGHT IN SCHOOL TODAY!
A FISTFIGHT IN SCHOOL!!
CHIP FLAGSTON! WHAT DID I TELL YOU ABOUT FIGHTING?
DIK BROWNE
© King Features Syndicate, Inc. 1971. World rights reserved.
YOU TOLD ME TO STAY COOL... KEEP MY LEFT UP AND CIRCLE MY OPPONENT...
AND WHEN I SAW AN OPENING TO THROW MY RIGHT!
BAM!
3·21
THAT'S HIS MOTHER CALLING NOW!
I FORGOT ABOUT THOSE BOXING LESSONS I GAVE YOU IN THE CELLAR
RING!

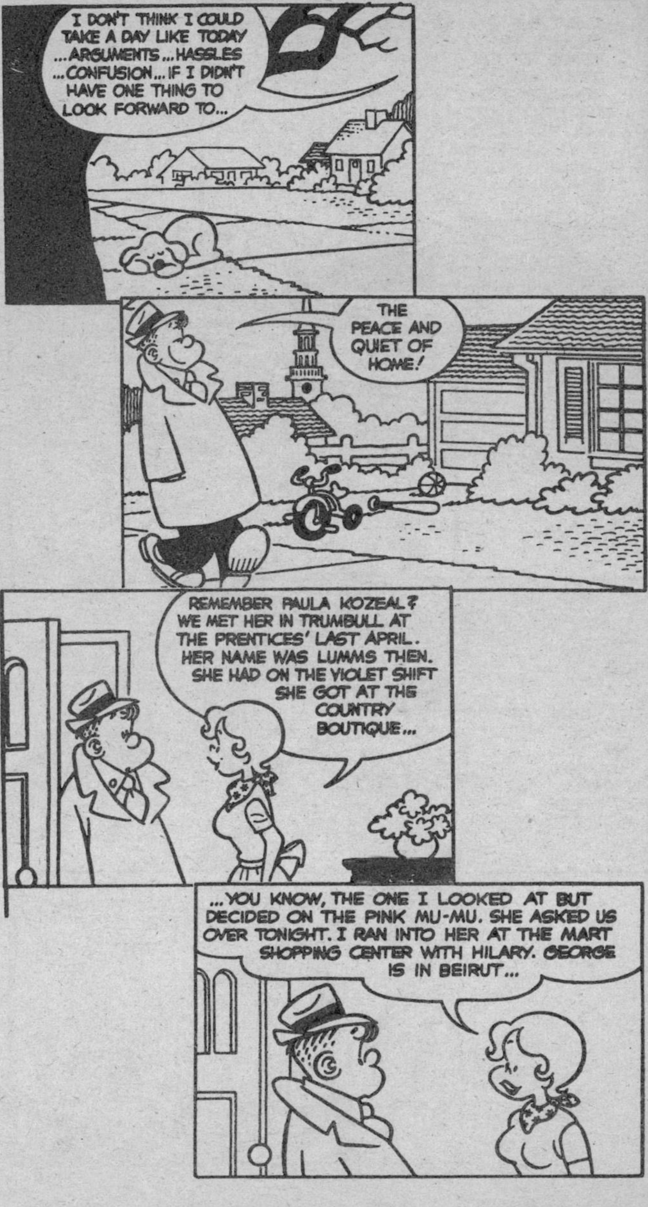
I DON'T THINK I COULD TAKE A DAY LIKE TODAY ...ARGUMENTS...HASSLES ...CONFUSION...IF I DIDN'T HAVE ONE THING TO LOOK FORWARD TO...
THE PEACE AND QUIET OF HOME!
REMEMBER PAULA KOZEAL? WE MET HER IN TRUMBULL AT THE PRENTICES' LAST APRIL. HER NAME WAS LUMMS THEN. SHE HAD ON THE VIOLET SHIFT SHE GOT AT THE COUNTRY BOUTIQUE...
...YOU KNOW, THE ONE I LOOKED AT BUT DECIDED ON THE PINK MU-MU. SHE ASKED US OVER TONIGHT. I RAN INTO HER AT THE MART SHOPPING CENTER WITH HILARY. GEORGE IS IN BEIRUT...

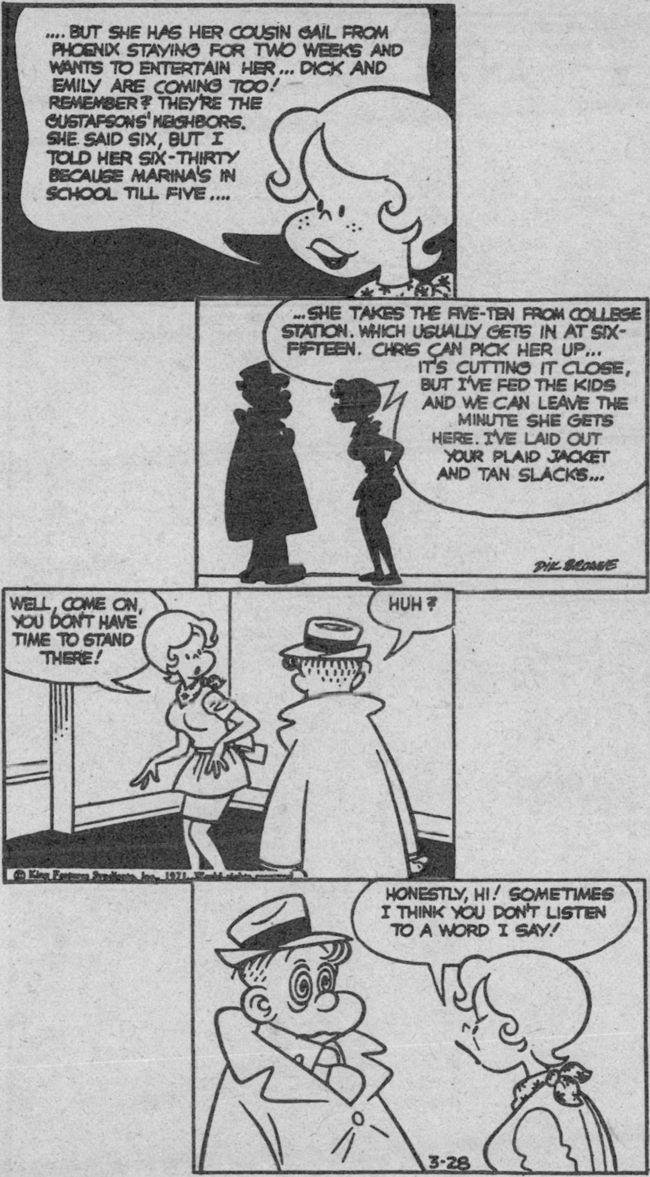
.... BUT SHE HAS HER COUSIN GAIL FROM PHOENIX STAYING FOR TWO WEEKS AND WANTS TO ENTERTAIN HER ... DICK AND EMILY ARE COMING TOO! REMEMBER? THEY'RE THE GUSTAFSONS' NEIGHBORS. SHE SAID SIX, BUT I TOLD HER SIX-THIRTY BECAUSE MARINA'S IN SCHOOL TILL FIVE ....
...SHE TAKES THE FIVE-TEN FROM COLLEGE STATION. WHICH USUALLY GETS IN AT SIX-FIFTEEN. CHRIS CAN PICK HER UP... IT'S CUTTING IT CLOSE, BUT I'VE FED THE KIDS AND WE CAN LEAVE THE MINUTE SHE GETS HERE. I'VE LAID OUT YOUR PLAID JACKET AND TAN SLACKS...
DIK BROWNE
WELL, COME ON, YOU DON'T HAVE TIME TO STAND THERE!
HUH?
HONESTLY, HI! SOMETIMES I THINK YOU DON'T LISTEN TO A WORD I SAY!
3-28

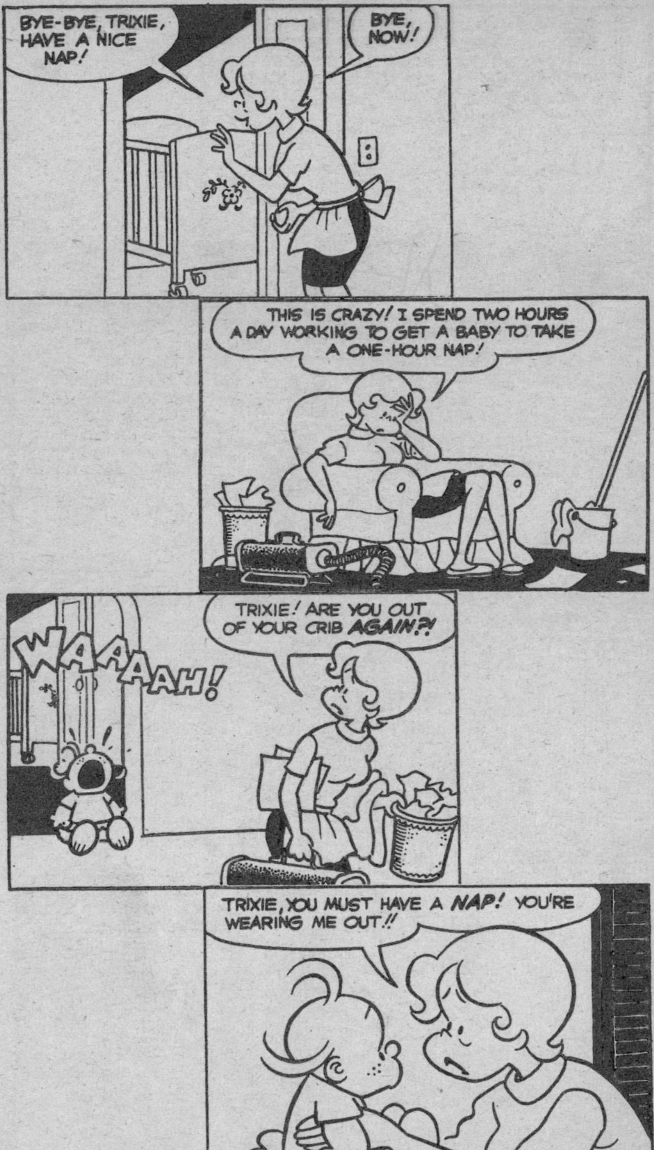
BYE-BYE, TRIXIE, HAVE A NICE NAP!
BYE, NOW!
THIS IS CRAZY! I SPEND TWO HOURS A DAY WORKING TO GET A BABY TO TAKE A ONE-HOUR NAP!
WAAAAH!
TRIXIE! ARE YOU OUT OF YOUR CRIB AGAIN?!
TRIXIE, YOU MUST HAVE A NAP! YOU'RE WEARING ME OUT!!

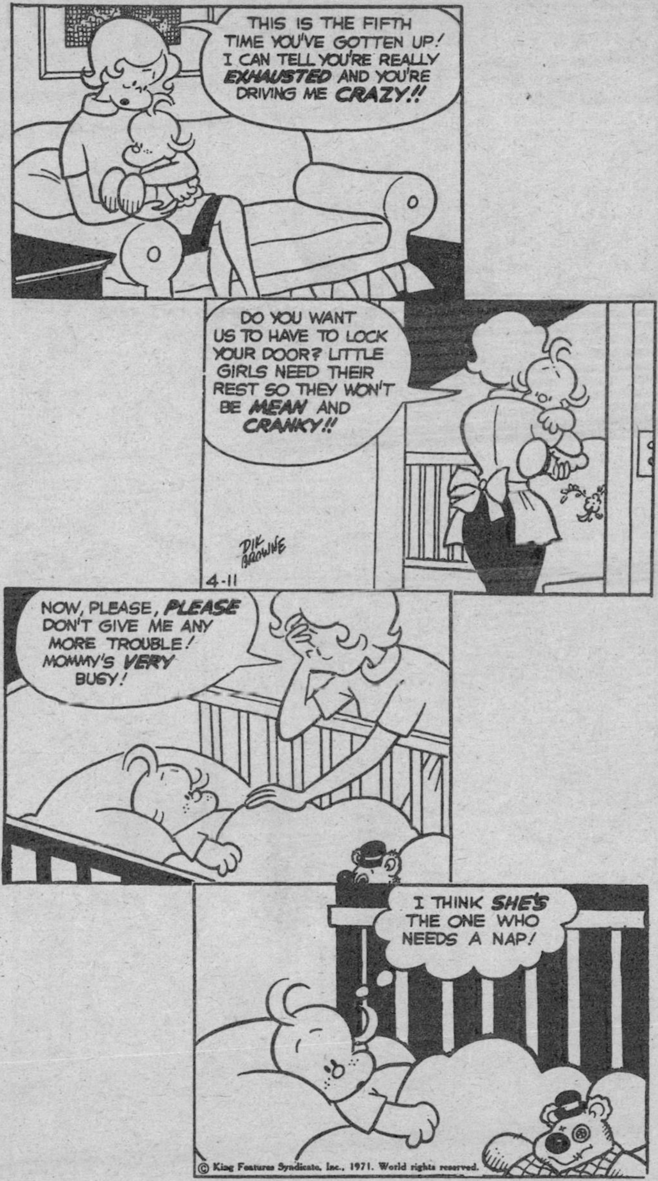
THIS IS THE FIFTH TIME YOU'VE GOTTEN UP! I CAN TELL YOU'RE REALLY EXHAUSTED AND YOU'RE DRIVING ME CRAZY!!
DO YOU WANT US TO HAVE TO LOCK YOUR DOOR? LITTLE GIRLS NEED THEIR REST SO THEY WON'T BE MEAN AND CRANKY!!
DIK BROWNE
4-11
NOW, PLEASE, PLEASE DON'T GIVE ME ANY MORE TROUBLE! MOMMY'S VERY BUSY!
I THINK SHE'S THE ONE WHO NEEDS A NAP!

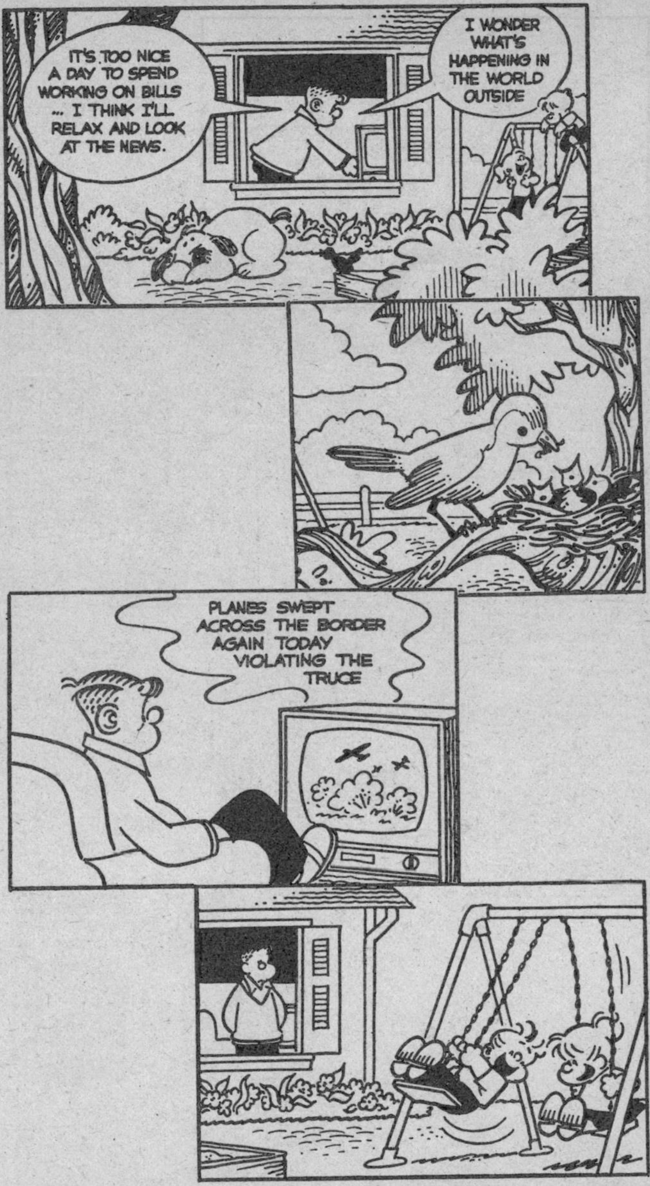
IT'S TOO NICE A DAY TO SPEND WORKING ON BILLS ... I THINK I'LL RELAX AND LOOK AT THE NEWS.
I WONDER WHAT'S HAPPENING IN THE WORLD OUTSIDE
PLANES SWEPT ACROSS THE BORDER AGAIN TODAY VIOLATING THE TRUCE

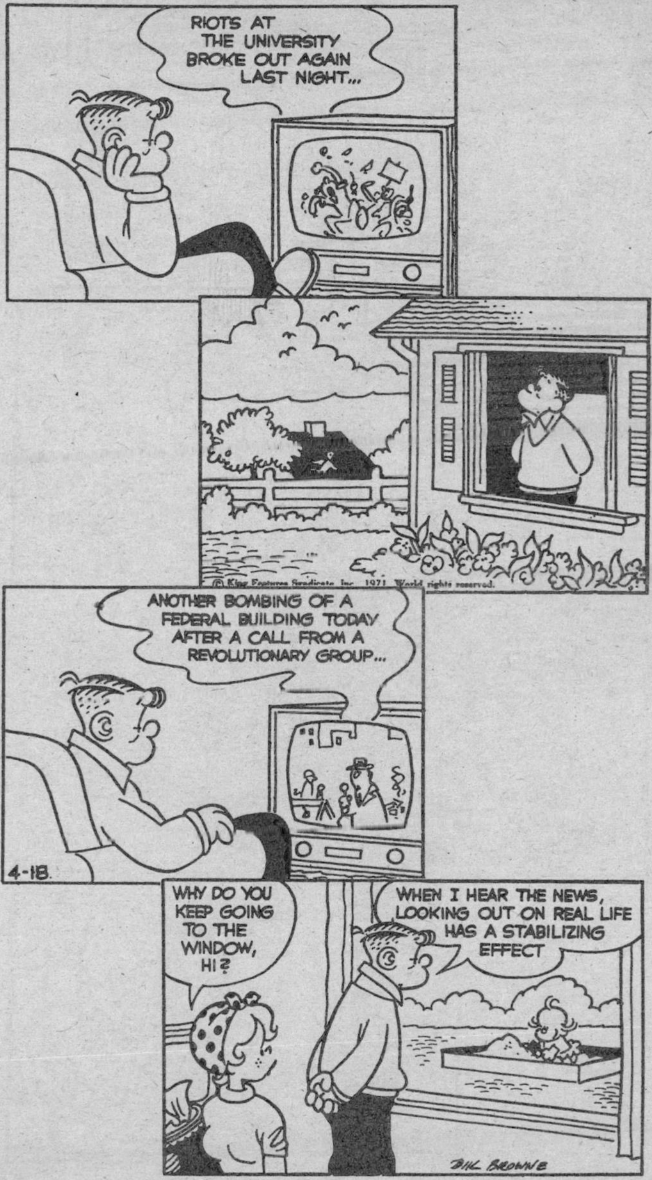
RIOTS AT THE UNIVERSITY BROKE OUT AGAIN LAST NIGHT...
ANOTHER BOMBING OF A FEDERAL BUILDING TODAY AFTER A CALL FROM A REVOLUTIONARY GROUP...
4-18.
WHY DO YOU KEEP GOING TO THE WINDOW, HI?
WHEN I HEAR THE NEWS, LOOKING OUT ON REAL LIFE HAS A STABILIZING EFFECT
BILL BROWNE

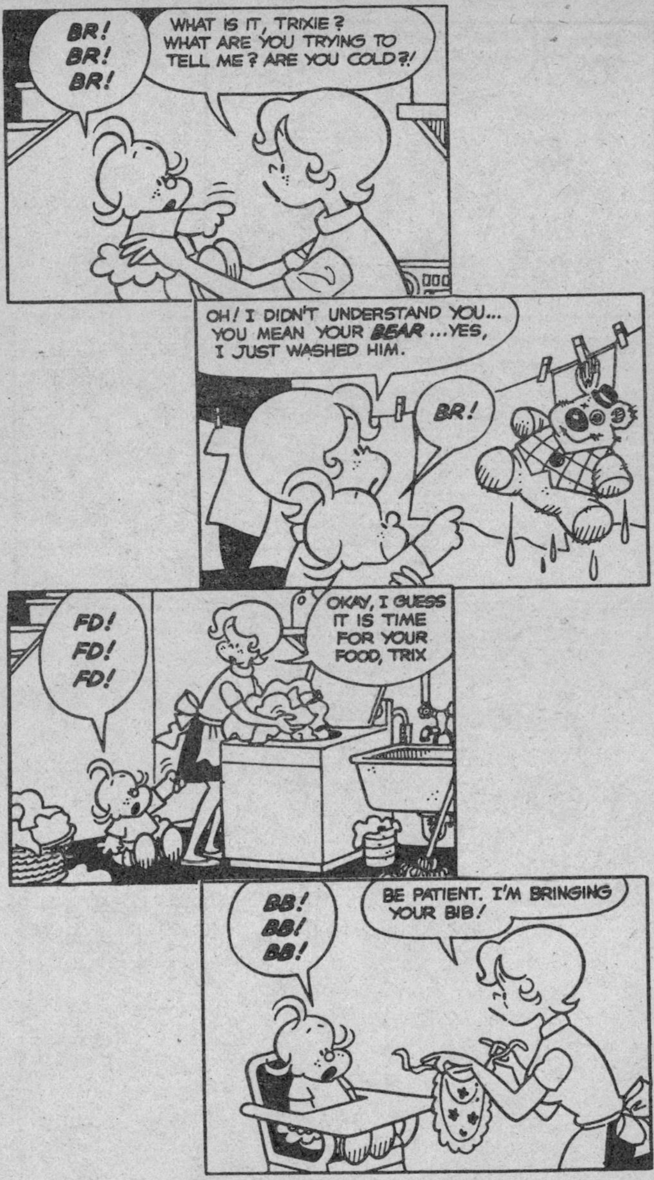
BR! BR! BR!
WHAT IS IT, TRIXIE? WHAT ARE YOU TRYING TO TELL ME? ARE YOU COLD?!
OH! I DIDN'T UNDERSTAND YOU... YOU MEAN YOUR BEAR ...YES, I JUST WASHED HIM.
BR!
FD! FD! FD!
OKAY, I GUESS IT IS TIME FOR YOUR FOOD, TRIX
BB! BB! BB!
BE PATIENT. I'M BRINGING YOUR BIB!

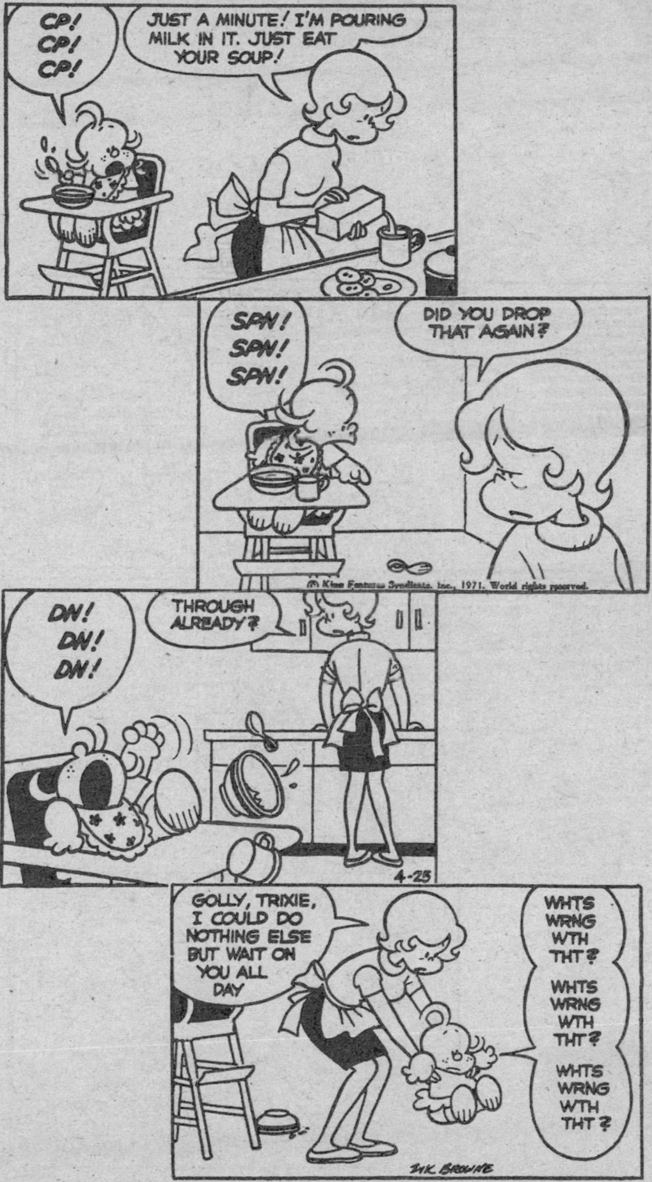
CP! CP! CP!
JUST A MINUTE! I'M POURING MILK IN IT. JUST EAT YOUR SOUP!
SPN! SPN! SPN!
DID YOU DROP THAT AGAIN?
© King Features Syndicate, Inc., 1971. World rights reserved.
DN! DN! DN!
THROUGH ALREADY?
4-25
GOLLY, TRIXIE, I COULD DO NOTHING ELSE BUT WAIT ON YOU ALL DAY
WHTS WRNG WTH THT? WHTS WRNG WTH THT? WHTS WRNG WTH THT?
DIK BROWNE

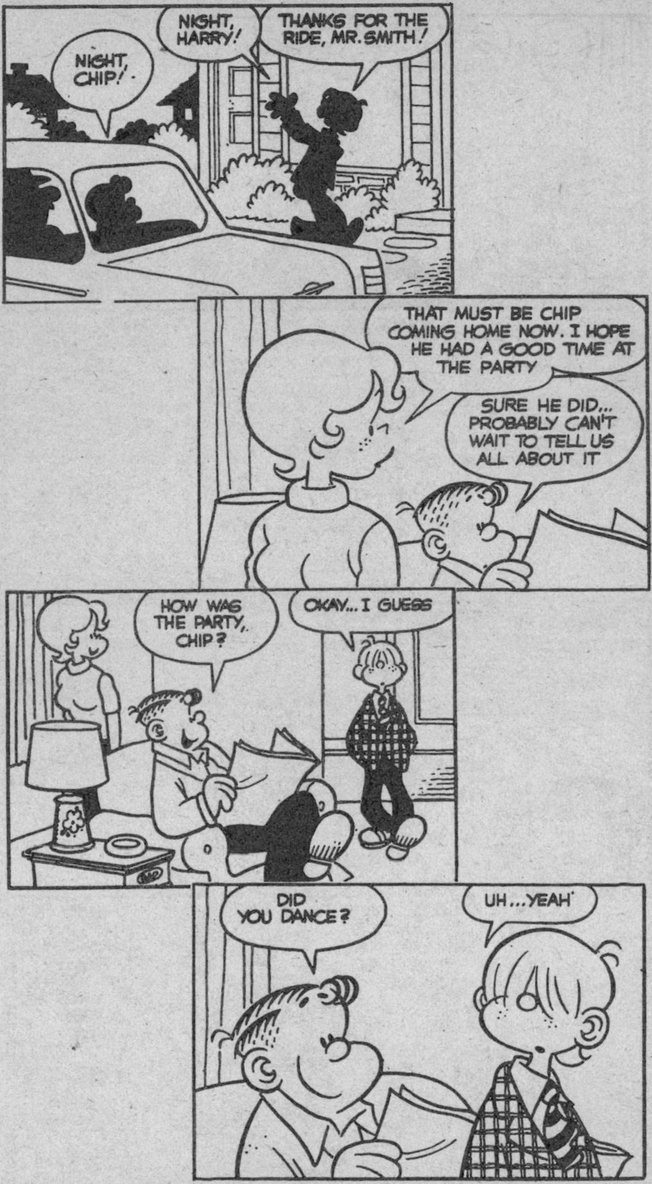

NIGHT, CHIP!
NIGHT, HARRY!
THANKS FOR THE RIDE, MR. SMITH!
THAT MUST BE CHIP COMING HOME NOW. I HOPE HE HAD A GOOD TIME AT THE PARTY
SURE HE DID... PROBABLY CAN'T WAIT TO TELL US ALL ABOUT IT
HOW WAS THE PARTY, CHIP?
OKAY... I GUESS
DID YOU DANCE?
UH...YEAH

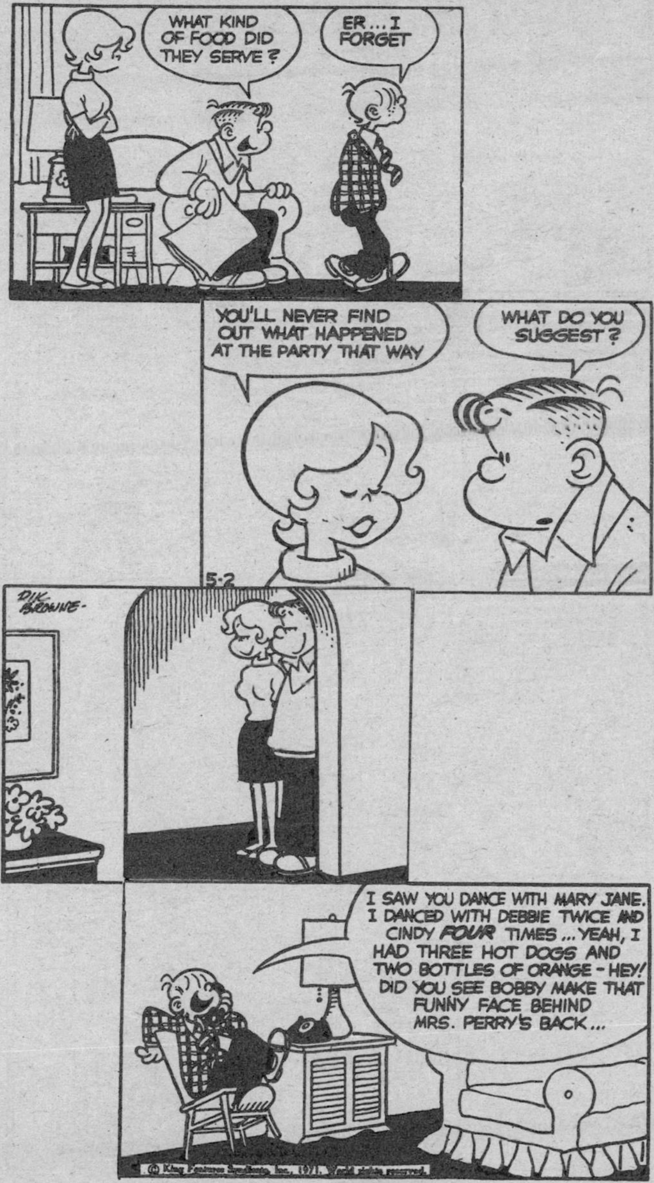
WHAT KIND OF FOOD DID THEY SERVE?
ER... I FORGET
YOU'LL NEVER FIND OUT WHAT HAPPENED AT THE PARTY THAT WAY
WHAT DO YOU SUGGEST?
5-2
DIK BROWNE
I SAW YOU DANCE WITH MARY JANE. I DANCED WITH DEBBIE TWICE AND CINDY *FOUR* TIMES ... YEAH, I HAD THREE HOT DOGS AND TWO BOTTLES OF ORANGE - HEY! DID YOU SEE BOBBY MAKE THAT FUNNY FACE BEHIND MRS. PERRY'S BACK...
© King Features Syndicate, Inc., 1971. World rights reserved.

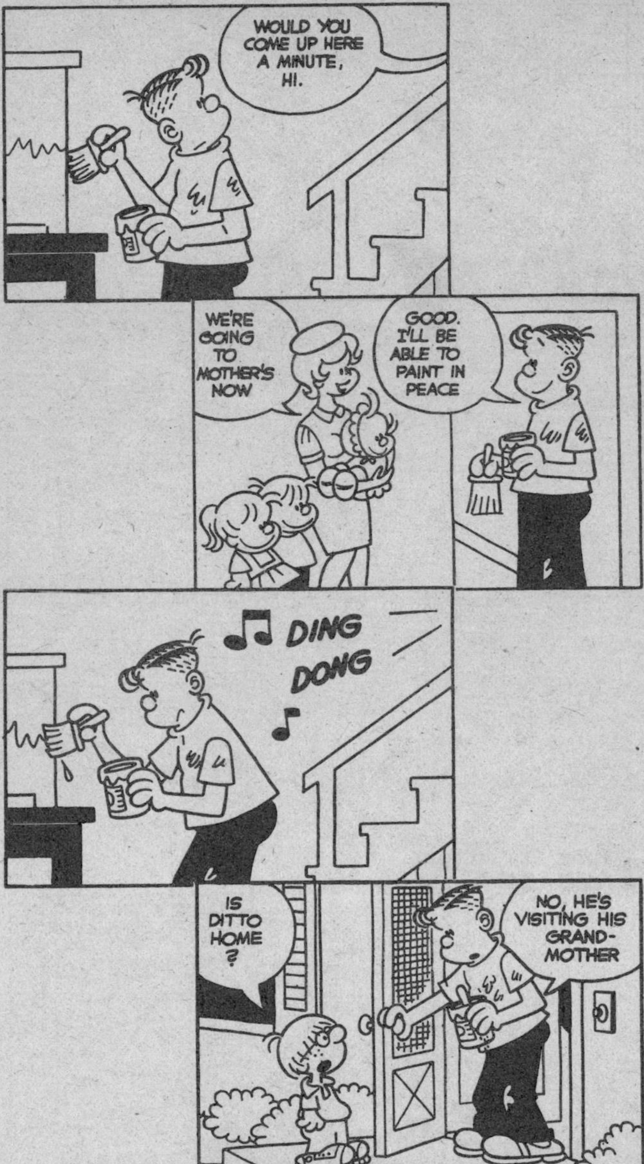
WOULD YOU COME UP HERE A MINUTE, HI.
WE'RE GOING TO MOTHER'S NOW
GOOD. I'LL BE ABLE TO PAINT IN PEACE
DING DONG
IS DITTO HOME ?
NO, HE'S VISITING HIS GRAND-MOTHER

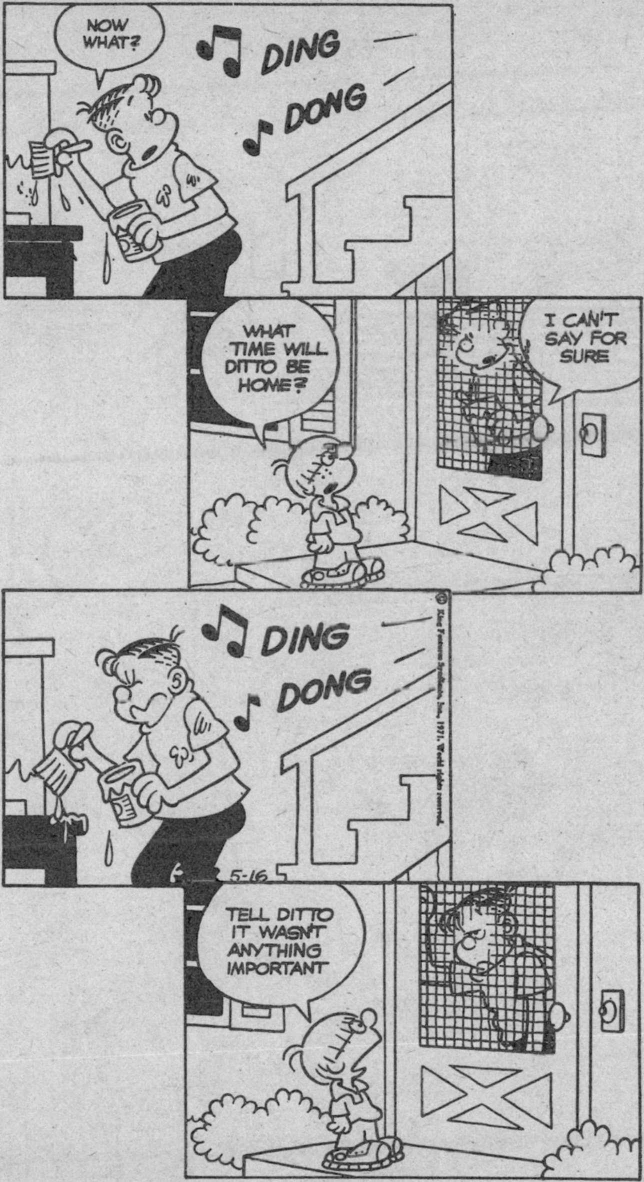
NOW WHAT?
DING
DONG
WHAT TIME WILL DITTO BE HOME?
I CAN'T SAY FOR SURE
DING
DONG
© King Features Syndicate, Inc., 1971. World rights reserved.
5-16
TELL DITTO IT WASN'T ANYTHING IMPORTANT

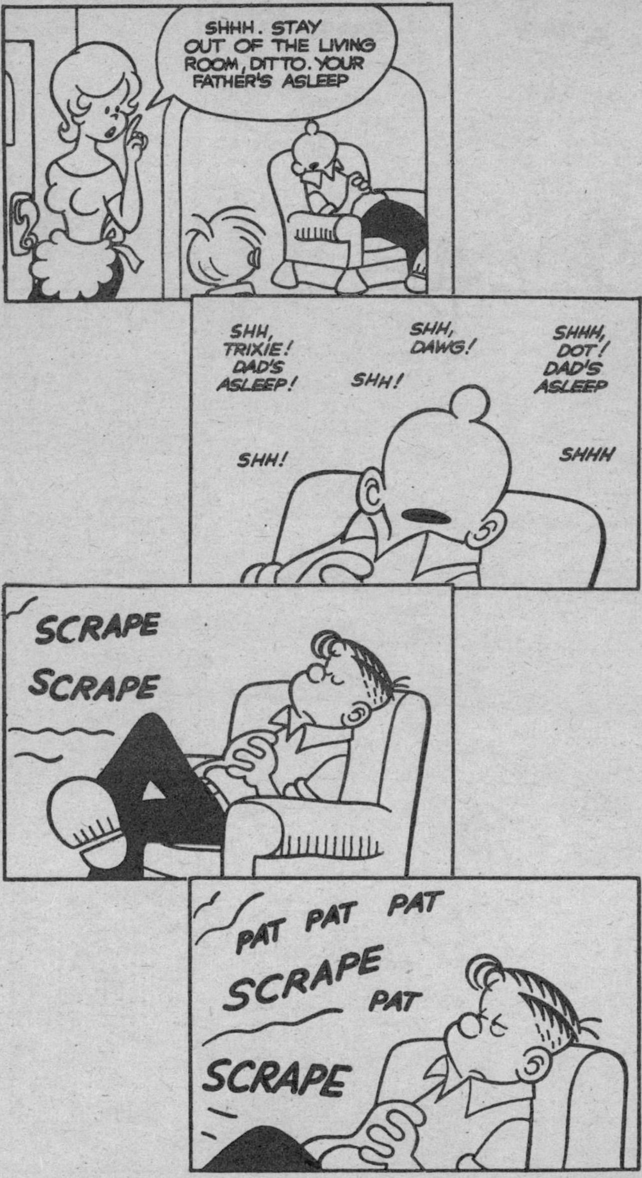
SHHH. STAY OUT OF THE LIVING ROOM, DITTO. YOUR FATHER'S ASLEEP
SHH, TRIXIE! DAD'S ASLEEP!
SHH!
SHH, DAWG!
SHHH, DOT! DAD'S ASLEEP
SHH!
SHHH
SCRAPE
SCRAPE
PAT PAT PAT
SCRAPE
PAT
SCRAPE

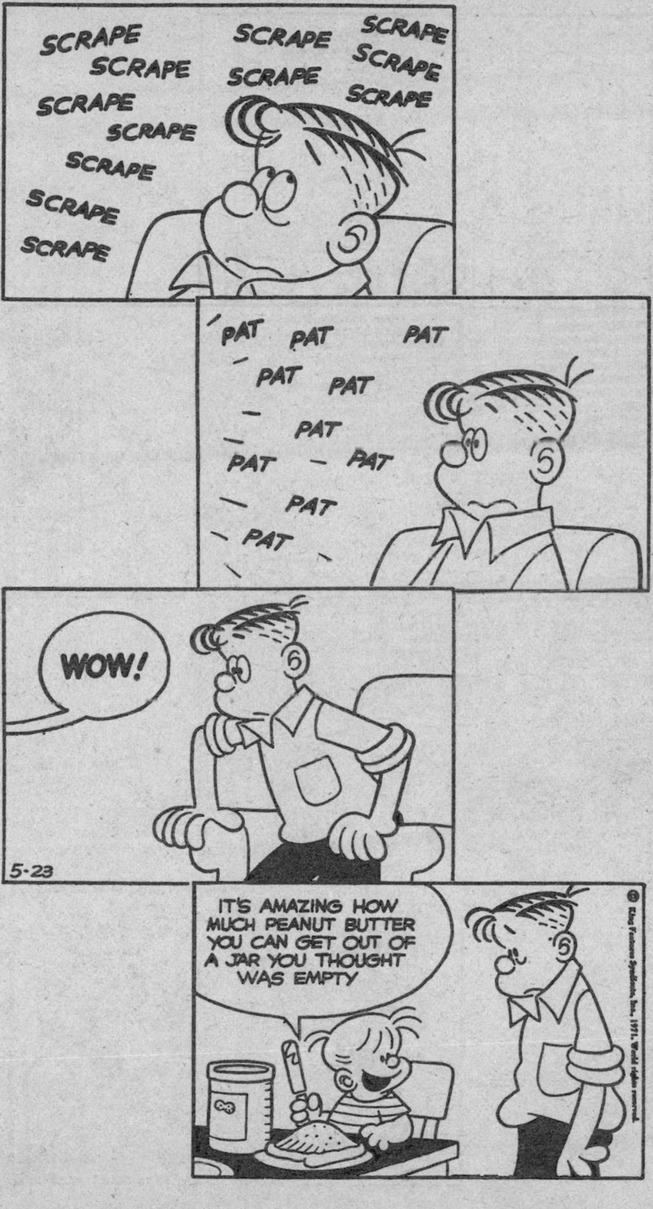
SCRAPE
SCRAPE
SCRAPE
SCRAPE
SCRAPE
SCRAPE
SCRAPE
SCRAPE
SCRAPE
SCRAPE
SCRAPE
SCRAPE
PAT
PAT
PAT
PAT
PAT
PAT
PAT
PAT
PAT
PAT
WOW!
5-23
IT'S AMAZING HOW MUCH PEANUT BUTTER YOU CAN GET OUT OF A JAR YOU THOUGHT WAS EMPTY
© King Features Syndicate, Inc., 1971. World rights reserved.

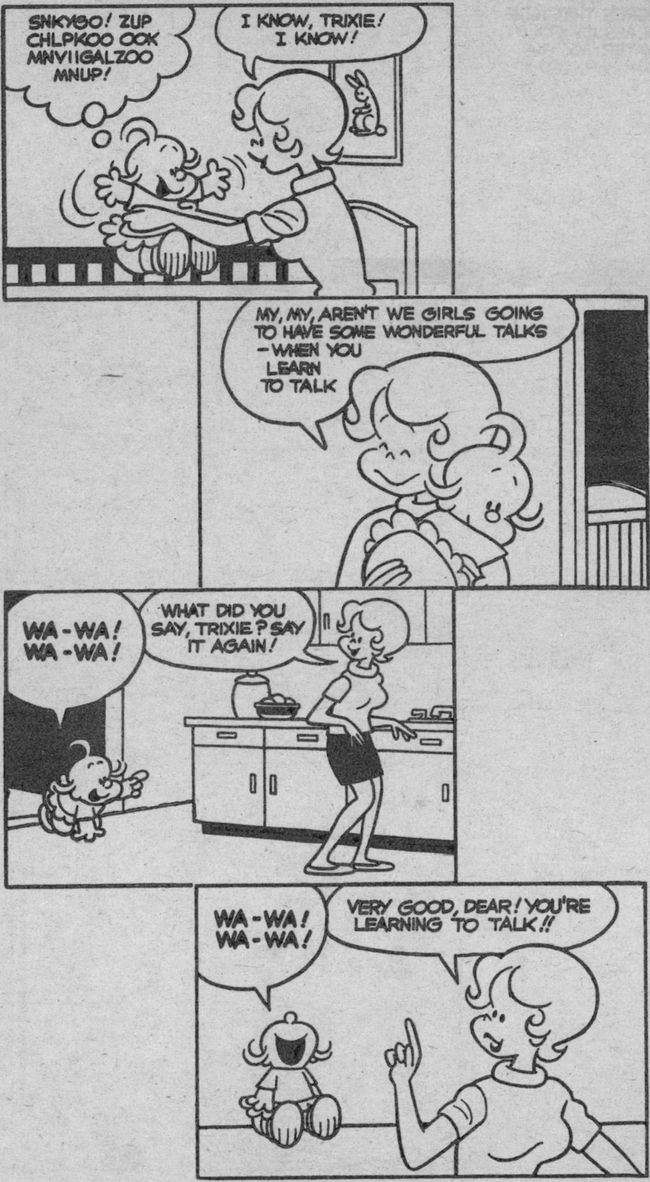
SNKYSO! ZUP CHLPKOO OOK MNVIIGALZOO MNUP!
I KNOW, TRIXIE! I KNOW!
MY, MY, AREN'T WE GIRLS GOING TO HAVE SOME WONDERFUL TALKS -WHEN YOU LEARN TO TALK
WA-WA! WA-WA!
WHAT DID YOU SAY, TRIXIE? SAY IT AGAIN!
WA-WA! WA-WA!
VERY GOOD, DEAR! YOU'RE LEARNING TO TALK!!

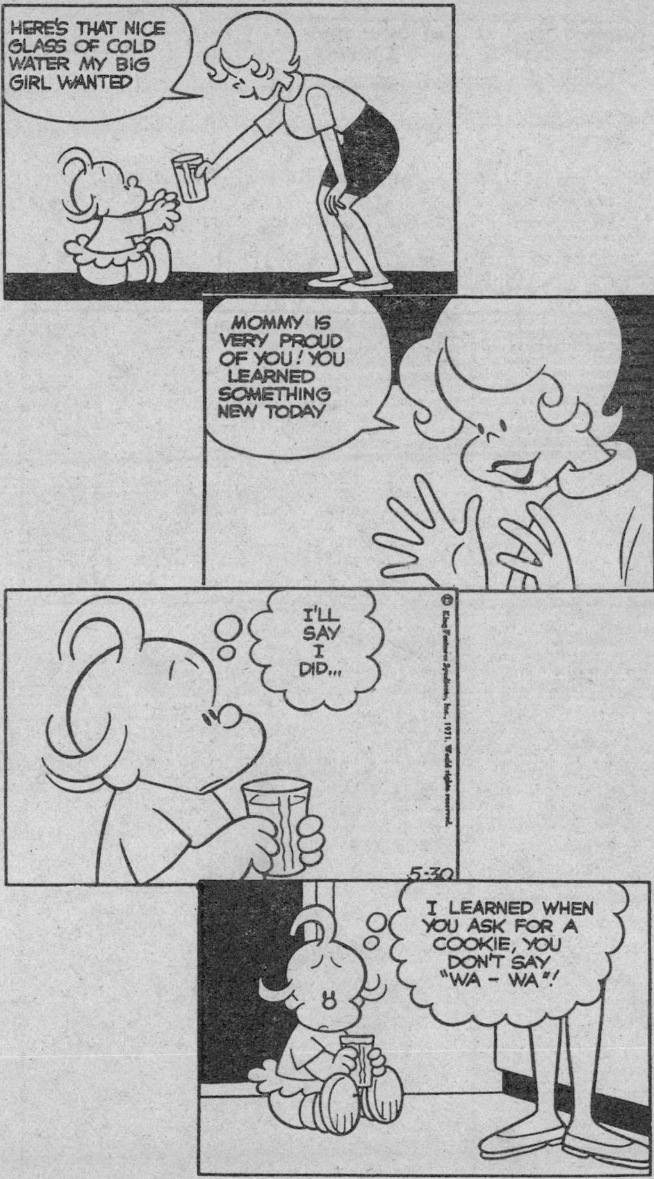
HERE'S THAT NICE GLASS OF COLD WATER MY BIG GIRL WANTED
MOMMY IS VERY PROUD OF YOU! YOU LEARNED SOMETHING NEW TODAY
I'LL SAY I DID...
© King Features Syndicate, Inc., 1971. World rights reserved.
5-30
I LEARNED WHEN YOU ASK FOR A COOKIE, YOU DON'T SAY "WA - WA"!

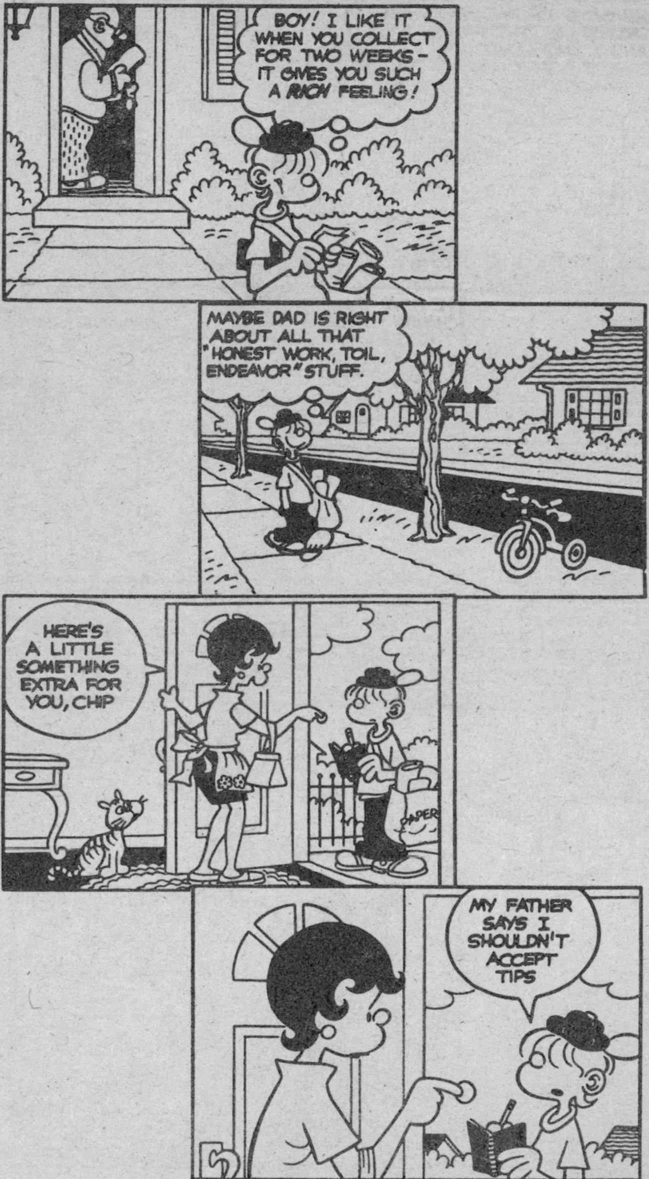
BOY! I LIKE IT WHEN YOU COLLECT FOR TWO WEEKS - IT GIVES YOU SUCH A RICH FEELING!
MAYBE DAD IS RIGHT ABOUT ALL THAT "HONEST WORK, TOIL, ENDEAVOR" STUFF.
HERE'S A LITTLE SOMETHING EXTRA FOR YOU, CHIP
PAPER
MY FATHER SAYS I SHOULDN'T ACCEPT TIPS

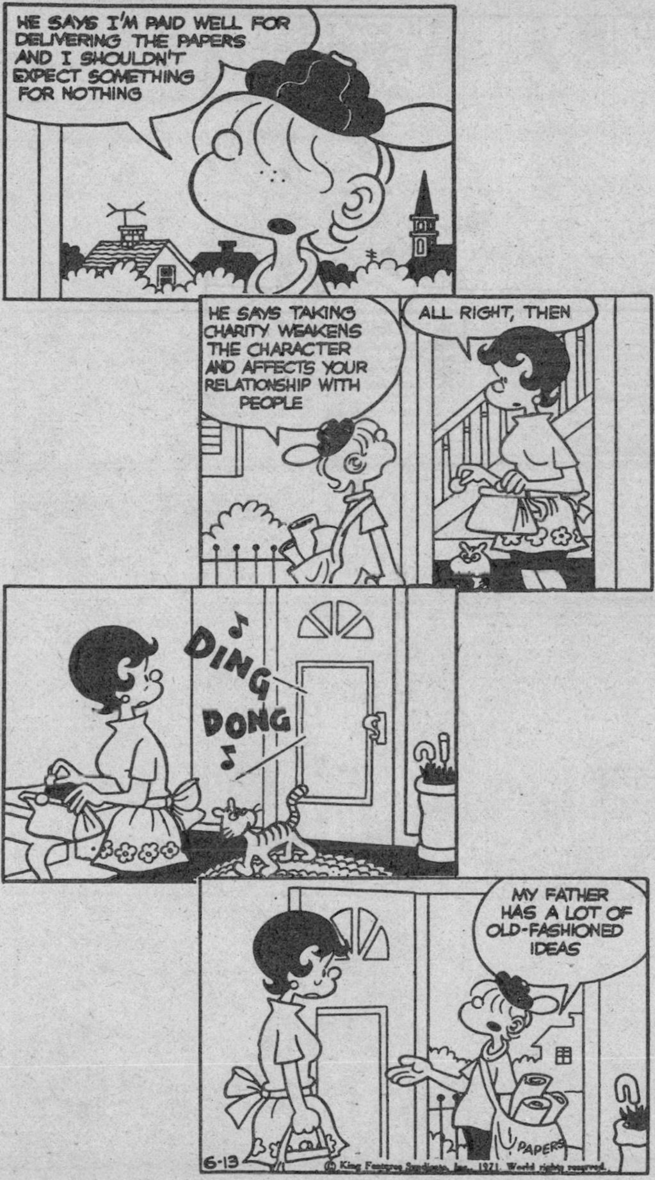
HE SAYS I'M PAID WELL FOR DELIVERING THE PAPERS AND I SHOULDN'T EXPECT SOMETHING FOR NOTHING
HE SAYS TAKING CHARITY WEAKENS THE CHARACTER AND AFFECTS YOUR RELATIONSHIP WITH PEOPLE
ALL RIGHT, THEN
DING
DONG
MY FATHER HAS A LOT OF OLD-FASHIONED IDEAS
PAPERS
6-13
© King Features Syndicate, Inc., 1971. World rights reserved.

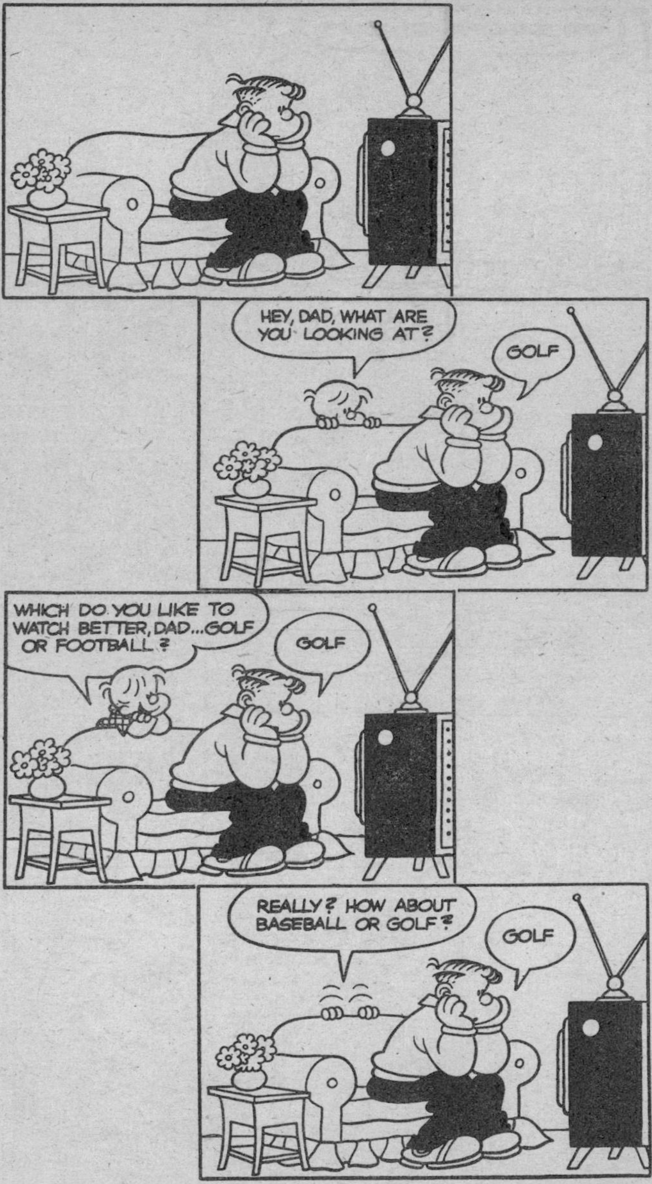
HEY, DAD, WHAT ARE YOU LOOKING AT?
GOLF
WHICH DO YOU LIKE TO WATCH BETTER, DAD...GOLF OR FOOTBALL?
GOLF
REALLY? HOW ABOUT BASEBALL OR GOLF?
GOLF

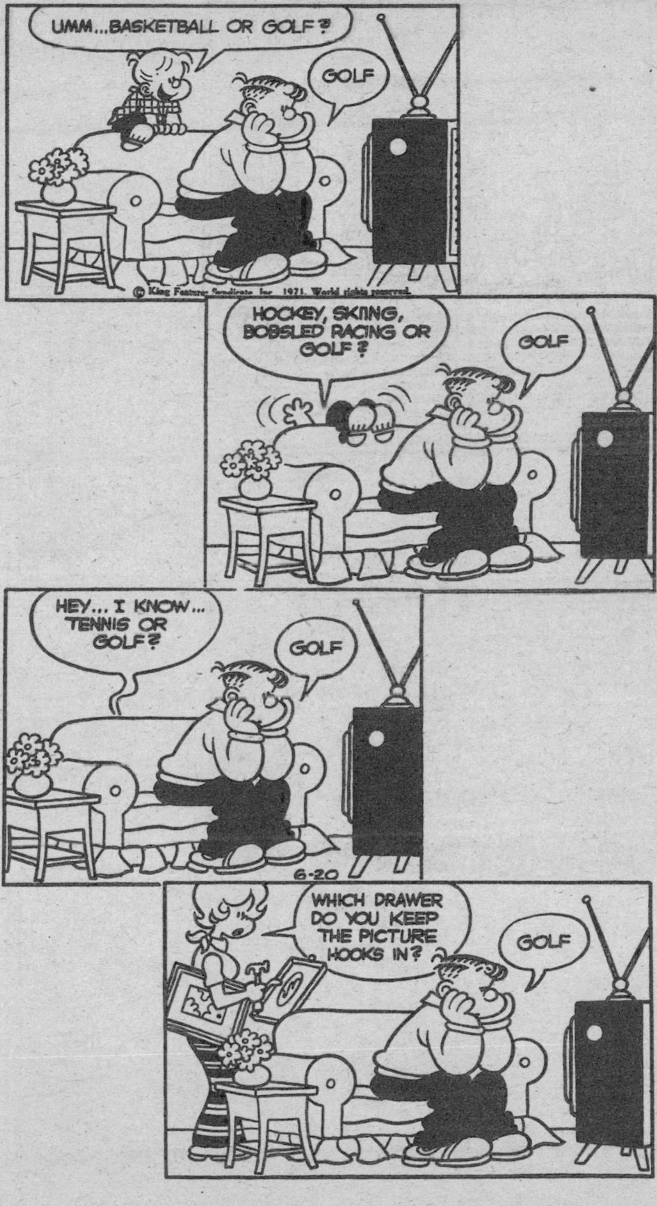
UMM...BASKETBALL OR GOLF?
GOLF
© King Features Syndicate, Inc., 1971. World rights reserved.
HOCKEY, SKIING, BOBSLED RACING OR GOLF?
GOLF
HEY... I KNOW... TENNIS OR GOLF?
GOLF
6-20
WHICH DRAWER DO YOU KEEP THE PICTURE HOOKS IN?
GOLF

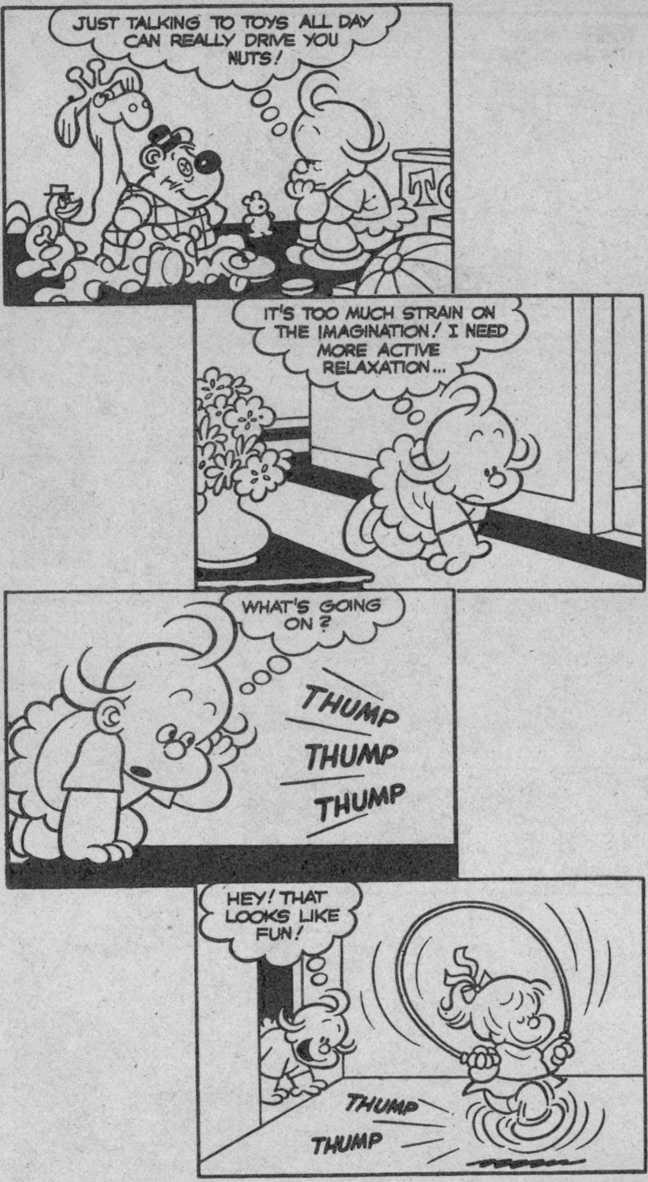
JUST TALKING TO TOYS ALL DAY CAN REALLY DRIVE YOU NUTS!
IT'S TOO MUCH STRAIN ON THE IMAGINATION! I NEED MORE ACTIVE RELAXATION...
WHAT'S GOING ON?
THUMP
THUMP
THUMP
HEY! THAT LOOKS LIKE FUN!
THUMP
THUMP

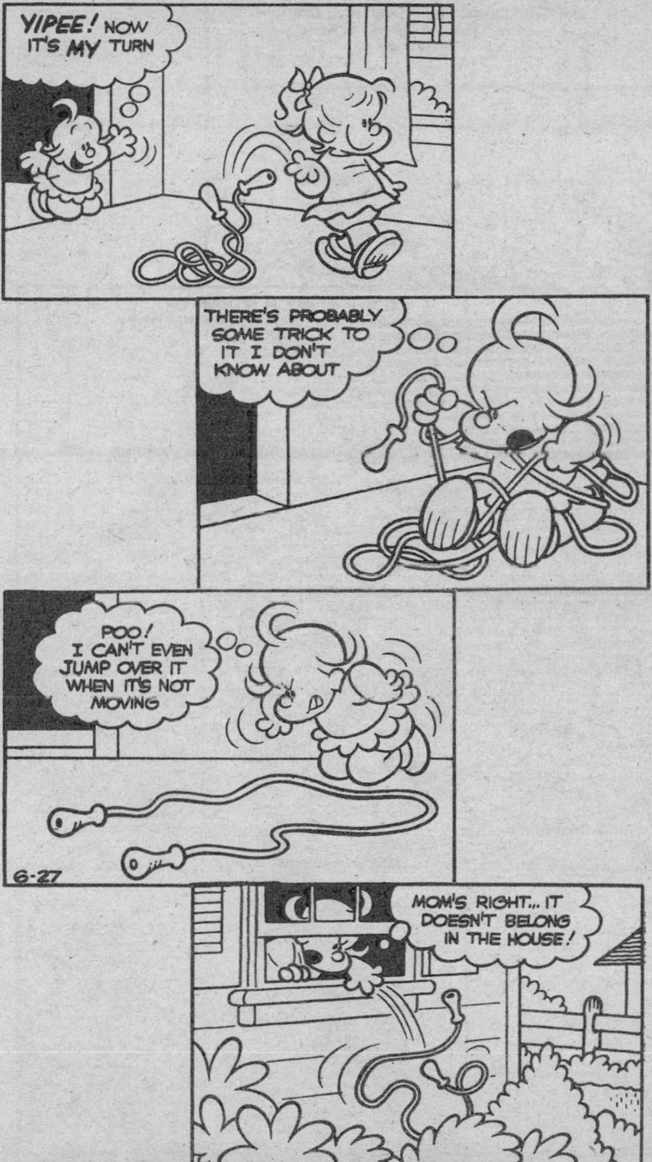
YIPEE! NOW IT'S MY TURN
THERE'S PROBABLY SOME TRICK TO IT I DON'T KNOW ABOUT
POO! I CAN'T EVEN JUMP OVER IT WHEN IT'S NOT MOVING
6-27
MOM'S RIGHT... IT DOESN'T BELONG IN THE HOUSE!
© King Features Syndicate, Inc., 1971. World rights reserved.

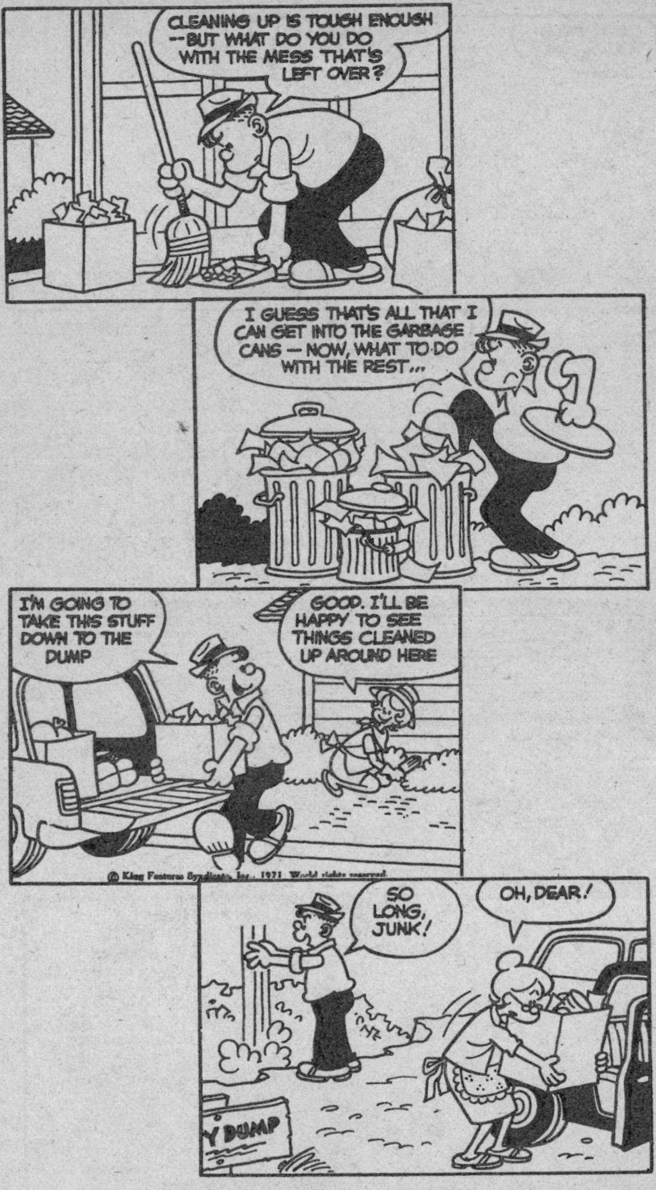
CLEANING UP IS TOUGH ENOUGH --BUT WHAT DO YOU DO WITH THE MESS THAT'S LEFT OVER?
I GUESS THAT'S ALL THAT I CAN GET INTO THE GARBAGE CANS — NOW, WHAT TO DO WITH THE REST...
I'M GOING TO TAKE THIS STUFF DOWN TO THE DUMP
GOOD. I'LL BE HAPPY TO SEE THINGS CLEANED UP AROUND HERE
© King Features Syndicate, Inc., 1971. World rights reserved.
SO LONG, JUNK!
OH, DEAR!
Y DUMP

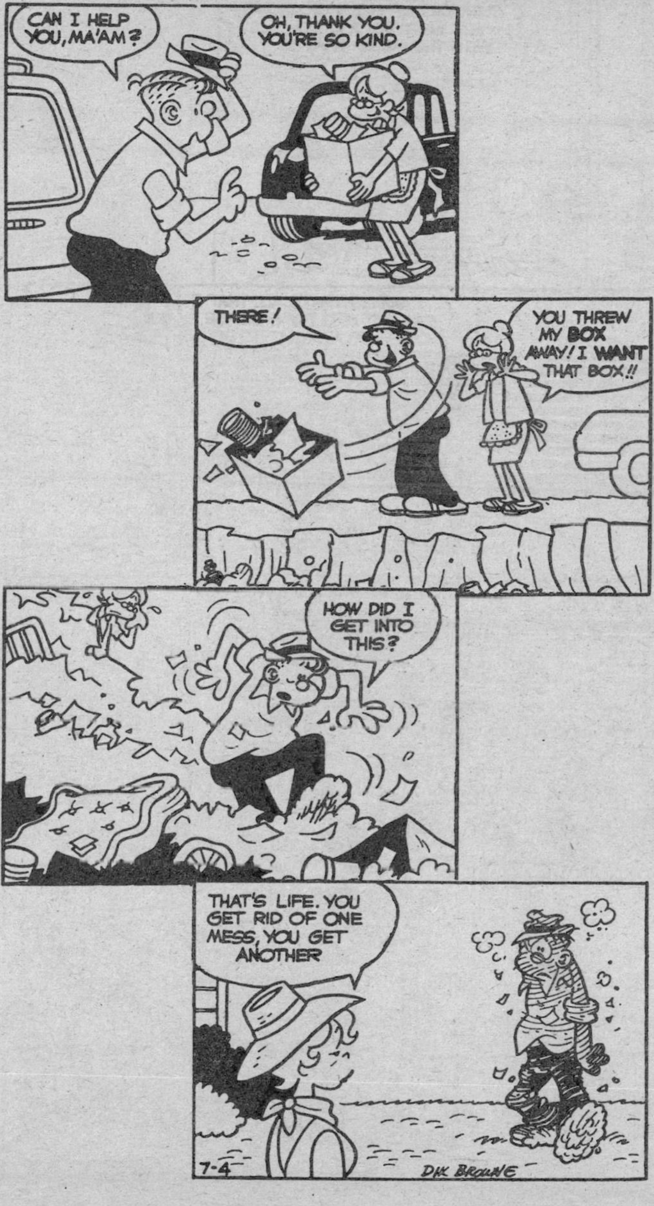
CAN I HELP YOU, MA'AM?
OH, THANK YOU. YOU'RE SO KIND.
THERE!
YOU THREW MY BOX AWAY! I WANT THAT BOX!!
HOW DID I GET INTO THIS?
THAT'S LIFE. YOU GET RID OF ONE MESS, YOU GET ANOTHER
7-4
DIK BROWNE

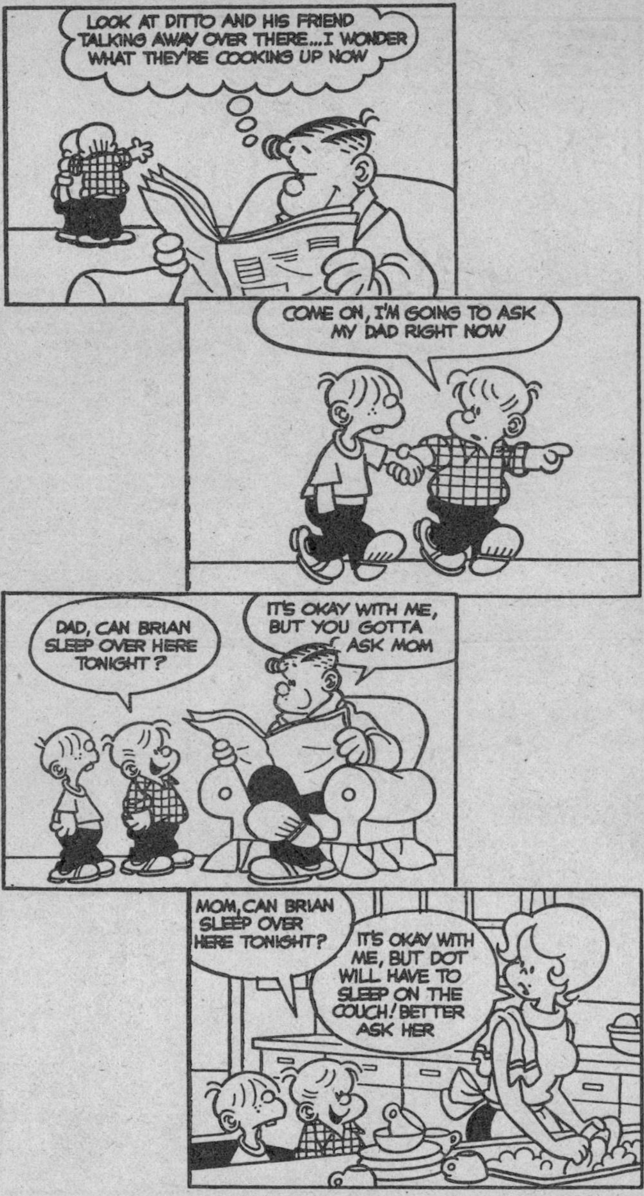
LOOK AT DITTO AND HIS FRIEND TALKING AWAY OVER THERE...I WONDER WHAT THEY'RE COOKING UP NOW
COME ON, I'M GOING TO ASK MY DAD RIGHT NOW
DAD, CAN BRIAN SLEEP OVER HERE TONIGHT?
IT'S OKAY WITH ME, BUT YOU GOTTA ASK MOM
MOM, CAN BRIAN SLEEP OVER HERE TONIGHT?
IT'S OKAY WITH ME, BUT DOT WILL HAVE TO SLEEP ON THE COUCH! BETTER ASK HER

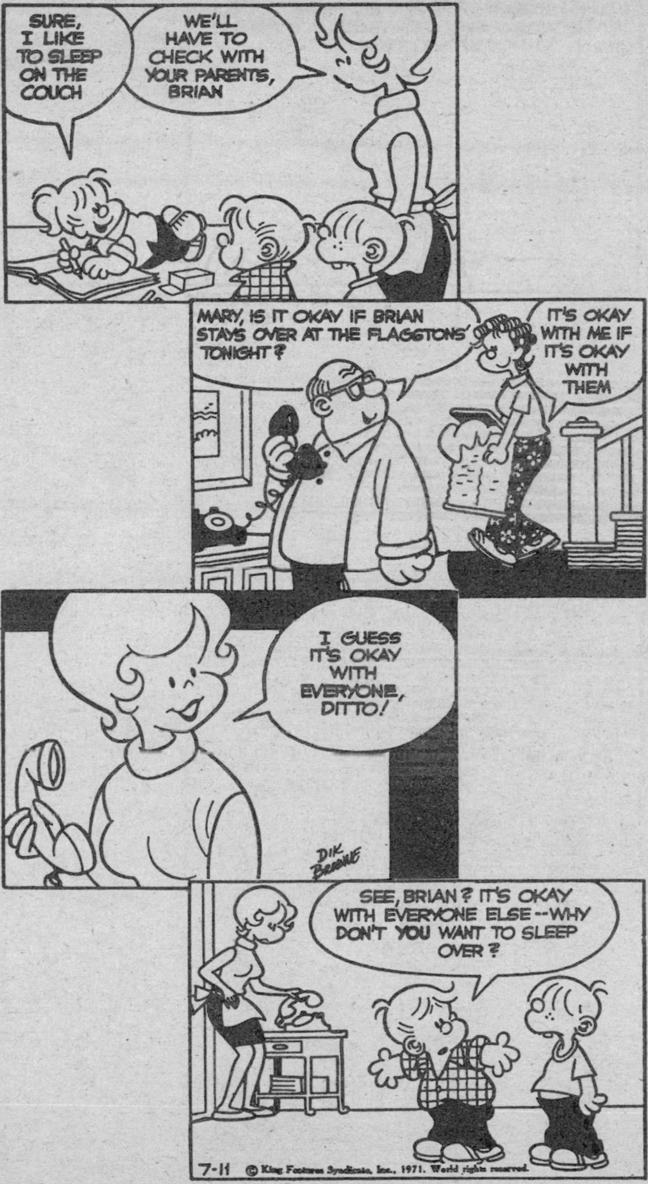
SURE, I LIKE TO SLEEP ON THE COUCH
WE'LL HAVE TO CHECK WITH YOUR PARENTS, BRIAN
MARY, IS IT OKAY IF BRIAN STAYS OVER AT THE FLAGSTONS' TONIGHT?
IT'S OKAY WITH ME IF IT'S OKAY WITH THEM
I GUESS IT'S OKAY WITH EVERYONE, DITTO!
DIK BROWNE
SEE, BRIAN? IT'S OKAY WITH EVERYONE ELSE--WHY DON'T YOU WANT TO SLEEP OVER?
7-11
© King Features Syndicate, Inc., 1971. World rights reserved.

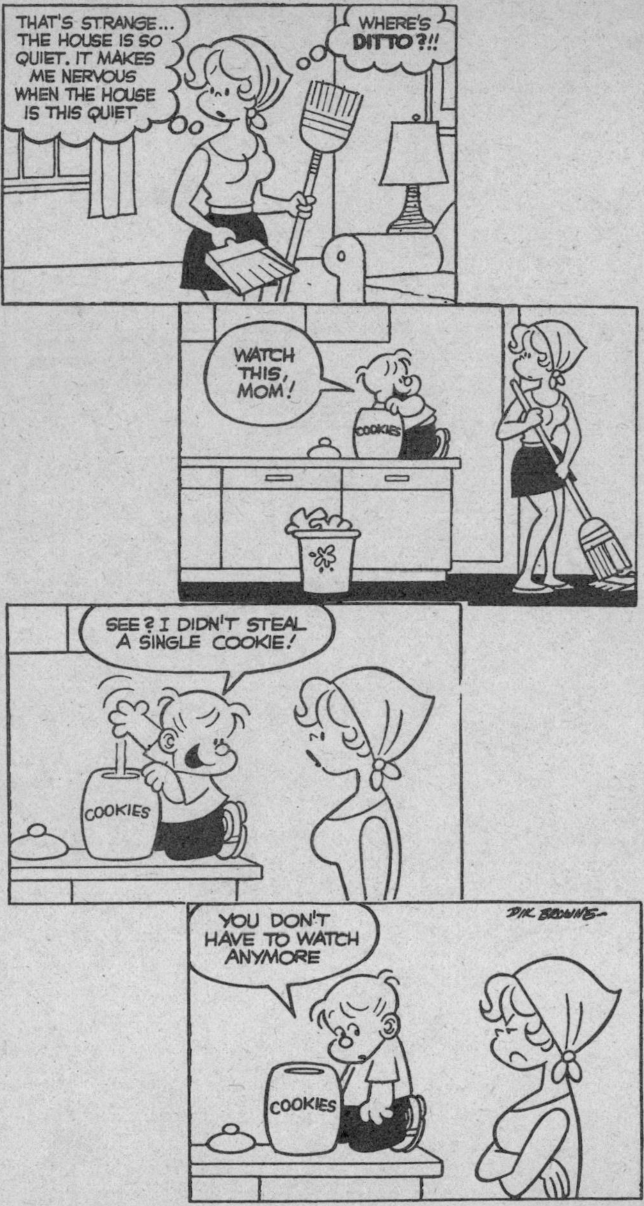
THAT'S STRANGE... THE HOUSE IS SO QUIET. IT MAKES ME NERVOUS WHEN THE HOUSE IS THIS QUIET
WHERE'S DITTO ?!!
WATCH THIS, MOM!
COOKIES
SEE? I DIDN'T STEAL A SINGLE COOKIE!
COOKIES
DIK BROWNE
YOU DON'T HAVE TO WATCH ANYMORE
COOKIES